THE SACRED VINE

BOOK ONE OF THE TENDRILS OF LIGHT SERIES

VICTORIA M. SORENSON

THE SACRED VINE. Copyright © 2024 by Victoria M. Sorenson. All rights reserved. No part of this book may be used or reproduced without written permission, except for brief quotations in articles and reviews.

Library of Congress Catalog-in-Publication Data has been applied for.

Editor and Formatter: Heather Hudec, with Simply Spellbound Edits

@simplyspellboundedits

Cover Art and Marketing Design: Rena Violet, with Covers by Violet

@violet.book.design

Map and Interior Design: Victoria M. Sorenson (Yours Truly)

ISBN:

Paperback 979-8-9916087-0-1

Hardcover 979-8-9916087-2-5

Ebook 979-8-9916087-1-8

This book contains themes of grief, loss, and overcoming cultural predispositions.

The Sacred Vine is a young adult fantasy set in kingdoms tethered by magic and mystery. Its story includes injuries, blood, death, and the loss of a loved one. I want my readers to know that their mental health is *essential,* regardless of age or gender.

I hope and pray that my stories help validate your feelings because even the not-so-fun emotions are crucial for moving forward during difficult times. I see you. I hear you. **You are loved.**

To include a wide variety of readers, I have decided to make my books **plot-driven, with no explicit language, and with closed-door romance.**

Glossary & Pronounciation Guide

Time Explained:

Lunation: One month has passed.

A single moon: One day has passed.

Thirteen Lunations: One year has passed.

Creator   kree-ay-tor

The consciousness born into existence out of darkness is responsible for the gift of the *Marked Ones*. It assisted in the making of the *Videira*, the sacred vine. All species and cultures recognize it as the higher entity.

Ligação Mágica   lee-ga-sow ma-jee-kuh

The green-and-gold swirls of tangible magic embedded into the soil, tethering the five kingdoms of Aksel to each other.

Videira   vee-dair-uh

The sacred vine of life is a sentient being that produces large green budding pods that bloom at the change of each season. The pods contain an infant elf child.

Marked Ones   markt wuhnz

Species or creatures endowed with extraordinary powers. They are gifted by the *Creator*, and it is still a mystery as to how they are chosen. They first came in abundance; now, their existence is rare.

Meir   may-eer

A luminescent orb is sent directly from the vine during the changing of seasons. It floats to the various doorways inside the elven villages with a lantern on their doorpost, signaling to the vine that the particular household is ready for parenthood. Once at the chosen doorway, it leads the expecting couple back to the *Videira* ceremony grounds, where it is absorbed into a pod—the pod then blooms, revealing the elven infant to the parents.

Pod   pawd

Large green buds connected to the *Videira*. They bloom at the changing of each season with the assistance of absorbing the *Meir*.

Gavinhas   gah-veen-yahs

The whisps of light radiating from a being's aura. It is one's lifeline to the *Ligação Mágica* and their existence. It is a living creature or species' ability to pass from this world to the next after death—what one would refer to as a soul.

Aura   or-uh

The energy encompassing each individual.

Mãe   ma-ee

A mother figure in the elven culture.

Papa   pah-puh

A father figure in the elven culture.

Xodó   show-doh

The current written language in the Elvish culture.

Reinos   ray-nohs

The spoken language used by all species in the five kingdoms of Aksel for communication.

Grato Amizade   grah-toh ah-mee-zah-jee

The holiday and celebration of the friendship and union between the kingdoms of Erebus and Alun.

Breeders of Thereon   **bree-ders ov thay-run**

Also referred to as *Breeders*, they were once dragons—now shrouded inside dark magic. Their souls, corrupted by greed and desire for power, were cut off from the *Ligação Mágica* by the *Creator.* They are bound to the blackened soil of Adara by an ancient spell cast by the monarchs of all five kingdoms before they fell. In order to hunt *Marked Ones*, they have found a way around the spell by creating soulless creatures to do their bidding.

Thereon   thay-run

Soulless creatures derived from any species are created by their *Breeders* and are consumed by parasitic dark magic. These beasts hunt the *Marked Ones* and bring them back to their creators.

Magic Spells & Information

Spell Casting Explained:

There are three requirements necessary to cast a spell.

First, the caster must speak the language of Reinos.

Second, the being must be within range of the *Ligação Mágica*, the origin of all enchanted magic.

Third, a source of friction is necessary to ignite the spell into existence—a finger snap is most commonly used.

All three of these actions must coincide with one another for a basic spell to work. All beings and creatures are able to cast a spell, but it is deemed not wise. The *Creator* is always watching, and it is a bad omen to use the magic source if it is not out of necessity.

Only *Marked Ones* have the ability to use gifted powers from the *Creator*; it is not to be confused with magic.

Spells Used & Their Definitions:

Puero- means to disappear: This spell is most commonly used for cleaning up small spills and messes.

Liguero- means speed; the elven species use this spell to pick up the pace when traveling through the dense forest of Alizeh.

Fogoe- meaning to heat; can bring forth flames to a fire or simply warm a bubble bath.

Fria- meaning to cool; you can freeze your dinner to save for a later time or chill your delicious pastry from the local baker.

Escureo- meaning to cloak or disguise; used to conceal one's identity.

Escudo das Almas- an intricate spell derived from the werewolf species, used to mask their soul's presence to outsiders.

For my lovely husband, Parker,
who has always supported my wildest dreams, knowing they will come to
fruition without a shadow of a doubt. Thank you for believing in me.
For my daughters Vivienne, Sophia, and Rosalie, I pray that you all find
your passion and pursue it with intense dedication and that your love of
reading never fades.

And for those who may feel alone
You are invited to join us inside my mystical worlds, full of magic and
mystery.
All are welcome here.

Prologue

An immense, black void spanned across all space and time.

Until a consciousness was born.

The five kingdoms of Aksel were then formed, their landmasses tethered to one another through magical properties. This magic flowed through the land, its visible wavelengths like vines anchoring all of existence. The iridescent green-and-gold swirls are referred to unanimously as the *Ligação Mágica*.

The consciousness synchronized with the land's magic, and a physical vine grew in the kingdom of Alizeh. This vine was like no other; as it grew far and wide, it became a sentient being that preserved the nature encompassing it. The tendrils produced pods, and a species known as elves began to bloom. The elves named their maker the *Videira*, and it started producing life four times a year, at the changing of each season.

A phenomenon unfolded; many species emerged from their creation, each endowed with extraordinary powers. Unlike the magic that permeated the land, these unique beings possessed capabilities that set them apart, sparking intrigue and fascination. They are known as the *Marked Ones*, chosen by the consciousness, later named the *Creator*, who blessed certain souls with gifts of power to create superior beings.

At first, they came in abundance, but as the hearts of those who inhabited the lands were filled with greed and corruption, darkness grew and tainted their spirits. The kingdoms began producing fewer species with gifted powers, and the *Marked Ones* became a rarity, coveted by the most heinous creatures.

A new monstrous beast formed, malicious in nature with a wicked desire to consume all power corrupting their souls.

They became known as the *Breeders of Thereon.*

Part One

Chapter One

Bless the vine and all things sacred! I was late. How I managed to get myself into the exact scenario I had been desperate to avoid was almost comical. Absorbed in my studies, I had flipped through pages of worn text, entirely in my own world. I often trekked through the various books on spells and our history's known literature, lightheartedly. But time had evaded me, as always, and a knot settled into the pit of my stomach as the ringing in my ears caused a slight headache to sprout at my temples.

This would be a day of reckoning.

The literature was spread across the kitchen table, books open at random sections, and my horde of notes mixed into the chaos. I left the buffet of knowledge and stumbled to the pantry, checking for the third time to see if something of sustenance had magically appeared behind the thin door. I reached around the small bag of flour in search of anything, and to my surprise, it rested upon an unexpected item. The crinkled, waxy paper was all too familiar, and before I had time to process the consequences, I unwrapped the treat. My stomach grumbled, and I shoved a stale, half-eaten pastry from the local baker down my throat.

Much to my annoyance, the old clock chimed on the wall, its ominous ticks growing in volume with each passing second. I poked the fire, killing whatever flame was left. The dying embers' last remnants of heat had me pausing a moment too long; the familiar scent of burning wood intensified, and the smoke filled the quaint living area.

I licked the remaining evidence of the flaky, sugary residue from my fingertips before quickly lacing up my boots.

An image of my twin's sullen face appeared in my thoughts, and my heart plummeted. *That must have been my sister's dessert hidden in the back of the cupboards.* But I was hungry, on the verge of hangry, and I didn't want my emotions to get the better of me. I'll deal with Ornella's insistent nagging later; there was someone else's wrath that was imperative to avoid. That reminder alone sent shivers down my spine; it drained what little color my complexion contained as I quickened my pace.

The moon's light peeked through the cottage's traditional elvish carvings, another reminder of the time. I passed beneath the crescent-shaped window and opened the heavy wooden door. It swung with a sudden urgency, catching on the cool breeze, and I briskly entered the surrounding wildlife. My vision took several seconds to adjust to the bright light emitting from the moon's surface, reflecting a spotlight onto our small village on the outskirts of the Woodlands.

I hadn't the faintest clue what excuse I would use for skipping ritual practice. My nose twitched as I used my two remaining brain cells to discover an answer. But I was only met with another twinge of pain as the headache made plotting an explanation impossible. During this lunation, I had studied in the comfort of our cottage while Ornella covered for my absences and lied to *Mãe*, convincing her that I had attended the rehearsals.

Bless my sister's pure soul.

I had my regrets about eating her pastry, but I'm sure she'd find the perfect occasion for me to repay her. Ornella was cunning in that way; she could make bread out of butter if given the opportunity.

My steps were nearly silent as I moved up the dirt path, the bordering flowers forcefully pushing through the last of this winter's frost, catching my attention. Spring was trying to make an early appearance this year. The nature encompassing me hummed with life as the plants of night woke from their quiet slumber, stretching their limbs. I would never get used to the luminescent glow of the thick pines and foliage; the enchanting sight was spectacular, the waves of magic tangible.

I entered the main pathway leading into the village and hid beneath my cloak's hood. The road was brimming with life, elves bustling to-and-fro. Their auras were faintly visible to my naked eye—a dull glow that ebbed and flowed with energy.

Faint whispers still traveled through the thick cloth, my stark raven hair revealing my identity as it spilled out from beneath my hood into the weather's crisp elements. Their words nipped at my ears, *Marked One*; they sneered in awe and envy. Unlike my twin, I was all but shunned for my gift. Dejection always found me, as it would with any outsider in this tight-knit community. I had bloomed from the vine like all my peers, but my unique ability to drain energy from any living entity and perceive their auras was the cause of my outcast status. Even now, I could feel the low vibrations of energy stemming from each passerby as I carefully avoided brushing up against them in the crowded walkway—not a difficult task, those around me naturally gravitated away from my presence, believing the rumors that I was cursed by both the *Creator* and the sacred *Videira*.

They viewed me as a predator disguised in sheep's clothing.

I did not mind their cold shoulders; I much preferred my own company alongside a hot cup of tea.

Standing before me was an old brick studio wedged between the multiple shops; its front windows open wide, music dancing out into the streets beneath the stars. This was my home away from home, my sanctuary from all life's woes.

All recognized *Mãe* here as Ms. Aster, the legendary musician who had traveled the dark seas and played her symphonies in numerous kingdoms. She was held in high regard due to her status as a pianist, but outside of her business, she was the single parent to Ornella and me. Residents were quick to determine an unpartnered woman as undeserving for being chosen by our sacred vine for parenthood, as it had never been witnessed or recorded by the priests before her. Judged for the very reason some admired her strength, *Mãe* had been willing to leave behind our way of life so easily to pursue her passions when she was young. Many claimed that she was not a suitable choice to be our caretaker. Elves rarely strayed from Alizeh. Our culture was deeply embedded into our homelands.

The sounds of a saxophone accompanied by intricate piano notes cut through my thoughts; the rhythm and tune swelled inside my chest as I recognized the stellar aptitude with which the pianist played. This was no beginner; even those with untrained ears could hear the raw talent exuding from inside the academy. I couldn't help the smile that tugged on the corners of my mouth as I listened.

Mãe was entertaining her students after class.

The weight of dread lessened as I stood at my usual spot beneath her business's entryway at the bottom of the narrow steps. Her lessons with her pupils had run late, an extremely rare and fortunate occurrence for me.

Maybe fate was on my side after all. Ornella still had a chance to meet me here in time. But the music that flowed overhead teetered off to a close, and I shifted from one foot to the other. I was doing my best to keep my expression easygoing, but the sounds of her students packing their instruments for the evening had me pacing back and forth as I chewed on my nails. I squinted into the multiple routes, eagerly waiting for my sister's silhouette to emerge from their shadows.

The sound of door hinges creaking open heated my ears and cheeks as the young musicians barreled down the stairs, gossiping about tomorrow's event.

"Ms. Aster chose me to play in the orchestra for tomorrow's ceremony." The girl's voice was high-pitched and shrill, much like the flute she held in her hand. They walked in unison, their matching green-and-gold uniforms tailored to perfection. I could only assume that was also *Mãe's* doing, inspecting every detail for tomorrow's event. Her students were an extension of her success.

As they filed out of sight, a head of white hair simultaneously appeared by my side.

"Ornella." I exhaled in relief. "What took so long?"

A frown immediately formed across her features, and her emerald eyes lingered on the collar of my garment, partially hidden beneath my cloak.

"Your shirt's backward *and* inside out." Her gaze thoroughly picking me apart within seconds. "Sayah, I can only help you if you put in some effort. Even your hair is a mess." She plucked at several strands of my flyaways, tucking them behind my ears. My twin examined me once more and sighed. "There's no way she's going to believe that you've been at rehearsal with me all day. You look like you just woke up . . . rub the sleep out of your eyes, will you?"

I grunted at her nitpicking and begrudgingly followed her instructions, cleaning my face with the hem of my cloak.

Our rite-of-passage ceremony was tomorrow, and today was the final day of rehearsal with this season's participants. The vine blooms four times a year, at the changing of each season. For elves, the ritual symbolizes the passing of our childhood and rebirth into mature adults, ready to offer our lives in exchange for peace and tranquility. Because two hundred thirty-five lunations had passed since our blooming, the superstitious villagers would notice if I did not participate.

Our existence was rare: two infants who bloomed from the same pod *and* were chosen to become *Marked Ones*.

It was unheard of. This swayed the elders to let me participate in the celebration despite their significant concerns.

I was doing everything in my power not to attend, but it pained me to see how much this upset Ornella. She pleaded for me to be present at the practices, but there was no possible way I would sit there and listen to how the entire village planned to overwork my sister for the rest of her existence now that we were both of age. Significant changes were going to be made, and that was a fact that I was sure of. So, I had promised her I would at least make an appearance at the celebration.

The elders had informed us that we would present our lives to the sacred vine as one; we bloomed from creation together, and our maker would bless us in the same fashion.

She waited with me now, her face etched in concern, her focus lingering at the top of the academy's banister.

"So, are you going to answer me or not—what took so long?" I probed, and there was an unexpected bite in my tone. I instinctively brushed my hair behind my ear and glanced at my feet. "Sorry; I'm just anxious," I whispered. She was the last being that I wanted to take my anger out on.

Ornella nodded, glazing over my unwarranted attitude. "I had to wait in line for these." Her feet teetered, and she clumsily held out two shimmering green gowns from inside the brown bag. "You missed a lot today."

A *tsk* of irritation from behind me instantly made the hairs on the back of my neck stand straight. I whipped my attention around to behold *Mãe* with her arms folded and her foot tapping on the top step, narrowing her gaze.

"How was class?" I squeaked, my voice an octave higher than normal—a detail that someone with pitch-perfect hearing wouldn't miss.

Her lips pulled back into a thin smile as she drummed the railing with her sharp fingernails, undoubtedly deciding my punishment in her brief pause.

"Today went longer than usual, but that was expected. We practiced with the choir for tomorrow's celebratory event." She slowly descended the steps, and her violet eyes bore into mine when she was at eye level. "How was your day, Sayah?"

The venom behind her question caused me to avert my attention to the street before us. Boisterous villagers trudged through the softly padded streets of soil; their excitement for the festivities did nothing to distract me from my growing panic. The cool night air filled my lungs as I deliberately took a steady breath. My eyes averted to *Mãe,* and I bit my lip, searching for an acceptable answer. "It went . . . well. My handwriting in *Xodó* is improving." I glanced up through my thick lashes, hopeful for approval, but her disdain was evident. The elvish written language was tedious; I knew several mature adults who had yet to master its complexity.

"Writing? I didn't realize that today's practice would include handwriting." Her head was tilted to the side, focused solely on Ornella. My breath hitched as I watched *Mãe* internalize every detail, from our clothing to the wavering of our voices. After several moments, she inquired about the obvious piece of evidence in my sister's grasp. "Why are you holding Sayah's gown?"

Ornella awkwardly shifted the bag in her arms, unwilling to look either of us in the eye. My sister was terrible at lying to our *Mãe,* but she was absolutely stellar at weaving her way around the truth with anyone else. I exhaled, praying to the vine that she would get on with it and reveal our sins. It was a miracle that *Mãe* hadn't noticed my absence until now. The ritual practices lasted one lunation, consisting of elders waving a fan in front of their upturned noses as they paced back and forth in the village's auditorium while diving even further into the history of our culture. All this so that the budding minds of my peers could find their permanent place in our society.

That was partially why I refused to attend; our fate was already chosen, and I resented that on my and Ornella's behalf. She might get under my skin occasionally, but I loved her and wanted her to receive the same choices offered to everyone else.

"I went to stand in line for the two of us at the seamstress; you know how Sayah hates crowds." Her emerald eyes flinched at the partial lie, making my heart sink further into the pit of my chest with guilt. I pinched the bridge of my nose to hold my composure.

I should have known *Mãe* would punish us both as Ornella squirmed underneath her scrutinizing stare.

A gush of cool air tickled my bare cheeks, and the vast array of stars caught my eye. The sun would soon creep along the horizon, causing the plants of night to withdraw from view and back into the depths of nature. "It's nearly time we leave to backpack to the vine, and I'm starving," I said with false absentmindedness.

Glancing over the streets, I took in the vibrant scenery, which was still lively during the odd early morning hours when the moon was prominent in the sky. This was one of the numerous reasons I adored our kingdom; the night was just as magical as the day. Street vendors lined the pathways, and conversations were never cut short because of a lack of sunlight.

"I'm exhausted and hungry myself." Ornella stifled a yawn, still clutching the heavy gowns. My face flushed, and I quickly snatched them from her.

"Let me carry these the rest of the way." I turned on my heel, avoiding *Mãe's* glare. She had always been that way, and her silence was louder than any scolding. I had absorbed the details of the families around me as I grew, quickly learning that there was some disconnect within my own. As a child, I was fascinated with my peers' family structure. Parents would loudly express emotion and reprimand bad behavior, annoyance plastered on their worn faces. Sometimes, they would laugh, chasing their little ones through the connecting pathways, tired yet aglow with joy. And you could see it in their hugs, the forehead kisses left atop the growing boys' and girls' heads. Their parents loved them, and it showed.

Mãe reserved her emotions for when I was behind the piano, performing.

Even now, silence invaded the space between us, the air stifled by our awkwardness.

The rhythmic soft shuffle of our boots padding along the forest floor did nothing to soothe the restlessness waging internally. *Mãe* would not let this be an easy punishment; she ruled our small cottage with an iron fist.

The crescent moon was well past the top of the pine's thick leaves, and daylight would inevitably come in the next few hours. As we put distance between us and the village's center, the music and laughter gradually faded from our hearing. Neon flowers budded high in the canopy, and I watched as their petals slowly revealed their ripe blackberries. Winter's breeze tickled my cheeks, and a sudden wave of grief overcame me. These were the last few moments of my childhood, and I was reluctant to let them pass by so casually. Time was inescapable, and even so, I clutched the brown bag tightly to my core as we neared our dwelling.

A hand gently rested on my arm, waiting.

Mãe stared at me, pulling on the hem of my cloak and me out of my thoughts. Her violet irises flickered with intensity, though the rest of her disposition displayed a false sense of calm. She was waging a silent war before me; I mentally prepared myself for battle.

"Ornella, go ahead and start supper." She nudged her with her free arm to head to our cottage, now only several paces away. "Sayah and I need to have a heart-to-heart."

I exhaled, slowly closing my eyes in defeat. Well played. Her strategy was to kill two birds with one stone. My sister was a terrible cook, a detail known by nearly half the village. Many had tried to teach her the basics, taking on what they thought would be a simple task. But Ornella lacked both the patience and focus needed to learn something new. She had managed to burn three roasts and nearly set someone's stove on fire, trying to recreate their easy-to-make chicken casserole. There was hardly anything she could use for ingredients, so this challenge was a great punishment.

I would be forced to consume whatever concoction was created. This was indeed diabolical, even for *Mãe*.

She grabbed the bag from my hands, her lip quivering as she headed inside our home to accomplish the near-impossible task of making a meal from scratch. With how bare our cupboards had been as of late; it was a huge risk letting Ornella use such precious spices.

Now alone with her, my pulse quickened. A heart-to-heart discussion with *Mãe* was never something that I looked forward to. It meant a punishment resulting in manual labor or, worse, conversing with the villagers. And after, I would have to relay my findings on what I had learned during the experience. This would be absolutely dreadful.

"Come." She gestured for me to follow. Dark-blonde hair gently swung back and forth in front of me, a golden river of soft waves rippling against her garments. *Mãe* led us off the main path to sit on our garden bench in the backyard. Her hands rested in her lap, and her shoulders curled inward.

For a moment, *Mãe* could have been mistaken for a small child.

Her lack of composure caught me off guard, and I took in the unusual display of her unfiltered expression. Wrinkles lined her violet eyes, which were heavy from exhaustion. A sharp pang of blame struck, and I sat beside her, patiently waiting for her to speak.

A puff of air escaped her lips, visible in the cold. "Why do you let others control you?" Her voice was sharp, agitated. *Mãe's* delicate hands gripped the edge of the bench. "I will never understand it, Sayah. I have fought tooth and nail for you to have the same opportunities as your peers despite the circumstances. And you carelessly throw them away."

My head snapped in her direction at the accusation, but her gaze was unmoving. It rested on a pot full of nothing more than old soil and dead leaves.

"By *not* participating, I am taking a stance," I alleged, my fingers forming into a tight fist. "Ornella and I should get to decide whether or not we wish to use our gifts." My voice turned soft, pleading. "It's never been a choice; not for *her*." My throat was suddenly dry, a lump forming.

Ornella's never had a choice.

My sister was the village's energy source and saving grace. She was always in the fields, saving the essential crops before they could wither away entirely from lack of sunlight or drought. Her presence was requested in the infirmary to give others the strength to endure their illness and survive. This was her daily life, and she had ultimately been robbed of her childhood because she was a *Marked One*.

A result of being blessed with the ability to give energy. She could not heal, though the villagers treated her as if she was their life source. Her energy manipulation simply sped up the healing process.

And I've had to watch her slowly wither away because of it. Using that much power daily came at a steep price. The light in her emerald eyes often dulled, and her natural rosy skin went pale from exhaustion. Everyone had a limit, and Ornella was far beyond hers.

The villagers all but disowned me at times, but at least I was left alone. She was not granted such luxury.

So, the thought of the ceremony and what it represented was maddening. I wanted the priests and elders who had abused her power to give

Ornella back her autonomy. She had been coerced into making adult decisions and missing out on what was most important during one's youth: the freedom to find out what type of life she wanted to lead.

Our future had been planned for us, making the power beneath my skin simmer with rage.

Mãe finally turned to me, her eyes burning with determination.

"I am going to help her, help the both of you." Her tone sent shivers down my spine. "So, I need you to trust me when I say it is essential that you both attend the ceremony tomorrow."

I sat up straight, now alert. "Why, what's going on?" I trembled. *Mãe* was a serious individual, but I could tell something was amiss.

"I'm sneaking the both of you out of Alizeh," she whispered as she scanned the nearby trees, wary of listening ears. "I've been in contact with an old friend in Erebus—he will let us stay with him until we get back on our feet."

I stood immediately, pacing, my thoughts jumbled as I tried to grasp the weight of her words.

I started biting my nails, a nervous habit I had yet to kick. "The elders will immediately notice our absence—and I can't believe I have to ask, but are we *allowed* to leave?" I probed. "And what of your academy? That is your life's work."

"Soon, you and your sister may not be allowed to do *anything*." She inhaled sharply. "There is much to discuss, but not out here, not now." Her gentle hands reached out and squeezed mine; the slight reveal of emotion was unusual, but I savored her touch, nevertheless. "Listen to me, Sayah, and you listen good." Her voice broke. "It has become apparent to me that those in authority do not have your or your sister's well-being in mind. I was in denial, but the truth has made its way to the surface now that your rite of passage is here."

A conversation from behind closed doors a few nights ago came to mind; *Mãe* had been clearly disturbed after the priests visited unannounced, their docile expressions unsettling.

I thought nothing of it at the time; they often called on Ornella when issues out of the realms of their control arose. Now, goosebumps ran up and down my arms at the ominous tension that grew with each passing moment.

Mãe clumsily dropped my hands, running her fingers through her locks. The smell of smoke reached our noses, and my frantic sister flung open the kitchen window, yelling in frustration as another puff of blackened fumes spread into the night's air.

"We better go help her before she turns our cottage into a pile of ashes." She jumped off the bench, running ahead of me, closing the distance to the backdoor. I could see Ornella's wide-eyed stare over the top of *Mãe's* head; both my sister and I towered over her petite frame. My twin and I had grown like weeds over the past summer, our gangly limbs now defined with muscle.

Before entering, she turned to face me and signaled by placing a finger over her lips.

She didn't want Ornella to know yet.

"What happened?" Her hands rested on her hips, expectantly waiting, repetitively tapping her toe on the ground. It was her go-to stance to display her frustration. "Are you hurt?"

Ornella's eyes were red, irritated from the smoke.

"No."

"Then clean this mess up," *Mãe* stated. She pulled the necessary supplies from the cabinets. We were not allowed to rely on spells for chores; she believed it made beings lazy and spoiled. All creatures and species used *Reinos*, the language for elemental spell casting; one only needs to be within a short distance of the *Ligação Mágica* for the spell to ignite.

And also have a *Mãe* that allows them to use spells.

But as *Marked Ones*, Ornella and I were forced to be an example to our peers.

Elemental magic is only to be used when necessary—do NOT openly steal the land's properties from our Creator.

That specific sentence had been ingrained into my brain, repeated so many times by *Mãe*, the elders, and the priests that it flashed across my mind as I helped my sister as swiftly as possible.

When *Mãe's* back was turned, I mischievously grinned at Ornella, who vehemently shook her head and mouthed, "no."

I responded by reciting the simple incantation, *"Puero,"* while snapping my fingers. The magic danced outside the kitchen window in reply to my synchronized call on the enchanting green-and-gold wavelengths.

Instantaneously, the mess disappeared, leaving our kitchen spotless.

That was when I noticed all my previous studies and necessary piles of scribbles were missing from the center of the round wooden table.

I panicked, scanning the tiled floor. During my time at home, while skipping ritual practice over the last lunation, I had done a bit of my own studying. All my notes on Alizeh's history had vanished along with Ornella's kitchen disaster.

"This is the exact reason I tell you not to use magic as a crutch for your difficulties; it never goes as planned." Her face had an *I told you so* look, and I clenched my jaw.

"We don't have time to waste—Ornella and I will need a few hours of rest before we head to the vine," I stated.

"You're participating?" My sister arched her brows in question.

"*Mãe* says that is my punishment."

I did not reveal to her that *Mãe* planned to leave behind the life we had built here in this picturesque village; that can of worms was to be dealt with later, by someone other than me.

My twin ogled at both of us but said nothing. Ornella was cunning and much like *Mãe* when presented with information. She stayed silent, but her emerald eyes gleamed with curiosity.

"You seem keen on punishing yourself lately, making my job as your parent much easier." Her back was again turned away from us as she put together a last-minute snack of fruits, vegetables, and dried meat from our cabinetry to eat.

The three of us sat at the circular table where our discussions were held. The table was somehow sturdy even past its prime, and the worn wood only gave the occasional splinter. I twirled my spoon in a circular motion, rummaging through the small portion of food on my plate. I focused on the crescent-shaped window above the door, waiting for someone to pierce the tension that filled the room with words.

"Will I still inherit your music academy?"

"*Sayah*," *Mãe* hissed. Her eyes were daggers, glaring at me. She dared me to say more, but I clenched my jaw shut, this time in fear.

Nothing is scarier than an elvish woman who's angry.

Ornella thoroughly enjoyed the drama as she scarfed down the last of the peas and carrots.

I finally threw my hands up in defeat, knowing *Mãe* probably wanted all the details fine-tuned before letting my sister in on our departure. *She* was the one we were smuggling out of Alizeh.

The less Ornella knew, the better.

"Finish your supper and rest before we make the journey."

I glanced down at her plate, which was already clean. *Bless the vine;* I wondered if she had any food on her plate to begin with.

Mãe always set the table and included herself, even when we didn't have enough to feed all three of us. Another downside to being a single parent was that there wasn't always enough nourishment to fill every dish. She often went without meals; it had taken me a long time to notice as I grew.

Her empty plate would always make my stomach feel full.

That was one way I knew she loved us, even when her emotions failed to show. She never complained, not once. Ornella and I never had to experience her whining and bickering like most adults do when there aren't enough gold coins to go around. *Mãe* would sit at the table, her face content as she inquired about the details of our day.

She loved us so much that she spared our ears bickering and our hearts guilt.

I quickly shoveled the food into my mouth to hold back the tears. *Mãe* watched as we licked our plates clean, consuming every last crumb.

Afterward, Ornella and I moved to the cot in our room. I left the door cracked, and from the bedside, I observed *Mãe* scrubbing the dishes clean in the sink, humming a sweet melody.

"She's really mad at you, huh?"

I flipped over and rested my head on the plush pillow, facing her. Ornella must assume that our heart-to-heart outing in the garden resulted in me losing the ability to inherit the academy and become the new music teacher. I wondered how she would react if she knew the truth.

Thankfully, my twin had no desire to take over the family's business. She preferred helping people tend to their crops and in the infirmary. That is what she wanted me to believe. The truth, however, was harsh, and my sister's emerald eyes bore into mine as she waited for a reply.

"Mad enough." I managed a response and flipped onto my backside.

I hated lying to her.

Mãe was planning our escape, from what exactly I was unsure. But I could see it slowly unraveling over the last several years. The priests and elders never used to visit and never dared to ask Ornella to give energy because she was just a small child. But as we grew, as *she* grew, their eyes shimmered with greed and desire.

Witnessing my sister's powers was a wondrous sight. It seeped from her fingertips while she walked by, caressing the vegetation and enchanting all who watched. Plants became vibrant, their stems standing straight and tall at attention.

"How do you think tomorrow will go?"

"Oh, I don't know." She moved her legs restlessly underneath the sheets. "But I am happy that you decided not to ditch, even if that was more of *Mãe's* doing."

A small laugh escaped my lips.

"I'll guide you during the ceremony, so you don't look like a complete fool." Ornella playfully nudged my shoulder.

"Oh, good. I had forgotten about that part." The grin that spread across my face was genuine as I twisted to face her once more. I pulled up the sheets, inhaled the smell of the soft fabric, and sighed. "We should try and squeeze in a quick nap."

She bobbed her head in agreement, clearly tired.

"The gowns for the ceremony tomorrow are beautiful, and they match the color of your eyes," I said softly into the dark after a few moments of silence.

Ornella's face briefly lit up with excitement. She loved everything fashion and the rare moments when *Mãe* had enough gold coins to spare for a few lipstick shades.

"Aren't they?" she gushed, squealing. I shushed her as she hid underneath the sheets. White strands of hair peeked out from beneath the quilted blanket. Her voice was muffled as she continued. "At rehearsal, they said we would be given access to professional hair and makeup artists. They are traveling from the city of Ascelin to help us prepare."

The startling sound of our bedroom door creaking wide open had us both seeking refuge under the quilt, giggling in unison.

"Girls, please try and get some sleep," *Mãe* said, her violet eyes nearly glowing in the dark hallway. "The journey to the *Videira* is only the beginning."

The door gradually closed, and my twin rolled and faced the window, immediately snoring. Ornella was always overly exhausted and, as a result, had the uncanny ability to sleep anywhere at a moment's notice.

I was alone with my thoughts, a gloomy place to be. The last day of winter was always melancholy, spring already invading my favorite season's space with budding flowers and fresh greenery. Winter never lasted long enough; it was the one time of year I felt at peace with who I was and the nature that surrounded me.

From above, I studied my hands at arm's length, the moonlight casting a white glow about them, before gazing out the window, my dull-grey eyes heavy with tears.

Clouds filled the night sky, covering the stars, and slowly descended upon the moon. I watched in sadness as I said my goodbyes to the one season that welcomed my gift, the one season I didn't worry about draining the energy of the plants around me, for they were already dead.

Chapter Two

During the wee morning hours, I dreamed of faraway kingdoms. Ogres tended to their farmland as fairies whispered mischievously in my ear. They braided vibrant flowers into my raven mane, the intricate hairstyle cascading softly between my shoulder blades. Multiple families of werewolves played in tall grass with their offspring, and mountain giants were off in the distance, herding buffalo and sheep in the kingdom of Alun.

My dream abruptly shifted, taking on a cold, dark landscape. I saw bleak mountains covered in ash and soot. Inside the elevated caverns were horrid creatures, once a vast array of species now cloaked in the same black mist, their eyes red with feverish desire as drool dripped from their mouths. Cages of iron hung from the ceiling, and those inside clung to its rusted bars, crying out in despair. Others who had been held captive for far too long lay on its metal surface, quiet as their hope for escape had withered into nothing.

The scenery then changed, and a pair of yellow eyes transformed into swirls of blood red, capturing my petrified stare. Their sharpness took in my presence. The creature lifted its head, now captivated by my being. Even in my sleep, I whimpered.

I abruptly woke drenched in a cold sweat.

Visions of flames surrounded by a dark abyss still lingered as I rolled out of bed, noticing that Ornella had already left the room. This dream had haunted me as a child ever since *Mãe* had started to read stories of lore from her beloved book of tales. Ornella had been spellbound, wanting to hear more about the vile creatures that resided in the kingdom of Adara and what lurked inside Mount Auberon. I assured her and myself that the dragons resided peacefully in their homelands along with the other cave dwellers. I repeated this as I packed my leather bag and braided my hair, before strolling into the kitchen.

"Ah, there's my *lovely* sister this fine morning." Sarcasm oozed from her words.

Ornella was waiting directly under the entryway's crescent-shaped window. *Mãe* had carved the window and the stars above the frame when we were still in our infancy. Passing underneath the sentimental design was a ritual in its own right.

"What's wrong?" I yawned, lazily making my way to the door. She was usually chipper the moment her eyes opened.

I, however, needed a cup of hot tea before anyone even tried to speak to me. I wasn't coherent without its warm fragrance, delighting all my senses.

"Where's my pastry?" Her accusation stung a bit. It was not wrong, but it still hurt. She stared blankly at me as if I could conjure the dessert out of thin air.

"Oh, I do feel a bit bad about that," I answered. "But it is probably sitting inside the royal throne room by now."

I eyed the lavatory, and she began smacking my back relentlessly while I bent over in a fit of giggles.

"It's not funny, Sayah!" She screeched in frustration. "I was saving that for breakfast!"

Ornella pestered me for several minutes outside of the cottage. My laughs turned to tears, and a heaviness that had been sitting on my shoulders began to rise off and away like the sun, slowly ascending into the clouds.

I craved more simple moments like these, where the biggest worry was how I would repay my sister for devouring her already half-eaten pastry. Instances that glittered like gold in the ever-sinking sand known as time.

As Ornella calmed down, I shielded my eyes from the sunlight originating through the tree line. We were each unexpectedly handed a small blunt object wrapped in cloth.

"A gift for each of you," *Mãe* stated matter-of-factly, and her violet eyes avoided our gaze. She cleared her throat, her hands on her hips while tapping her foot on the floor. It was tradition for the parents of those participating in the ritual to give a parting gift to their child; it signified good fortune and luck on their voyage to adulthood. I did not expect such a gift; though she had her own business, and the taxes in our village were incredibly steep.

The surprise in my features must have been evident as she narrowed her eyes.

"Well, go on then, the both of you," *Mãe* urged. "We haven't got all day."

Ornella opened hers first, and she audibly inhaled.

"I—I can't accept this." She choked back tears as she remained frozen in the middle of the pathway. The sun's rays outlined her white hair, and her emerald eyes glimmered.

It was easy to see why everyone loved her.

And because we loved her, we had to leave Alizeh. Ornella's happiness and freedom were worth all the gold coins, the academy, and every single delicious pastry from the local baker.

My head snapped up at the sound of *Mãe* speaking again.

"I am allowed to gift my two daughters whatever I wish." Her eyes darted to my hesitant fingers. "Sayah, it's not going to bite; go ahead and look." I could feel her stare as I peeled back the cloth.

There were three items in my possession.

It contained a pouch full of gold coins, a map, and a journal with a letter addressed to me tucked inside. Before interjecting about being gifted *Mãe's* savings, I read her letter first.

Sayah, my moonflower,

I am so proud of you and all that you have accomplished. Your desire to read and learn about the world around us is truly inspiring. There is yet to be a pianist who can move beings' hearts as you do when your fingers dance along the ivory keys. Both you and your sister are the biggest blessings in my life. I am so grateful that I was sent a Meir from the Videira, and I followed the orb to you and your sister's pod on this day so many moons ago. How rare it is for a single pod to contain two healthy infants. For that, I am genuinely thankful.

I can only imagine how hard life has been for you, having bloomed from the vine as a Marked One. Regardless of what your peers and those in the village may say, you have been blessed by our sacred vine, the Creator, and the magic that takes root in this world. I am positive that you and your sister were meant for great things. Do not be afraid to embrace those around you, my daughter. You only need to show others how gentle and kind your touch can be.

I have gifted you a map of the five kingdoms so that when life leads you in new directions, you may blaze your own path. This journal is yours to keep and write down as many adventures as possible, as I know it is difficult to recall all in memory. The last item I have for you is a pouch of gold coins. I have spent years saving for you and your sister so that when the time came, I could gift you the life I wished I could have given you from the beginning. Accept my gifts and follow your passions. If you truly want to take over my music academy someday, you have my permission and gratitude when I say it is yours.

Love,

Mãe

The empty plates.

That was all I could think about as a sob escaped my lips.

During all those years, she went without meals so we would have a bright future and a fresh start.

The paper blurred in my vision, and tears fell onto the parchment paper.

Why would she do such a thing? I already knew the answer, and my lip quivered as I nodded my head in thanks and slipped the heart-filled words into my pocket.

Mãe never expressed such raw emotion, and it was out in the open between the lines made of ink and feeling. This letter must have been prepared for some time now, before knowing that we would leave Alizeh. My vision still burned, and a lump had formed deep in my throat. The cold wind that whipped at my face did nothing to cool my now-heated cheeks. Memories of her sitting at the table during supper with an empty plate flooded my thoughts, and the gold inside the pouch felt overwhelmingly heavy.

Mãe tenderly squeezed my shoulder, pointing her chin toward the main walkway. I placed the items into my pack.

Some things were better left for the heart to interpret in its own language.

My throat was unexpectedly dry as we left home and headed towards our village's main entrance. I took one last look at our cottage. Our dwelling was modest, but the feeling of warmth oozed from every nook and cranny. The plants around us seemed to be saying farewell; the large oaks shook their limbs, and their mostly bare branches fluttered in the wind. Other families could be heard locking up their lodges to join us on the day's trek to the *Videira* as the sun spread its light over the horizon.

The center of the village was already full of life; it would be a monumental day for many. Elves and other beings gathered to celebrate not only the changing seasons but the new lives that would bloom. Spring was crucial for the many farmers and beings whose livelihood relied on their bountiful crops.

And tonight, I would finally witness such wonder and enchantment.

I hesitantly walked on the crowd's edge, careful not to draw any attention. Ornella was beside me, painfully unaware of those we passed as they gossiped. It was the year the *Marked Ones* would join their place amongst the adults in society.

I pinched my cheeks and made a silly face at several older women, blatantly standing on the sidewalk's edge, squabbling about their disdain for my presence at the ceremony grounds. Their shrieks had Ornella's gaze snapping in their direction, looking for the cause of worry. She grinned and rolled her eyes once she knew I was to blame.

"Making childish faces at the villagers won't improve your reputation," she crooned.

"But it does make me feel better, and my happiness is important too," I smirked as we walked through the crowded streets. "No matter what I do or say, I can't convince them I'm not the monster they've painted me to be."

She simply frowned, her brows creasing together, deep in thought.

Not all villagers disliked us, but we were never treated as ordinary. Some absolutely adored Ornella and fawned over her like she was the rarest gem. However, she did have her fair share of jealous observers who coveted her ability to give energy. Most of the village ignored my presence, certainly told to by the elders, I had no doubt.

What an odd pair we were, the black sheep and the crown jewel.

All storefront windows had been painted with pictures of our sacred vine of life; swirls of green and blooming pods filled my vision in almost every direction. Lanterns were placed above dwellings that excitedly anticipated the *Meirs* that would arrive tonight in search of new parents—this was how elves let the *Videira* know that they were willing to take on a child of their own. Only about a dozen or so infants bloom at a time, so if the sacred vine sends a *Meir* to your home, it is considered one of the highest honors a couple could receive. They would follow the *Meir*, a glowing orb, back to one of the various pods attached to the *Videira*. The pod absorbs the *Meir*, shining luminously before each petal recoils back to reveal an infant elf cradled inside.

This is why *Mãe* being chosen as a parent for the two of us remains more of a mystery. There were alleged rumors that her door had remained bare, and all lights were off in her cottage on the night we bloomed three hundred twenty-five lunations ago. No lanterns were hung at her old dwelling before she had moved to this village on the outskirts at a minute's notice.

The sun had crested over the treetops in the east, displaying a vast array of colors as its beams of light made their way across the foliage. The flowers and plants of the night were back in their hollows and crevices, their luminescent glow fading. *Mãe* led the way through the masses to the entrance of our village. The archways had been carved to resemble growing vines along their wooden posts.

"Are you two about ready?" *Mãe* asked, her voice nearly lost inside the crowd's excitement.

"Ready as I'll ever be." Ornella's lips didn't quite manage a smile.

A loud popping noise rang out, and those who were gathered by the gates cheered. Flower petals fell from the sky like confetti as we began to march toward the *Videira*, northwest of our current location. If we jogged and stayed as a group, we would make it to the ceremony grounds before evening. Elves harnessed the *Ligação Mágica* when traveling to the vine to quicken our pace. Generally speaking, it would take us three moons to make the journey there without casting a spell.

But with the help of the land's magic, we quickly and stealthily moved through the trees without disturbing the nature around us.

I placed my fingers through the swirling tendrils of light, their green and gold unattainable. An invisible barrier encompassed the *Ligação Mágica*, making it impossible to grasp fully. It glittered like light around my skin, an ethereal experience. My eyes closed, and I prayed.

Please, Creator. Protect my family; help me keep my powers under control.

My chimney smoke-colored eyes flew open wide; I was now ready.

"Ligeuro." No sooner than the spell was spoken from my lips, I was off, bounding through the pines like a fawn using its legs for the first time. I had practiced saying the elementary spells my entire existence, and only now had I earned an approving nod from *Mãe*. Today would be the single day she permitted our use of magic. Ornella was beside me, her emerald eyes bright and joyful. Her waves of white whipped around her face as she laughed, enjoying the freedom at which we moved.

The illusion was shattered, however, when I noticed the elven military moving quietly with us among the tree's shadows. They were more likely present for the village's protection as we progressed a large distance in a short time. Their armor clung to their body like a second skin, the same subtle, warm green-and-brown tones of the encompassing foliage.

Mãe was behind us; I could feel her presence near.

We managed the rest of the journey in the comfort of each other's silence, Ornella occasionally humming a soft melody whose tune lingered now in the songs sung by the nearby birds.

And out of nowhere, it appeared.

The *Videira* was only a few hundred paces away; the massive trees made the perfect camouflage for the vine that stretched across Alizeh's soil.

I couldn't help but think this would be the first and last time I would witness such a magnificent event.

As our group entered the grounds, I mindlessly plucked a pubescent flower from a nearby tree, tossing its pink petals. Ornella and I observed them slowly spin in the air as they descended to the ground while most of our peers assembled by the nearest tents.

A mysterious feeling had awoken inside of me, something dark. It crackled inside my heart, a fire scorching across an already withered landscape. My vision blurred as I dazed about the elves before me—their faces bright with unfiltered happiness. This emotion went unnoticed by all, as the birds still chirped, and the air was filled with a weighted intensity. The magic was dense here, near the *Videira*.

The petals gradually turned to an ashen black beneath my feet—and I walked over their newly made graves before anyone could see.

Chapter Three

The *Videira* was an enchanting sight to behold.

As we approached the sentient being, the magic that stemmed from its trunk and the earth around us became vibrant with color and active throughout the forest's soil, traveling up the tree trunks and vegetation. A vibration, first soft, became apparent as we strolled through the ceremony grounds. I exhaled, taking in its massive size that stretched miles across our kingdom. Up close, the vine was a translucent green, with orbs of light swirling inside the trunk, which was as tall as our cottage. The spinning clouds of bright color constantly moved, like the fluttering wings of a butterfly in flight. Its display of life and magic transfixed me as I stood on its outskirts.

Movement from one of the many tents beside the ancient platform caught my attention as I waited with the dozen other elves participating in the rite-of-passage ceremony. An elder dressed in traditional elvish attire stepped into view. His tan robe stopped short at his ankles, and the several badges displayed over his heart showed me his rank was important. The male made his way over to our group, walking with unassuming confidence.

"Good afternoon, children of the vine." He bowed, and we reciprocated the gesture. With his hand he signaled to one of the larger shelters in the back of the grounds, where there was less activity bustling from tent to tent, preparing for tonight. "This is where you will bathe and change into your ceremony attire. Both family and volunteers for this season are waiting inside. They shall help you prepare your mind, body, and spirit for the renewal of your soul."

His eyes brightened, and he scanned each of us. "After the rite, you will have passed through your youth. The *Videira* will have transformed you."

I strolled next to Ornella as we approached the large camp. I made eye contact with the tenured elder, who narrowed his eyes.

From behind, I heard him say to our group, to not one elf in particular, "Today is a day of rebirth. May your image be one of positivity and light as you will now be recognized as contributors to our kingdom."

Ornella rolled her eyes at the elder's comment, and I peeked over my shoulder to see him enter the tent opposite ours, near the platform. "As if I didn't already contribute to society," she mumbled under her breath. She crossed her arms and frowned. "I'm tired of being constantly reminded."

"That was absolutely directed at me." I rubbed my temples, perplexed. "What do you think they will have me do to contribute? Maybe clean out the horse's stalls? I can see that being an option."

Whatever task I am given, it will not be pleasant. But perhaps *Mãe* will have snuck us out of Alizeh by then, and I won't be forced to do the remedial work.

I wondered where she was now, scanning the faces around us, searching for her familiar violet eyes.

"Shush before you give them any ideas." Ornella pinched my cheek, and a slight smile emerged across her weary face.

We slipped through the tent's cloth to find several bathing stations in the corner. The thin makeshift walls made me uneasy; we would bathe near the boys, who were also preparing for this evening. I bit my lip and tried to focus on anything else.

A large group of volunteers entered the space as we changed into robes. They all stood behind the young adult they would be assisting tonight, and I watched several women bicker about who would have the privilege of tending to Ornella.

I felt small, grasping that no one would stand behind my bathing station. The volunteers began to work, starting the baths and ignoring me in the process.

This was my first time on the verge of tears in many lunations. There were no jokes to help me cope with the massive feeling of dejection now invading my heart.

My feet felt planted on the floor, and time moved sluggishly. Ornella was too preoccupied with the volunteers trying to rid her body of our journey's filth. Tears ran down my cheeks as I gritted my teeth.

Today was my ceremony day. My day to cleanse my essence and renew my soul.

Why, then, did I feel like the filthiest elf that ever existed, like the mud and dirt that now covered my skin, had somehow absorbed into my core?

I straightened my shoulders and exhaled before starting my bath. Power began to hum beneath my skin, responding to my anger. Several women glanced at me. Their auras were slightly dull, already tired from their task-filled afternoon.

The most imperative thing at this moment was remaining calm.

"*Fogoe*," I uttered the spell and, in chorus, snapped my fingers. The sudsy water started to heat. My breathing calmed as I numbly stared and watched the bubbles grow in size.

As I went to step in, *Mãe* appeared, abruptly whipping back one of the tent's makeshift walls; the other contestants squealed as they were briefly exposed to the adjacent room.

Expressionless, she scanned the makeshift bathing quarters and stealthily walked over to my station.

"Wait." Her hand gently pulled me back out of the water. She examined several jars with unknown ingredients before her hardened gaze met mine. Her violet irises were dark, swirling with anger and determination. "You forgot the herbs and oils for your bath."

I merely nodded, my mind silent. The shaking of my limbs had ceased, a detail I was suddenly made aware of as I entered the hot bath. Several bubbles popped gently against my skin, and I sunk deep into the sudsy water for coverage. My hands fluttered over my chest as I willed myself to take slow and steady breaths. The threat of losing control of my powers was now at bay. I would get through this, and *Mãe* was here to help me.

She scrubbed at my skin fiercely, and I was positive she was trying to remove the flesh from my bones along with the dirt and sweat.

"Please, can we be finished? The other girls have already moved on to their hair and makeup." I remembered what Ornella mentioned about stylists coming from Ascelin, and my heart dropped. There was no possible way that they would come close to touching me.

The bubbles in the bath had all popped, and I inspected my wrinkled hands, which had been sitting in the water for an extended time. I started biting my nails out of habit.

Abruptly, *Mãe* slapped the top of my hand, and I winced.

"Quit that, Sayah. Only children chew on their fingers." A bucket of cold water was suddenly dumped over my head, and I groaned.

A towel unexpectedly appeared inches before my face, and I snatched it, eager to leave the cold bath behind. After I was in a fresh white robe, we were escorted to the last remaining vanity in the next room.

I hesitated before sitting on the stool, studying my features in the mirror.

The seven or so girls next to me all wore matching shimmering emerald gowns and were nearly identical to one another. They sat poised in perfect unison while various stylists whispered compliments in their ears. The girl's cheeks were painted pink, and the smiles emitting from their expressions looked painful. Ornella's white wavy locks perfectly complemented the subtle shades of the usual light-colored hair, and their skin glowed with warmth from constant sunlight.

My raven hair was a stark contrast, and my grey irises did nothing to contribute to my naturally pale skin tone.

Mãe laid out various beauty products on the countertop before us, and I rested my eyes as she began to work.

For once, the silence between us wasn't awkward as she applied a cream to my forehead and cheeks. I wondered what I would look like with such expensive products caked onto my face. We did not have extra gold to keep such luxurious items in our home, so this was a once-in-a-lifetime chance.

"What are you thinking about?"

I listened to the sound of her shuffling around products, looking for something.

"Who do you know in Erebus?" I asked in a hushed tone. The question had been eating away at me from the instant she mentioned she knew someone outside of Alizeh.

It wasn't a secret that she had traveled when she was young. But our conversation in the garden was the first time she openly admitted to me that she had a life outside our kingdom. One I knew nothing about.

She sighed, and I cringed in response, expecting to receive an earful.

"His name is Ulfred; he is a good friend of mine." *Mãe* began to apply another cream to my lips. "We were in a band together and played mostly concerts in a small town called Flykra. It's in Erebus. He lives in a small cabin beside the town's lighthouse and is one of the few I still am in contact with."

My heart skipped a beat, and I absorbed every word, committing them to memory.

The next question I knew was crossing the line, but I needed an answer.

"How did you manage to contact him?"

I heard the catch in her breath, the momentary lapse in composure.

"What I am about to tell you stays between us." She tapped my shoulder, and I opened my eyes. Her intense stare was unwavering as it met mine. "Do you understand?"

My head bobbed up and down, and she braided flowers into my hair as I focused on the floor below me.

"I used the *Ligação Mágica*." Her voice quivered as she continued. "It was risky, I know. And I can't tell Ornella anything because they watch her every move. The only person that is not monitored in our village is you."

I met her eyes in the vanity mirror, confusion lining my features in the reflection.

"The priests are afraid to synchronize with your wavelengths. They think that connecting with you will drain them of their energy."

I furrowed my brows, blind-sighted by the news.

The *Ligação Mágica* interconnects all living things. The more bonded by memory two beings are, the stronger that connection is, and the easier it becomes to synchronize with their wavelengths.

Distance is nothing more than an illusion for two fully bonded souls.

"I don't understand." Thousands of questions formed, eager to leave my lips. "Why can't you tell Ornella?"

Mãe knelt at my feet, her already petite frame now far below mine.

"Because, Sayah"—her slender hands caressed the sides of my face as she spoke—"the magic in the soil is a double-edged sword. Yes, it is convenient for cleaning up spills and messes. But the more you use its properties to cast spells, the easier it becomes for others to synchronize with you too."

I sharply inhaled and gripped the sides of the vanity's stool.

That was why she did not want Ornella and I to cast spells. She hid the fact behind the ruse that we were the example set for our peers. That it made us lazy and incompetent.

The truth was much more disturbing.

"This is why you do not see others using magic so freely. It is not for the sake of respecting the *Creator*; it is because you make yourself a target to the world around you if you take that chance."

"They've been spying on everyone? For how long?" I asked in disbelief. I scanned the area and noticed all the vanities were now empty. Ornella had vanished along with the others.

Mãe stood, neatly dusting off her knees. Her expression was now emotionless as she waited behind me in the mirror, gently squeezing my shoulders.

"From the second you two bloomed from the vine. Ornella the most; that is why I cannot confide in her. Not yet." I followed her observation to the back of the room, where several soldiers' shadows stood outside our tent. We made eye contact in the mirror again, and she tenderly smiled. "What do you think?"

I blocked my reflection by hovering my hands in front of my line of sight. "Wait! I don't want to see until I have my dress on."

Careful not to reveal my transformation yet, I stood away from the stool, my backside sore from sitting too long. I quickly changed into the shimmery emerald dress, identical to all the others. *Mãe* slowly zipped up the back, and I waltzed over to the full-length mirror set up at the end of the row of vanities.

I saw a young woman staring back at me, timid but beautiful.

Night-blooming water lilies had been woven into my midnight hair, cascading down my shoulders. Paired together, they reminded me of my favorite night sky. The flower's scent added to the special occasion, and its fragrance reminded me of my evening strolls beneath the stars. She had kept my makeup natural, just soft undertones of nude colors to accentuate my full eyelashes and pink lips.

"I look pretty. Thank you, *Mãe*."

She stepped forward, and I anticipated she would tell me the same.

"Sayah, today is your day of transformation." She paused to clear her throat before continuing. "In life, you do not need to be the most skilled, sharpest, or even the best-looking elf in the room." I watched a tear trickle down her cheek in the mirror's reflection. "But you must promise me you will be the most resilient."

My lip quivered, and a small cry escaped as I nodded.

Most parents tell their children they look dashing and embrace them before saying their good luck wishes and prayers.

But my *Mãe* was different; her expression once again brutal, cold.

I caught my timid expression in the mirror and changed it to that of a determined warrior. I would be the most resilient of all my peers and face hardship with grit and perseverance.

Their fear would not define me.

A giant hum sounded the alarm, and the vibrations from the *Videira* let us know the shift in seasons was taking place. Winter was fleeing, and spring prepared for its grand entrance.

It was time for the ceremony to begin.

Chapter Four

I *will not show weakness; they cannot shatter my callused heart made of pure grit and severed feelings. The rhythmically beating flesh inside the cage that is my chest is nothing more than hardened stone.*

For my family, I would stand before the masses and endure their scrutiny. I can do this.

This is what I repeated to myself as I exited the tent and met Ornella standing in an orderly fashion with the other participants.

We formed a line beside the tent, just beyond the view of the waiting masses next to the platform. Made of carved stone, it was strategically positioned mere inches from the *Videira*. The ceremony grounds contained what was left of the remnants from our past, a historic relic created by our ancestors. Several priests stalked toward us; their smiles were bland as they waved the line forward.

"What do I need to do?" I whispered to Ornella. She walked in front of me, and I focused only on the movement of her hair. Orange marigolds were intricately placed throughout, forming a gorgeous waterfall of flowers.

How fitting; they represented the sun's warmth and light.

She squeezed my hand for reassurance and turned her head to the left so I could hear. "Follow my lead and mimic my movements."

Our single-file line stopped at the edge of the stairs. My heart accelerated seeing how many beings were in the crowd. Ornella ascended the few steps to the top of the large stone, and I followed swiftly behind her.

I placed my hand over my heart, a gentle reminder. It was made of solid stone, the same material beneath my bare feet. No amount of callused stares or harsh words could move me.

We formed a circle around the forgotten language, the swirls of intricate symbols engraved into the center of the stage. The vibrations from the vine stopped, and I held my breath. The priests found their queue to enter the ritual, bow to the vine, and then to the masses for their patience.

"Our sacred vine prepares for a bountiful harvest this spring."

A young priest, only a few years older than me, spoke, his voice quite large for his petite frame. He was dressed in a light brown robe with small accents of green and white. His eyes were kind as he met our stares and gave a silent nod of approval before continuing.

"The *Videira* has blessed us with many children this season; I am thrilled to announce that twenty-seven pods were counted last night and are ready to bloom."

The crowd murmured excitedly; twenty-seven was the highest number of pods to bloom in a season since nearly the vine's creation. If all pods successfully matured, that is. In rare instances, a *Meir* would lead a couple to their pod, and the infant inside would be still, entering the world lifeless. Their souls had already moved on to the next, but the chosen parents would mourn their child's passing in this world for the rest of their lives.

Elves live for several hundred years, so the thought of mourning a child for that long was heart-wrenching.

The only peace was knowing that their souls would be forever intertwined and that they would meet again in their soul's next existence.

A soft breeze began to move toward the vine, pushing past those of us standing on top of the platform. We watched in awe as the magic from the kingdom was pulled in its direction.

Swirls of yellow and green tickled my skin and glided through my hair. The thin veil that separated the *Ligação Mágica* and my skin had vanished; I had not known that the magic of our world could be physically touched; the sensation was euphoric.

The enchanting scenery entranced my peers, their eyes glowing with a childlike wonder. Ornella's mouth was agape next to me as the *Videira* glowed brightly. The dense forest trees began to rustle, and I squinted into the shadows to see past the warm glow.

What I thought was a large ogre pushing through the twigs and brush was actually a giant black bear. The woodland creatures gathered at the edge of the ceremony grounds, all to observe the changing of seasons from winter to spring—wild animals filled every nook and cranny of the surrounding forest. Hundreds of deer gathered beside families of cougars and foxes; mice, squirrels, and rabbits peaked out from their burrows and holes. Birds littered the dense canopy; it was a miracle their weight did not break the branches of the pine.

The air around us grew still, no sound uttered over the piercing quiet. An abrupt gust of wind came from all directions, whipping and lashing at our skin. The frigid cold lasted seconds, and even so, I worried I might lose feeling in my fingers from frostbite. Our *Videira* began to vibrate and shake the earth, glowing brighter than I thought possible.

A wave of warm air produced by the vine blew past me and back into the landscape, pollinating the all-encompassing nature. The caress of the swirls of magic tickled my skin, and I had already forgotten the icy air from moments ago.

Alizeh's winter flowers were nothing compared to the beauty of spring's vegetation. The greenery that surrounded us bloomed in seconds. An array of colors now took hold of our woodlands, and the yellow-and-green magic again enveloped the forest floor, synchronizing all living things.

Spring was in full bloom, winter already a distant memory.

"Our sacred *Videira* has again blessed us with the joy of spring. Let us rejoice and praise both the *Creator* and our vine."

The priest raised his hands, permitting the masses behind me to express their delight and thanks for a successful shift in seasons. They erupted into cheers of bliss, laughter, and celebration, which lasted several minutes as I stood anxiously awaiting the next part of the ceremony.

Elders dressed in white robes embroidered with green leaves at the ends of their sleeves walked onto the platform, holding several crowns. They were made from white lotus flowers to signify our purity and rebirth.

"It is time for the changing of seasons for our children, as all will now recognize them as young men and women."

We faced the crowd, and an involuntary blush rose to my cheeks. The priest made a point of gesturing toward my sister and me.

Heart of stone, Sayah. I chanted the words in my mind until they became a softspoken whisper. Their sharp stares and sneers could slice through to my core, but my heart had already solidified.

This time, an elder came forth to speak, his grey beard tickling the collar of his robe. "This ceremony is special. Among the participants, we have two sisters who bloomed from the same pod and were blessed by the *Videira* and our *Creator*." He then paused for effect. "The rare *Marked Ones*."

I withheld from rolling my eyes at his over-exaggeration. The man had enunciated nearly every word, explaining our importance. However, Ornella bowed, so I followed her example. Sounds of excitement could be heard rippling throughout the crowds. After lifting our heads, we stepped back into the circle with our peers. What a relief it was when we were instructed to face inward once more.

Several significant vibrations emanating from the vine shook the earth. All the elders on the stage stepped forward and bowed to the masses before speaking in unison. "Let the ritual commence."

A symphony of music began to play, and I noticed several of *Mãe*'s pupils included in the orchestra. I knew she must be proudly watching her students, and the thought flashed a temporary grin across my face.

The elder came forward; the badges on his tan robe seemed too loud for the rest of his attire. His bold voice broke everyone's trance from the elegant music that played quietly in the background.

"Admon, son of Theos. Please step forward and touch the sacred *Videira* so our maker may bless you."

Admon was a sharp-looking elf who sported a military uniform. His light brown hair cropped at his shoulders was neatly combed, and the usual stubble on his chin had been shaved for the occasion. He was quite handsome. The young man stepped out of the circle and met the elders beside the vine, who nodded for him to proceed. A small flash of light pulsed from within when his hand touched the vine's flesh, and a quiet hum could be felt.

The elders placed a crown of white lotus flowers on Admon's head, and he went to stand at the front of the stage to face the audience.

"Admon has made the transition from boy to man. Let us rejoice in his acceptance." There was a quick applause and a pleased look across the priests' faces.

The ceremony continued as several names were called, and I watched as our circle grew small in the center of the platform. This was the tricky part—the ceremonial dance.

All the other participants were in complete synch, their feet perfectly timed with the music that flowed onto the platform. I did my best to keep up, but their sharp movements increased as the circle tightened and sweat creased my brow as the seconds turned into minutes.

Suddenly, there wasn't enough air in my lungs; my vision blurred as I twirled. If Ornella and I were not called soon, I feared I might pass out on stage in front of everyone.

My heart stopped when I heard the priest harmoniously announce our names: "Ornella and Sayah, daughters of Aster. The *Marked Ones.*"

The added status to our names again felt unnecessary, and when I glanced over at the elders, their eyes were like daggers piercing through me. Their glares showed no kindness, and I could feel they would not hesitate to take out the threat to the *Videira* if something were to go wrong. The knot in my stomach tightened as Ornella, and I approached the vine.

A heart of stone; I had a heart made of stone.

Murmurs could be heard above the soft melody of the orchestra still performing. I hesitated, greeting the vine up close, awkwardly bowing. My mind was frozen, fearing what might happen if I touched it and accidentally drained our maker of its energy. The elders on either side of me and my sister were tense, and I could see their hands flexing from the corner of my vision. Faces were etched with worry, some emotions bordering hatred. But the more I was within the sacred vine's presence, a wave of calm trickled over me as I focused on the swirls of colors flowing throughout its awareness.

Ornella nudged me with her elbow to break my trance.

"Both daughters of Aster, please step forward and touch the sacred *Videira* so our maker may bless you," the head elder announced, followed by a deathly quiet.

We placed our palms on the *Videira* and waited for the expectant flash of light to be followed by a hum of approval. I cleared my throat, still trying and failing to recover from the dance I had not prepared for. Seconds ticked by, and I wiped the sweat off my forehead and glanced at Ornella. She was frowning.

The vine was not acknowledging our presence.

Oddly enough, neither my twin nor I was the first to panic. The elders looked as if we had committed a great sin, failing to hide their grimaces behind placid smiles. Confusion swept over the crowd like a plague, and I could hear feet shuffling on the forest floor.

I wondered what *Mãe* was thinking while staring at her daughters' backs. The two children she had paved a future for at her own expense were now in a dangerous situation; if the vine refused to give us a blessing, we would be viewed as unworthy.

We could be exiled, or worse.

I could hear shouting as an odd sensation tickled my fingers, and I looked to Ornella as she impatiently shifted in her emerald gown, meeting my shocked stare with her own. It was painfully quiet, and I realized the orchestra had been abruptly cut short. One of the elders dressed in white whispered something to the short priest, and as he made his way to us, an overwhelming awareness came over me.

Ornella's expression was agape, and this alluring consciousness coursed through our veins as we became one with the *Videira*. A bright luminescence flowed throughout the sacred vine, and its entire being began to glow from its roots to its canopy. The white light traveled into our hands and limbs, and the symbols carved into the ancient platform began to shine with a scorching intensity.

The enchanting display lasted several seconds before dissipating, creating a shock wave in its wake that was felt throughout the dense forest. The vibrations that originated from the vine were so intense that I could hear several cries from the crowd as the ground became unstable.

Overwhelmed by the *Videira's* response, I quickly retracted my hand from its presence. Ornella mimicked my movements, and we turned to face the elders for clarity on what had just happened. Everyone wore the same expression, their mouths agape as the vibrations from the vine quieted, and my skin's ethereal glow faded to its standard pale shade.

I found the courage from somewhere deep inside to face the crowd.

To my disbelief, the masses before us expressed the same emotion: amazement and wonder. A rush of emotions overcame me, and I placed my hands over my lips to keep them from trembling.

This was not the reaction I thought I would be met with. I wasn't prepared for acceptance.

The villagers who feared me gazed into my dull, grey eyes as if I could somehow bring hope and peace.

The elders' expressions were a mix of confusion and worry as they panicked, trying to salvage the rest of the ritual.

"Look at how our *Videira* has blessed us! We should praise and rejoice in its gift to all elven kind: Ornella and Sayah. It has been several generations since our species was blessed with *Marked Ones*, and our sacred vine wants to acknowledge such wonderful creations," the short priest shouted, his arms raised high.

My sister and I are more than our gifts; my thoughts mirrored my expression, and I frowned at the priest's declaration.

An unsettling feeling sat in the pit of my stomach as the crowd erupted into cheers. Ornella stood with hands clenched into fists at her sides. The elders carefully placed the ornate flower crowns on our heads, and we were ushered to the front and center of the platform with the rest of our group.

My vision shifted and transformed as I studied the crowd, not fully comprehending the imagery before me.

The scenery was rich in color, everyone oblivious to the tendrils of vibrant light that intricately surrounded each individual outside of their auras. Confused, I looked to Ornella, but she only held a tight smile, fists still clenched in irritation at the priest's comments.

My power tingled suddenly at my fingertips, and a feeling of fullness spread to every inch of my body. I examined my palms, and in the peripheral, shriveled petals floated down to the platform.

I closed my eyes and focused on the beautiful orchestra that restarted their concert. The music grew more potent, and the background noise vanished as I enjoyed the sweet melody.

Ornella grabbed my hand and squeezed. My eyelids fluttered open to a once again silent audience. Her smile faltered, and her grip began to cut off my circulation.

"Your crown!" I whispered with urgency. The orange marigolds and her crown had nearly tripled in size. I had never witnessed flowers so large and vibrant.

She shook her head and bowed to the crowd, pulling me down in the same motion.

My view now directed at the stone, I noticed the ground was strewn with dead petals. I instinctively reached up to touch the top of my head. What was left of the flowers from my crown fell away to the stone beneath me, void of color and life. The night-blooming water lilies *Mãe* had woven into my hair were mere ashes.

I had failed to contain my emotions, and apparently, touching the vine had only intensified the process nearly tenfold of what I was usually capable of.

The young priest jumped into action, standing directly behind Ornella and me as he raised his hands above his head and toward the sky. "Behold! Another beautiful display of their gifts; what divine powers meant for the well-being of all of Alizeh! Let's give both sisters another round of applause!"

There was nothing that I could do or say as the masses cheered. We were not tools, and we did not exist merely for the benefit of others. I would convey this if I had the ability to voice my opinion aloud.

But I remembered how, moments before, the masses would not have hesitated to exile my sister and me if the *Videira* had not given us a formal blessing.

Those in authority already knew this, and I was beginning to fully comprehend how much power they indeed had over our lives.

Ornella squeezed my hand again, and the power ebbing through our bodies quieted. She was the yin to my yang, and whenever I couldn't shut off my energy manipulation, she would give her own until my power's hunger was satiated.

I was living with an angry beast inside me, always ravenous.

Immediately following, we were ushered off the platform in an orderly fashion. Here, we would now wait in preparation for the ceremonial feast. My thoughts began spiraling; *what would happen now? Mãe* told me that I must attend this ceremony to appear unassuming. I had zero idea how we would sneak out of our village once the ritual was all said and done.

The shimmery emerald line of gowns moved forward. We were headed to the other side of the vine, where the feast would be held. The answer to the question invading my thoughts was quite clear as the elders stood before us, their eyes slanted in disapproval.

We will not be leaving Alizeh anytime soon.

"I think it is time we are acquainted." The elder with the badges hanging on his chest stepped forward. His hazel eyes were full of judgment as his glare lingered longer than necessary. "I am Elder Josias, head of the council. It is nice to meet all of you formally."

Elder Josias bowed, and we reciprocated the gesture. He led us to a path underneath the vine. We paused at the entrance to the short tunnel; the captivating swirls of color above us were magical.

However, all the enchantment was lost when he pulled Ornella and me briefly to the side.

"Sayah, it is so nice to meet you finally." His words sounded rehearsed. "I heard you did not attend the ritual practices, which is understandable." He stopped walking directly in front of me. I had never seen an elf with eyes like that of a snake, yet here he stood. "Your path in life has already been chosen by the *Creator* and the *Videira* when they blessed you."

I cocked my head to the side in confusion as he spoke in riddles. "What do you mean?"

"Has no one told you yet?" He glimpsed at the military guards, shooting them a disapproving stare. "It appears that I will be the one to inform you. After the ceremony has commenced, you are to report to the city of Ascelin to receive proper training on your energy-draining abilities. You will be stationed there as a cadet in training until further notice."

I was speechless.

The embellished dream that I would inherit *Mãe's* academy was a lie. I suspected they had yet to inform her of this decision.

I spoke through a clenched jaw, matching his intensity. "Does our *mãe* know about this?"

Elder Josias snickered, leaning down to whisper into my ear, his reply oozing with venom. "I'm sure that you will inform her. And if you use your powers without permission again, you should expect consequences. I do not care that you are an esteemed *Marked One.*"

His threat was perfectly timed, as our *mãe* and others rushed to our side. Her violet eyes were bright and proud, making my own water. Sweat formed on my temple, and my palms were clammy.

To protect our family, I would do whatever was necessary.

That included being forever bound to the invisible chains of authority. I nodded to Elder Josias, remaining obedient. He grinned and gestured for my family to continue forward.

Ornella had said nothing the entire time, but tears now painted her cheeks. She had endured this her entire childhood, the wrath of those in control.

And now that our childhood was over, it was my turn.

Chapter Five

Military personnel were stationed every few paces from one another; how I had not noticed their overwhelming presence was a mystery. All I could focus on were their hardened expressions, the suits of armor that clung to nearly every inch of their skin beyond their necks and faces.

Reality started to set in as we casually strolled to a long rectangular table, already brimming with food. My appetite had abandoned me as my family sat in our chairs, the traditional elven food warm and fresh. Their delicious smells of meat and cheese wafted under my nose, and typically, I would stack my plate to the rim.

Mãe filled her dish with scalloped potatoes, vegetables, and a thick turkey leg. She seemed unaware of those around us, who gawked and stared. It was difficult to ignore their gossip, and I could hear the words *Marked Ones* make their way into a conversation every few minutes.

I sat and watched *Mãe* fill her plate with her favorite side dishes, oblivious to what had transpired between Elder Josias and me.

I sighed, tossing a bread roll and roasted duck onto my saucer.

Elves began to filter into the makeshift dining space, and I would have enjoyed a meal outdoors if I hadn't felt a pair of eyes monitoring me. Elder Josias sat two tables down and had the perfect vantage point.

I picked up the bread roll and scarfed it down quickly. I wanted to tell her I wasn't hungry, but that had never been a luxury we could afford. When you don't know when your next meal will be, when you grow up in a house with often empty cupboards, you don't get to say those arrogant words aloud.

A distant memory of *Mãe* sobbing on the kitchen floor surfaced, cradling my sister in her arms while she apologized repeatedly for having nothing for us to eat. So, I chose the blandest food I could find and ate my feelings.

I consumed all that my stomach could manage, and it wasn't until my sister placed a hand on my wrist that I noticed my tears soaking the napkin in my lap beneath me.

"You can stop now; you've had enough." Her voice was gentle, a soft murmur. I wiped my mouth clean of crumbs using my wet napkin and placed it back into my lap.

Mãe sat silently from across the table; she had stopped eating.

Her expression was once again detached, cold.

"When do the *Meirs* arrive back at the vine?" I asked, my voice scratchy and dry. I reached for a glass of water and gulped it down eagerly.

"Soon, typically at sunset." She squinted, studying my face. "Are you all right, Sayah?"

No, I was not okay.

I was told my purpose would be to join the military; I wasn't a fool. They were planning on using me as a weapon—for what and why, I did not know.

But now was not a good time to mention it, not while *Mãe* had a plate full of delicacies. I wanted her to have a chance to experience such luxuries;

this was all that I could give her right now. I quickly stuffed multiple bread rolls into my pack. Eyeing the rest of the food, I looked up at the weight of *Mãe's* glare.

"Do that again and see what happens." She still had a fork in her hand, and I gulped. "You've made poor choices recently, and it seems to me that another heart-to-heart needs to happen, doesn't it, Sayah?" Her fork was pointed at me, the closest weapon of choice on the table.

I was lucky the knives were out of her reach.

She blatantly pointed with her utensil to a table where the priests and elders sat. "They're watching. Put the bread back on the table, and do not add fuel to their fire."

Bless the vine, she was right. Elder Josias smirked from where he sat as I put each piece of bread back on the table. Luckily, no one else was watching; they were too absorbed in each other's company.

I turned to my side; Ornella had been oddly quiet. She was picking at the food on her plate, pretending to eat. I raised a brow, wondering why the sudden vow of silence.

"Did you . . . see it, Sayah?" Her eyes never left her plate. Her long white waves created a barrier between her face and mine. The larger-than-life marigolds had been removed from her hair. "There were these odd-looking rays of light outside everyone's aura."

Ornella could also perceive other beings' auras; our energy manipulation gift was similar. The huge difference was that I steal energy while she graces others with it.

"I did." I glanced over at *Mãe*, who was pretending not to strain her ears to hear our conversation. My elbows rested on the table, my chin on my fists, as I leaned forward. "It's probably best we save this conversation for the journey home. The sun is starting to set, and the *Meirs* will be arriving soon."

Mãe's expression relaxed, and I received a quick nod of approval.

A group of young children playing at the front of the table caught my attention as they tried to catch fireflies with their bare hands. The sun had set behind the trees, and the moon hung delicately in the orange-and-pink sky, its light reflecting off the empty dinner plates. I glanced around at the other tables, observing the sudden change in atmosphere.

Mãe straightened, craning her neck to try to see through the dense forestry. "They're here." Her violet eyes glowed with anticipation in the dark.

Ornella and I twisted in our seats, looking in the same direction. Others around us had joined in, scanning the surrounding foliage. Considering the size of our gathering, the crowd was silent; a whisper was hardly audible over the chirping of crickets and the occasional call of an owl.

"There, I see one!" A man from the table behind me had nearly knocked over their drinks in eagerness. Elves inside the ceremony grounds conversed in excitement as small lights in the distance contrasted against the shadows of the dark forest.

"Those look like fireflies." I scanned the area, unconvinced.

"It's the *Meirs*. The pods are about to bloom!" Ornella squealed.

Mãe shushed us, as it was customary to welcome the infants into this world peacefully. We sat on the edge of our seats as the first of the glowing orbs made their way into the clearing.

Several elven couples entered the ceremony grounds, blushing with joy, their eyes not leaving their *Meir* once on the way to the vine. The *Ligação Mágica* swirled around the chosen individuals, and I felt it was our *Cre-*

ator's way of showing joy and blessings. The *Meirs* floated like stars sent from the heavens to lead the way. Several elves patted the newly blessed partners on their backs as they hurried past the tables to congratulate them on their journey to parenthood.

My gaze was transfixed as the orbs of light slowly descended into the matured pods and became one with the *Videira*. The new parents knelt before the vine, waiting in anticipation for their child to bloom.

The pods' flesh began to glow a vibrant green, triggering the petals on each pod to curl back one by one, revealing a crying infant cradled inside its soft interior. The couples held their baby close, and several midwives stood beside the *Videira's* root system.

A tenured midwife stepped forward after the newly joined families entered their tents just outside the ceremony grounds. She was holding a clipboard and wearing a maroon-colored robe. An emblem of the vine was sewn onto her chest.

"I am pleased to announce that all twenty-seven pods bloomed successfully this year. There are eleven boys and sixteen girls. All have been confirmed healthy and are now in the care of their chosen parents. Please be respectful and give them space during this exciting time." She nodded to the elders and priests, who softly clapped and beamed at the positive results.

The crowd quietly celebrated, and gossip about who was blessed with an infant this year became the center of all table discussions.

"Was that the baker and his wife, Dalhia, I saw? They have prayed to the vine for several years to be chosen." Ornella smiled. "I am so happy for them."

"I think it was. I wonder what it feels like to be blessed by the vine with a child." My eyes lingered on *Mãe*, who was cleaning up her dishes. I thought of a young version of her, led by a *Meir* to the vine without a partner. What it must have been like to have been chosen by the vine and walk in front of the masses alone. My heart momentarily ached.

"What is it like—becoming a parent?" The question was nearly inaudible as it escaped my lips.

She froze, carefully considering her words. Several seconds passed, and there was a look in her violet eyes that I couldn't quite place. "It *was* scary—at first. I wasn't sure if I had the ability to take care of an infant, let alone two. But from the instant I laid eyes on the both of you, I knew I was meant to be a mother." She recalled, "You two were sunflower and moonflower for many moons before I finally decided on your names."

My throat bobbed. She hadn't called me moonflower out loud for many lunations; the last time I could remember, I wasn't old enough to tie the laces on my boots.

She blinked, and emotion swirled deep inside her violet irises as she took our hands from across the table. *Mãe* gave a gentle squeeze.

"Regardless of what anyone thinks of me, I know the vine gave me a family because I needed one. If it weren't for the two of you, I wouldn't have tried so hard with my academy. I owe all of my success to being chosen as a parent." Her hand shook in mine. "You both gave me a purpose; thank you."

I bit my lip to keep it from quivering. Her unscripted words effortlessly moved my heart; the thin thread tethering me together was dangerously close to snapping. Parents usually express their feelings when giving gifts, after their child is fully dressed in ceremony attire, or even after the ritual, congratulating them on entering a new stage of their lives.

But here *Mãe* was, reaching out to us over a table of messy plates in front of strangers, displaying her feelings for all to witness.

A family walked behind us, and Mãe let go to wipe her tears away. "Let's clean up our area before heading back."

I nodded, following her lead. As I removed the dishes and silverware at the end of the table, my vision still played tricks on me. Every so often, I would notice the magic tendrils surrounding each elf. I also began to see that *Mãe* was right. None dared to use spells besides the elders and priests. They had cleaned up their table in seconds, synchronizing with the land's magic swirling along the grass without a second glance.

I had always been fond of the magic encompassing our kingdoms. Its familiarity was comforting and a way to feel connected to nature. But now, the magic was just an extension of those who wished to control us. Something that was meant to be beautiful and good twisted into a weapon.

Elder Josias caught my attention as he left his seat. His brows furrowed, and a frown tugged at the corners of his features. Dread crept up my body as I watched him stroll over to the guards stationed beside the pods.

It wouldn't be long now—I would leave the ceremony grounds with the military and fulfill my purpose to the kingdom of Alizeh.

I needed to warn *Mãe* of what was coming.

But before I could speak, Ornella interjected.

"What's happening?" She pointed at the *Ligação Mágica*.

The usually calm swirls of green and gold were in a frenzy. Their movement was jagged and rapidly growing distressed. *Mãe* jumped from the table, where all the noise around us had abruptly stopped.

The masses waited, watching in wonder as the magic of our kingdom acted in an odd manner. The hair on the back of my neck and arms stood, and I listened for any sound inside the dense forest full of animals and creatures.

There was none. It was silent.

A few moments passed, and something sauntered within the brush at the edge of the ceremony grounds without disturbing a twig or branch.

They all came out into the open, and we stood frozen. Creatures cloaked in black had entered the sacred grounds during a harmonious occasion. This species was unknown to me, and none matched any descriptions from my previous studies. Not one creature was alike, yet they were similar. Their sizes immensely varied, making it hard to make out specific details in the moonlight. But each one was blanketed in a black magic that ebbed and flowed along their skin.

A group of military guards quickly rushed between the unknown creatures and the families just a few paces away. Their swords were drawn, and some held daggers. I scanned the area, taking a defensive stance, and noticed archers in branches of the forest, their arrows pulled and ready to fire when given the command.

"Exit the ceremony grounds at once," a soldier ordered. "You do not have permission to be here. If you do not comply, we will use force."

The creature before him lifted its arm, pointing directly at the soldier's chest. Multiple guards formed a battle stance, prepared to defend the surrounding elves and the *Videira*.

"You will not receive another warning; you are ordered t—" The guard crumpled to the ground, gasping in pain. He winced, removing his hand from his abdomen to reveal a gash oozing with blood.

Gasps and shrieks rang through the air as the guard coughed up the red liquid onto the grass, becoming lifeless. His aura faded until it completely vanished from my sight.

Chaos ensued.

My heart pounded as I ran toward the vine in the opposite direction of the threat. Ornella's hand found mine, and screams of terror were trailed by the sickening thud of bodies falling to the forest floor. The vile creatures moved in unison, their silent attacks quick and deadly.

"Where's *Mãe*?" Ornella's voice trembled. We were a few paces from the vine.

"I don't know." I frantically scanned what was now a bloody battlefield, where more soldiers began to charge the cloaked beings before falling to the ground in despair. Arrows flew through the air, some tragically meeting an innocent victim trying to escape. I spotted her dark-blonde hair near the tents outside the ceremony grounds, where the infants and their new parents rested. Three ghastly creatures followed her.

Realization hit me like a ton of bricks, and I met Ornella's stare as we hid behind one of the empty pods intertwined with the vine. "She went to protect the children." My voice came out a strangled mess.

That was what *Mãe* always did. She cared for others before considering her own well-being and protected those needing protection.

And the infants were Alizeh's future, their souls innocent and vulnerable.

My body shook, and my knees were close to caving in. I squinted back and forth between Ornella and Mãe's location, finding my resolve.

"We have to help her," I said aloud, more for myself than my sister.

She nodded as we peeked out from behind the *Videira's* foliage. Our sacred vine had sensed something was amiss, and its defense system of poisonous thorns started to multiply, wrapping around the vine's exterior. Elves were naturally immune to the poison, as we were created from the same source. Several families were with us now, their whimpers and cries intensifying while we hid inside the vine's protection.

The ceremony grounds were painted red, the blood of our kind seeping into the soil.

"If we don't leave now, we will be stuck inside the vine's armor," Ornella whispered beside me.

We could stay in the vine's protection, almost ensuring our survival, or risk everything for *Mãe* and the newly bloomed.

Before I could change my mind, I squeezed past the dense vegetation of thorns and out into the open, where I was vulnerable to attacks.

A sea of still figures was strewn across the sacred landscape. Moans erupted from the mouths of several elves, still alive, with weakened auras. Our military held no ground. The creatures turned vicious, exposing their fangs; they attacked like rabid dogs. The fight inched closer to the vine, near the tables where we had dined earlier this evening.

"I have to help them." Ornella jumped into action, running to the nearest injured. She held a man's hand, and I watched as the power left her fingertips, cradling his aura until it was reenergized. She quickly observed the battleground that was closing in on our location. "Go on ahead; I'll be all right here." My sister nudged her head in the direction of the tents.

"If necessary, I can run back under the vine's protection. Hurry, Sayah, please help *Mãe*." The panic in her voice was evident as creatures moved toward the tents. Our military was exhausted from failing to pierce the impenetrable black mist that shrouded the enemy. Their swords, daggers, and arrows were useless.

"The second they pass the tables, promise you will go and take cover," I instructed, waiting for her to nod before racing toward the tents; I left Ornella to fend for herself.

The vine's shield would soon be impenetrable, and I did not know if she would make it underneath its foliage before that happened.

Without a second thought, I reached out to the *Ligação Mágica*, which was still in complete disarray.

"*Ligeuro*." I spoke the spell into existence while snapping my fingers.

Bounding forward, I used every ounce of my focus to dodge through the battlefield, containing a disarray of soldiers, vile creatures, and fallen victims. A soldier's blade accidentally caught my arm, slicing through my skin. Wincing in pain, I rolled outside the edge of the sacred grounds, placing a palm over the wound for pressure.

The tattered fabric of my dress was filthy and stained various shades of brown and red. My bare feet were caked in dirt mixed with the blood of my fallen kindred. I whipped my head around toward a distant scream in the direction of the group of tents nestled in the trees.

Soldiers had been discarded on the ground in front of the tents. A fresh wave of panic rose in my chest as I ran inside, concerned with what I might find. But to my relief and confusion, the tent was vacant. Their cots lay turned over; various items, such as blankets and food, were scattered on the floor. I thoroughly checked the other nearby shelters to ensure my findings were the same: all empty.

Mãe must've helped relocate them; that was the only solution I was willing to accept.

I swiftly bandaged the cut on my arm and left the tent to examine the forest for clues as to where they might be.

The moon was hidden behind the clouds as I examined the nearby brush. Anxiety crept up my skin as I found nothing. I was positive I had heard a scream moments ago. The only visible light emanated from the frenzy of green-and-gold magic running along the shrubs and soil.

The Ligação Mágica can connect me to Mãe and tell me her location.

I did not care if it made me vulnerable; this was an emergency, and I was desperate. With my fingertips fully immersed in the land's magic, I tried to call out to her. Nothing happened. Frustrated, I tried several times more, closing my eyes and repeatedly saying her name.

Still nothing.

I screamed, pulling at my hair as I kicked the dirt beneath me. "Why won't it work!" My sobs carried through the quiet nature. I crumbled to the ground, defeated. All I wanted was to help *Mãe*. A river of tears flowed onto my lap, mixing with the dirt on the shimmery fabric. I wept inside the shadows that enveloped me underneath the tree's condensed canopy.

A pulse began at the center of my palms and traveled down the length of my hand into my fingers.

The power that ebbed and flowed beneath my skin tingled, and I instinctively reached for the magic again. This time, I didn't say her name. I thought of how her face was content with joy as her hands danced along the ivory and ebony keys sitting at her academy's grand piano. The sound of her humming a tune while washing the dishes. I visualized her essence, who she was to Ornella and me. A teacher, renowned pianist, our *Mãe*, who fought tooth and nail to give us everything. She was the courageous woman willing to leave all she had worked for behind.

Then, I felt a slight tug, a pull from the magic, as my thoughts synchronized and traveled through the intricate pathways; I envisioned *Mãe* running through the trees, pacing herself with multiple couples cradling their infant children. They raced forward, sprinting away from some unknown threat. *Run faster*, I urged, frantic that whatever was chasing them would soon catch her.

Her violet eyes went wide, and her head twisted in my direction. It was as if she was looking straight at me before the image inside my mind collapsed.

I blinked, standing, now aware of *Mãe's* presence. I sprinted to her. My soul was tethered to hers, and I felt its tug on mine, guiding me in the right direction as I avoided tree limbs and stumbled over rocks. I snapped my fingers once I had a clear visual of the forest encompassing me.

"*Ligeuro.*" I repeated the spell and was off.

The closer I was to her presence, the more substantial our connection grew. I heard another cry as I homed in on their location, disregarding the sharp rocks beneath my feet as I scrambled to find them.

And quite abruptly, she was there, backed into a thick pine as one of the vile creatures towered over her petite figure. In the distance, I saw the families carrying infants fleeing toward the city of Ascelin, where the rest of our military was dispatched. I prayed to the vine they would remain safe and be intercepted by the military shortly.

My focus turned back to *Mãe,* who was in immediate danger.

"Which one is it?" a dark, gravelly voice spat at her.

Her eyes narrowed on the man, and she spoke through clenched teeth. "I'll never tell." She threw a dagger in his direction and simultaneously dove to her left into the bushes.

He caught the blade with his bare hand, unfazed by the blood now dripping from his palm. "I won't ask again." The stranger leaned forward, glaring into the brush where she now hid. "Which one of the infants is a *Marked One*? I saw the beacon of light and felt its presence."

At his words, I halted and crouched behind a tree. None of the infants that had just bloomed were declared *Marked Ones*. The elders or priests would have announced if any had possessed gifts, rejoicing in yet another blessing for our kind. No, this man was mistaken.

Unless . . . by a beacon of light, he referred to when my sister and I touched the vine. I inhaled, placing both of my hands over my mouth in shock.

That would mean he was searching for Ornella and me.

I tensed at the sound of the friction from the man drawing his sword. His movement was so quick it was nearly undetectable as he pulled *Mãe* out from the shrubs and held the blade pressed against her throat.

"No!" I panicked, revealing my position, and threw myself at the man's feet. "I am the one you're looking for; leave her alone—please," I begged, fully bowed in compliance. "I will do whatever you ask of me as long as you promise to spare her life."

I peered upward and met the stranger's glare.

He was the shell of a man, a lifeless beast. Once, perhaps an elf or werewolf, I could not tell. The dark magic clung to his pale skin like a parasite; his eyes were the only remnants of where his soul still resided. His right eye was green, and the left a golden hue.

However, unlike the others, he could speak. The tendrils of light surrounding his heavy black aura were a startling silver.

Mãe put herself directly before me, shielding my body from his blade. His eyes were shockingly bored as we cowered.

"You are not my target." His attention averted to where the families had fled, irritation now lacing his tone. "And now my prey is escaping."

At that moment, my heart shattered into a thousand shards.

His movement again was untraceable; there was a split second of silence before his sword pierced *Mãe* straight through her chest. A gargling noise left her mouth, followed by a gasp as he sheathed his weapon.

He kicked her before stepping over us as if we were no more than the soil beneath his boots. I cradled her in my arms as she breathed haggard breaths. Before leaving, he turned his head to the side. Inside the black mist, I could see him smiling.

"I left you alive so that you would have to watch her die." He shrugged his shoulders, uncaring. "I don't like when people ask me for favors." And just as sudden as he had come, the stranger disappeared into the night. We were left alone, deep inside the wilderness.

I tended to *Mãe* and desperately tried to stop the bleeding. But we were soon sitting in a puddle of red, my hands stained as I comforted her. Her moans of pain were unbearable, and she did not respond to my voice as she twitched inside my embrace.

I shook through the sobs and tightly pressed her cheek to my chest, my tears soaking her warm hair. "I'm so sorry," I repeated over and over into her ear. I rocked her like a child, listening to her body fight for air as she no longer winced.

My regret and guilt were all-consuming as I stroked *Mãe's* golden hair and hummed a soft lullaby, blanketed by the shadows of night.

The whimpers that escaped her lips were nothing more than a whisper, and soon, her breaths began to shorten until they stopped altogether.

I felt her soul rip from my own, leaving this world as she moved on to the next.

Mãe left me, taking with her all the joy and love that had remained inside my heart with her.

Death was not at all like I had imagined; it was quick and underwhelming. She was unable to talk in her final moments. We did not have a heart-to-heart, and I was startlingly aware that I was alone, shaking as I held her fragile figure.

I sat in a daze until I awkwardly moved her to a patch of soft grass, kissed her cheeks and forehead, and placed her rigid hands over her chest. I hovered over her grave, suspended in time. *Mãe* looked like an angel resting on top of the soft grass.

Except her face was too stiff, and all the color had drained from her cheeks and lips. Her expression still held the remnants of pain, the last feeling that she felt, the last experience that she held.

The sun slowly rose into the morning sky and began to peak through the pines.

Until something inside of me snapped, and I dug my fingers into my palms, piercing my skin. Anguish consumed me as I came to the awareness that *Mãe* was gone. I let my powers take control, they seeped out of my body, a trickle gradually shifting into a raging river of hate powered by revenge.

The last thing I can recall is my head snapping to where *Mãe's* murderer headed in pursuit of a *Marked One,* and I took a step forward.

The foliage around me fell limp, losing its vibrancy and color. The forest critters shrieked and ran in all directions, seeking shelter from my wrath. My mind went black with fury as I siphoned the energy of every living thing around me.

That was when the true chaos began to rain down on the kingdom of Alizeh.

Chapter Six

None received mercy,
The destruction that followed was born from her misery,
Wrath consumed all living things,
Enveloping the wilderness inside her raging fury,
The land beneath her feet was now forsaken,
She blindly forged a warpath on the hunt for revenge,

Nature, however, was eerily silent,
Mourning the death of her beloved children.

Part Two

Chapter Seven

A soft melody had pulled me out of the darkness. A hazy vision of fingers dancing up and down the ebony and ivory keys, growing in intensity; it was a bittersweet song full of mourning.

I shuffled forward, my mind an empty abyss. We paved our way farther into the greenery, blindly moving as the sun and moon alternated overhead.

Mãe was gone.

The only truth that was absolute. Pain coursed through every inch of my body, and I wasn't entirely sure if it was from mental or physical exhaustion. How many moons had passed, I did not know. The world surrounding me was laced in black.

Ornella was the one who found me—after the attack.

I had no recollection of the time following *Mãe's* death. My eyes had abruptly fluttered open to see a pair of emerald irises hovering inches above me, still inside a deserted forest. Her expression was contorted from grief, and I knew she was aware of *Mãe's* passing. I had traveled most of the way to Ascelin, draining the energy of all the encompassing vegetation in my path.

We did not return to our village in the Woodlands, and we managed to escape without being detected by our military. When I inquired about the second wave of soldiers, she said we had traveled too far east to be on their radar. It was a selfish decision on both of our parts. Ornella was having a more challenging time with not going back, expressing that she could greatly aid the wounded in their healing process. But knowing that we were what the creatures were after, we couldn't. It would be detrimental if we led them straight to our kindred.

The monsters cloaked in black were after *Marked Ones.*

And if I was being completely honest with myself, I was running away. I wasn't prepared to face the world I knew with *Mãe* no longer in it. The last time I had stepped foot in her academy, our old cottage, and walked the narrow pathways to and from the various shops, she had been there, full of life. I did not want to ruin those sacred memories with ones that were bleak and full of anguish. This departure had been planned, but now it was complicated.

We were being hunted.

The only thing that put me at ease was that the *Ligação Mágica* was no longer in a frenzy.

Ornella eventually spoke, her voice raspy and hoarse from crying. "Sayah, hold my hand." She extended her own after a brief hesitation.

I examined her skin, covered in a layer of dirt. My bloodshot eyes squinted in the sunlight. "Why?" I asked, my voice unfamiliar.

"We are still leaving breadcrumbs." She twisted around to the landscape behind us, and I copied her movements.

My powers seeped out of me like poison. There was a trail of lifeless trees, sucked dry of their vitality. The freshly bloomed flowers and spring greenery had recoiled in on themselves, desperate for rejuvenation. I had created a path of withered and dying plants leading straight to our location. The world looked how I now felt with *Mãe*'s permanent absence—dark and void of all joy.

"Ah, *those* breadcrumbs." I noticed Ornella's trail of overgrown plants and the vibrant scenery of nature she painted when she walked. "I'm not the only one leaving clues. Mine just aren't as pretty." I gestured toward the flourishing landscape behind her, but she said nothing.

After the realization, we held hands and pushed forward. Our touch calmed the power that ebbed and flowed underneath our skin, daring one of us to release it from its confinement. The instinct to survive kept us upright and moving.

Ornella had salvaged our packs from the ceremony grounds before coming to find me. The creatures attacking our kind abruptly stopped after I went to find *Mãe*, disappearing into the woods. In the confusion, she grabbed our belongings and followed behind shortly after.

I wondered how long it took before the elders grasped we weren't coming back.

We passed several farms and avoided populated villages, which proved convenient as we stole several crops for nourishment. My gardening and hunting skills were amateur at best, but I made do with what I had.

My twin had never looked so pale, even when she overworked herself using her powers. Her usually sun-kissed skin blended into her long white waves. She was much like the wandering souls from our childhood bedtime stories. Lacking purpose and drive, forever cursed to flow within the magic that tethered together our five kingdoms.

The landscape around us had slowly changed to flat land with the occasional rolling hill. We needed shelter for the night now that we were close to the Woodland's edge. There was a winding creek up ahead beside a small, abandoned barn. This would accommodate our needs for now.

Ascelin was close. We would likely arrive at its gates tomorrow afternoon.

"This spot is good enough." I peered down at what was left of the rags we now wore. The clothes we had previously traveled into the *Videira* were inside our packs, a small blessing for which I was more than grateful. Suddenly, I was aware of my stench, and I itched to wash the filth off my body and to get out of these blood-soaked clothes. I gagged at the thought that I had worn them for so long.

"We should wash up first." I nearly choked on bile as I spoke.

The creek's water level was high from recent rain and cold from the night's drop in temperature. We scrubbed our skin raw, cleaning off the grime and remnants of the tragic event that occurred. After drying, I put on the only clothes to my name. It was a pair of fitted cargo pants and a fitted T-shirt I usually wore for hiking. Ornella wore similar attire. As I laced on the boots that had been stored inside my pack, I immediately felt recharged. I was indebted to her for retrieving our possessions.

"Thank you." My heart was still heavy. We sat at the creek's edge, staring into the stars.

She didn't answer, and we rested for the first time in several moons.

The situation still didn't feel real. My head was bursting with pain, but it was nothing compared to my constant agony.

Ornella moved from her frozen position next to me and began to comb the tangles out of my matted hair. It reminded me of when I would gripe and groan when *Mãe* brushed the tangles out of my mane after a long day of playing in the garden behind our cottage. If I had any tears left, they would have run down my cheeks.

She tugged on my scalp, braiding my hair down my back. When she was finished, I did the same for her. The tangles in her hair were not as bad as mine had been, and I did my best to use my fingers to comb through her white waves gently.

"What were those creatures?" Her question startled me, breaking the long silence. Ornella pulled her knees into her chest while waiting to hear my thoughts.

I bit my lip, thinking. "I don't know. But I am quite certain that they did not originate from Alizeh."

She considered. "What if the black mist was a spell? Could it have possibly been a known species, disguising themselves using *Escureo*?"

"No, I doubt it." I rubbed my chin and exhaled. "Spells don't last that long; they would have been revealed eventually."

An unwarranted memory flashed across my vision, and I squeezed my hands into fists. "I saw one of their faces close up. At first, I thought it was lifeless, but its aura was black and still intact. And the mysterious tendrils of light we've been noticing were silver."

The man who had murdered *Mãe* was of an unknown origin. I was determined to expose this monster for what he was and make him pay for his crimes, for taking away the most beautiful soul.

We had both studied the different species in our kingdom growing up. There were primarily plant-derived beings and those who thrived inside our dense, leafy, green nature. None of those studies mentioned any creatures cloaked in a mysterious black mist with parasitic qualities.

"While in the city, we could check their library for information," I suggested. There would be a wide selection of books, and knowing exactly what we were against was important. Perhaps these vile creatures had a weakness of some kind.

"I'm not sure that's a good idea, Sayah," she whispered. I turned to her, and Ornella would not meet my gaze.

"Why? That's all we've got to work with right now. We're not exactly in the position to be picky." As I questioned her, I studied the *Ligação Mágica*. It was flowing with ease and still showed no sign of distress. My shoulders relaxed slightly, knowing that the mysterious creatures were not nearby.

"Because not only do we have to be careful of an unknown creature hunting us, but we also have to watch out for the guards. And we could be targeted if anyone finds out we are *Marked Ones*." She stood and held out her hand to help me up. "Let's sleep a bit before heading into the most populated area of Alizeh."

I had forgotten about the military. They would want to capture both Ornella and me so they can use us for what they view as our purpose in living. To be at the beck and call of all elven kind. *Mãe* was no longer around to protect us, and now that the vine had blessed us in front of everyone, it would be acceptable to have us fulfill our duties as adults.

We had never traveled outside our village, let alone our kingdom. The *Creator* only knows how others would react if they discovered we possessed powers. We had been under the protection of our military and those in authority throughout Alizeh.

Now that we were trying to escape from their iron grasp, who knows who else would want to buy, sell, or trade us for large amounts of jewels and gold?

Power was what was coveted the most in all the five kingdoms. More than all the treasures and luxuries one could obtain.

If one had control over the *Marked Ones*, they could forge a new world—new kingdoms.

"All right, you have a valid point. A few, actually." My face was now level with hers as I met her stare. "But if the opportunity presents itself, we should at least try. Their library's history collection is huge compared to what we had in our village."

We took shelter from the cool night air inside the nearby barn, its faded red paint peeling off the soft wood in giant flecks. I used my arm as a pillow, still holding hands with Ornella with my free hand.

The power still coursed through my veins, pulling at whatever energy was near. My sister was turned away from me, though I could hear her quiet sobs every so often as I stared up into the shadows on the ceiling.

"I'm so sorry," I quietly pleaded. I wished to take away her pain; I wanted to turn back time and make the right choice. If only I had used my powers to drain that vile man of his blackened aura to save *Mãe* from a horrible death.

Reality fell upon me, and I choked on my tears through haggard breaths.

I did not save her, and my sister still did not respond to my apology.

Chapter Eight

There were elves in every direction, and I naturally recoiled at the size of the masses. I was still draining energy, my powers trickling out as they gently tugged on the auras of those nearby. However, luck was on my side, as most just yawned or stretched while I hurried through the crowded streets.

The city was alive; a gentle hum traveled through the ground, and the massive, towering buildings nearly touched the clouds. The elves here wore different clothing, regal garments meant purely for fashion. There was no need to wear work boots or the sturdy material in our village on the Woodlands' outskirts. Although detailed and adorned with lace, I blushed at the sheerness of the fabric surrounding me. I had expected a more diverse crowd here in Ascelin; it was our main seaport for all imported and exported goods. Only elves shuffled about to their destinations, oblivious to the impending threat that had mysteriously invaded our kingdom.

We stayed in the shadows of the looming skyscrapers, scouting out a place to rest before heading to the port. Guards were stationed at every other corner, alerting us. Somehow, I had to avoid the military's detection and being caught by those who attacked us.

I was too proud to admit out loud, but I was frightened to board a ship and cross the Dark Waters. Our kingdom was known for its hospitality and secure borders. The elven army was massive simply because our kind could live for several hundred years. However, most of our military guarded the *Videira* and the outer borders, leaving small villages like ours with little to no protection.

I couldn't fathom how the mysterious threat had snuck into Alizeh undetected and wiped out a large group of soldiers in such a short time. The strong military presence must have resulted from this, but as I surveyed the citizens enjoying their afternoon, it was obvious that they were unaware of any danger. Outside of Alizeh's protected boundaries, the risk to our safety was concerning, to say the least.

We walked in the cover of the crowds in search of an unknown destination. The buildings were identical, accented in green and gold, with large circular windows. Bridges weaved through the skyscrapers above us, connecting the structures to form an intricate design. It was a maze without a beginning or end.

"Can we please just take a peek inside?" I looked up at the sign above the shop's doorway. There was a picture of several books stacked on top of one another. A library. Thank the vine for something familiar to me. Ornella glanced at the incoming waves of beings; her features wary at the guards accompanying them. She nodded, and we took cover in the safety of the various books.

The door jingled as we entered, and I stifled a disappointed sigh.

This was, in fact, a library, but nothing like the one back in our village. Looming before us was a labyrinth of shelves that continued to a second level of identical rows of literature. All the walls were pristine white and lacked decoration; there was no originality in sight. I couldn't help but compare the bland scenery to the enchanting bookstore that resided back in the Woodlands; yes, there were books stacked high on every tabletop corner, but the rich scent of old, worn books that sat atop furniture painted a vast array of colors drew in readers of all kinds by the droves.

This establishment had a large desk behind which several librarians sat as they busied themselves with paperwork and customers.

Ornella entered the library and began scanning the monotonous rows of shelves. I followed. We reached a section labeled *creatures, species, and biology,* and she started scanning the bindings of the books.

"Did you notice how often the land's magic is used for spell casting here?" I asked as I started my search.

"Yes, it is odd." Her emerald eyes were still decorated with dark circles, but the spark of unwavering determination made me admire her that much more. Even in exhaustion, she could find the will to keep pushing forward. After everything we had endured. "Especially with how it is preached in our village only to use if vital or during monitored practice."

But here, the swirls of green and gold were pulled to and from, and the residents cast spells as if it were muscle memory. Ornella did not know that the magic was being used to spy on our species, the synchronized waves of magic tethering us together a double-edged sword.

I had decided to wait to tell her more until we left our kingdom's borders.

"Do you know what we should be looking for, specifically?" The books before me were labeled *Species in Alizeh* and *Rare Creatures Inside the Five Kingdoms of Aksel.*

"Anything to do with rare magic, dark magic." Her eyes slid over the literature with care as she continued. "Books on black magic are banned, but there has to be information on a creature with a similar description to the ones we encountered at the vine."

I furrowed my brows. I loved to read. More so than Ornella. In all the books I had read throughout the years, I never encountered a volume that mentioned so much as a single passage about dark magic.

The bulky black-and-white clock on the wall chimed; it was almost noon.

"If the vine decides to bless us and we find any information, we should quickly head over to the seaport." My hands skimmed through the pages of the various texts, not skipping over a single word.

"You still think we should head there?" Ornella now faced me with a large book opened in her hands.

"Yes." My reply was immediate. There was a reason *Mãe* thought we could find refuge in Erebus. For selfish reasons, I needed to know more about her past and what she kept hidden from us. I wanted to cling to what was left of her; I was desperate.

Something deep in my bones told me we would find answers in Erebus's small, frozen landscape.

My eyes started to water, and I blinked away the pain. A little voice in the dark corners of my thoughts whispered venomously over and over: *She's not here because* you *hesitated, Sayah. You failed to protect her when she needed you most.*

Ornella's book abruptly closed, pulling me out of my momentary despair. "We can plan to hide in Erebus for now," she responded. "It's not as if we have anywhere else to go."

We combed through the shelves to no avail. No books on any species cloaked in black were found, and anything related to dark magic was forbidden. Literature containing information on magic severed from our world was considered blasphemous.

A long sigh escaped me; I would have to resort to requesting outside assistance.

"I'll go and ask for help." I shrugged, placing my hands in my pockets. She closed yet another book on creature biology. Her irritation radiated off her being, and I prayed to the vine that her annoyance was not directed at me.

Before she could reply, I turned my heel and headed to the front counter, not wanting to find out. Ten or so librarians sat behind the counter as customers waited to check out their reading material. I mulled over how to ask the question without alerting the librarian of my true intentions.

"Do you have any books on . . . an extremely rare or unique species? Not located in the *creatures, species, and biology* section?" I despised my naturally awkward demeanor, as the librarian paid me no attention and flipped through several paperwork packets.

"No, everything we have on species is in that section. Perhaps you skimmed over the book you are looking for." Her boredom stung as she pushed her square glasses up from the bridge of her nose.

The other curators also ignored me, immersed in their daily routines and tasks. A line of customers grew behind me, heightening my anxiety. I chewed on my nails, unwilling to walk away without something useful to tell Ornella.

"Can you give me a description of the species you're looking for? Or what kingdom they reside in?" The librarian snapped; her tone laced with irritation.

"All that is known about the species is that they are aggressive and are cloaked in a black mist." My arms were now crossed, a frown playing at the corner of my lips. There was no need for her to be so rude.

The librarian's eyes darted to me for the first time, and she carefully laid her papers down. "Dark magic is forbidden." Her gold eyes whirred excitedly, but her expression was emotionless. "Why are you looking for such a creature?" Several librarians were now staring at me as heat flushed my face.

"It's—for research. I'm writing a book on legends and fairytales." The lie fell flat as it left my mouth.

Out of the corner of my eye, I noticed one librarian, a dwarf, whose gaze lingered as the others went about their work.

She exhaled, clearly finished with our conversation. "If you are looking for books on fairytales and such, they are in the fiction section. But even those do not contain anything related to dark magic." With a wave of her hand, she gestured toward the shelves on the right side of the building.

"Thank you," I mumbled, slowly making my way over to my twin, shoulders slumped. I hated being the bearer of bad news. She was hunched over a book with her head in her hands. Her braid was falling out as she tugged on her scalp in frustration.

"Anything?" Ornella's hope fizzled out at the sight of my deflated appearance.

"Perhaps a different, less regulated and monitored kingdom would have more information." I had no idea why I thought we would find any information in the largest city inside Alizeh, where they monitor our every move through magic.

If we wanted answers, they must come from an outside source.

The pile of literature that my sister had acquired was heavy in my arms as I went to return them to their proper origins on the shelves. One of the curators took me by surprise as I swiftly turned the corner, nearly dropping the novels in my shaky grasp.

The dwarf's hooded eyes darted around, scanning the area, and she shoved a small, thick book under my arm to conceal it from prying eyes.

As I turned it over, the woman spoke in a hushed tone. No title or author was listed on its faded purple leather binding. "All I can give you is a few minutes," she stated. The strong scent of a hibiscus flower stemmed from her clothes as she popped a peppermint into her mouth. The smell filled my nose, making me a bit queasy.

I gasped as I flipped through the novel's brown pages. "Are these journal entries? I can only read the excerpts that are in *Xodó*." Historical works were printed, never handwritten. This novel had to be at least several centuries old. "Is this information factual? It is not recorded by a scholar or published authentically."

Her thin lips pressed together, and several wrinkles formed on her forehead. Her forced exhale caused her nostrils to flare in annoyance as she looked at both ends of the shelves to ensure we weren't being watched.

"This is recorded by Alizeh, one of the first to bloom."

I nearly choked on my inhale. How did something so ancient exist? And how did a mere dwarf, who is not our species, have access to something so primitive? I had my doubts that this was indeed what she said it was as I once again flipped through the worn parchment paper.

If what she said was true, this was the most valuable item in our kingdom's history.

"You have until noon to put the book back in this exact spot." She grunted as she pointed to the end of the shelf, the weight of her words only beginning to set in. "That is when I go on my lunch break. If you do not return the book by then, we will all face the consequences."

I checked the clock and held back the bile that threatened to come up onto the floor. Ten minutes.

When I glimpsed back to where the librarian stood—she had vanished.

Ornella nearly bumped into me as I ran back to the table, snatching the top book on the heap of literature in her arms to hide the cover of the journal.

"Hey!" she retorted, changing directions to follow. Her annoyance turned to concern when she sat across from me at the many tables. She studied my features, her fingers drumming on the countertop. "What's wrong?"

The clock again chimed on the wall, another minute passing.

Only eight remained.

"We have until the clock strikes noon to review the contents of this journal, and there's a high possibility it contains information on the forbidden dark magic." I carefully started skimming the journal's contents and was shocked it did not fall apart at the seams. The age of the journal was a mystery, but the familiar swirls of a forgotten language sent goosebumps down my spine. They were the same letters carved into the stone platform inside the ceremony grounds. A spell must be used to keep the book in pristine condition, and guilt invaded my thoughts as I knew what the librarian would face if caught.

Ornella squeezed in next to me, and as we began to scan the pages, another issue was brought to light. In response, she mumbled ill of the vine under her breath, and I nudged her with my elbow. It was forbidden to speak negatively of the vine and was even known to cause bad luck to befall you if you repeated such profanity often. I had to agree with my sister on this one, though.

"It's written in the ancient dialect." She hissed into my ear. "Even if we find the right passage, how would we know what it says?"

The symbols seemed to swirl on the pages, my thoughts blurring as the panic set in. My eyes darted to the oversized clock, taunting me as the sound of its hands ticked with each passing second, a constant reminder that we were almost out of time—five minutes.

About halfway through the journal, I stopped on an illustration of a hand-drawn dragon that seemed to be encased in black. At the bottom of the picture, someone had deciphered a small passage into *Xodó*, thank the vine.

"*Breeders of Thereon*," I quietly read the translation aloud. "*They are dragons corrupted by greed and their desire for power; their links to the magic and land around them have died and faded to black.*"

I flipped through several more pages, desperate to find another in *Xodó*. Sweat dripped from my forehead, and my eyes pulsed from the strenuous mental load. My sister placed her finger on a page, bookmarking the drawing of a creature cloaked in black, my heart skipping a beat.

This was what we had been searching for.

"*Our world's Creator renounced the abominations that are Breeders of Thereon, severed from the magic permeating all five kingdoms. The corrupted dragons then discovered that consuming Marked Ones would replenish the magic severed nearly tenfold. Worried about the slaughter that would ensue with this newfound information, the beings in all five kingdoms came together, and a forbidden magic was used to bind the dragons to the land by which they were created—a last resort to keep those gifted with powers from facing a fate worse than death.*

"Still, binding the corrupted souls in place did not stop their greed and desire. In retaliation, they began to breed their creations by using dark magic to give birth to the vile creatures known as Thereon. The Thereon are soulless, enslaved to their Breeders as they crave the darkness from which they were twisted and shaped. Consumed by their desire, they viciously hunt and capture Marked Ones for their masters to devour inside the kingdom of Adara, where the dragons reside."

As I finished reading the long passage, the clock chimed on the wall, threatening to doom us all. I prayed to the vine that my sister had absorbed every word I read aloud to her.

Our time was up. I nearly knocked over my chair and jumped out of my seat without looking at the aftermath. My feet thudded on the carpet as I rounded the corner once more. Sweat formed on my brow as I breathlessly put the book back on the shelf where instructed. The librarian appeared, her face neutral from the other side of the shelves, pulling the piece of history off the ledge and sliding it into her robe's pocket.

"That was close," she alleged to no one specific. "Did you find what you were looking for?"

My head bobbed up and down, and I gratefully bowed to her. "Yes, thank you."

"Don't make it obvious!" The stout librarian grimaced at me as she twisted away to head to the door, lunch in hand.

"Wait!" I pleaded. "I have to know, why did you help us?"

The woman paused, and her chubby fingers brushed back her hair as a playfulness danced in her piercing eyes. Tiny tendrils of light emitted from her being, the same light that encircled all life.

She cleared her throat.

"A truly great librarian carries all books of knowledge. Our duty is to share information, regardless of opinions. The truth is neither kind nor caring. But what you do with that material very well may change the future. And I will always share it." The dwarf wore a half-smile before heeding a warning. "There are those who wish to destroy what history remains, and I have made it my burden to share what is left before it is all gone."

The grin quickly faded from her lips, and the kind woman disappeared amongst the shadows cast by the endless rows of shelves.

Ornella rushed to my side; her face full of concern.

"Did you make it in time?" she inquired, and the sounds of heavy footsteps coming our way made us jump, only to peer around the wooden shelves to see a group of classmates pass by.

"I hope so." My eyes adjusted as I focused on the dark corridor the librarian disappeared into. She didn't have to help, but she did.

I should have asked her about the tendrils of light when I had the chance.

Something deep in my soul told me she would know.

Chapter Nine

*B*reeders *of Thereon.*

My mind flipped over the discovery as we approached the enormous seaport. *Mãe* read bedtime stories to us, and only a handful of times did they mention dark magic.

I never imagined that such vile creatures could exist or that one could be cut off from the magic that permeates the five kingdoms. My eyes followed the swirling green-and-yellow magic that stirred beneath my feet as it entered the ocean's waters and flowed gently with the current.

How tainted must a being be to have their soul permanently banished from using magic by our *Creator*? The uneasy feeling in my stomach was more than just hunger. *Breeders of Thereon* sent their creations to hunt the *Marked Ones* for their consumption. The thought of being devoured by a corrupt dragon made my throat dry.

Cold chills ran up my spine.

"Do you think they're real?" I asked.

Ornella was frowning at the list of departures from our port, examining when the next boat to Erebus would leave. "I do because she was willing to risk her life to share it." The worry lines etched on her face only increased as she stepped away for others to take a look at the long list. "There's more going on here, I'm sure of it."

My shoulders tensed, and I began to pick at my nails. She was right, and she didn't know everything yet.

The elders and priests carefully watched Ornella's every move. I couldn't inform her. Not until we were far enough away from our kingdom that even if they found us through her wavelengths there was nothing that they could possibly do.

Hunted by both our kind and creatures who should only appear in night-mares.

I mulled over her words and nodded in agreement. "I wish we could have talked to her. She might know something about the whisps of light around being's auras."

When our hands touched the vine, the world became vivid and bright. I felt in tune with the magical forest and its inhabitants. No longer was I an outsider to its mysterious beauty; now, my sister and I were a part of its intricate design.

And I needed to understand why.

"What she did could have her executed. That was no ordinary journal, Sayah. We should keep our distance from her." She grasped my hand and led me toward the ticket booth. "There are bigger problems that need to be solved." My twin exhaled before pulling at the hair on her scalp. "No ships sail to Erebus from this port."

"What?! That can't be." I ran over to the board, skimming my fingers along the boats and their departure times. Ornella was right, none to Erebus.

"What do we do now?" My sister chewed on her lip nervously.

Scanning the area, which was now beginning to crowd with people loading onto the vessels for departure, I joined the line for tickets anyway. "I do know that we can't stay here. I'll go ask someone how to board a ship to Erebus," I said with as much confidence as I could muster. "The longer we take to leave the kingdom, the more time the military has to spot us."

She nodded, frowning.

The elves directly in front of us were from Ascelin; their snooty designer clothes were a dead giveaway. I needed to ask someone who didn't look like they would immediately answer my request with their own set of questions.

Elves naturally stayed near the vine; it was our way, our culture. But now that I needed to escape, this was a natural deterrent. When buying tickets to other kingdoms, we would be allotted a pass for a set number of days. If you stayed past your allotted time, you could end up in jail.

There were even rumors that you could be sentenced to Cadell's Chamber, but those were ridiculous childhood lies told by your friends to scare you. Not that I had any. I usually listened to my peers play games and gossip from my corner in the shadows, where they thought I belonged.

"Let me find the right elf to ask." I patted my sister on the shoulder before walking forward. Anxiety crawled along my skin, threatening to release what little control I had over the powers still slowly seeping from me. Walking through crowds should be easy, but I felt like a shark preying on an unsuspecting school of fish. This had to be done, and Ornella would not always be there to hold my hand, figuratively and literally.

The burly man who stood in front of me in line looked like a seasoned fisherman: tanned, wrinkled skin, worn clothes, leather boots. But the look in his eyes as he scanned the horizon, knowing what lay beyond our dark waters and untamable seas, told me he was safe. He wouldn't ask questions he knew he didn't want answers to.

"Sir, do you know why no ships are departing for Erebus ?" My voice was muffled amongst the loud beings surrounding us.

His keen eyes studied my face a moment before answering. "Look around." He vaguely gestured to those in line and at the port. "What species do you see?"

I didn't have to, and I narrowed my eyes at him. "Elves, I have two eyes that work quite well." My voice was clipped.

His smile broadened, seemingly pleased. "Exactly. The captains of these vessels are also elves, and your kind likes to stay in or near your sacred vine. You won't find anyone here who will sail you to where you want to go."

"My kind?" My face heated. "I know what you're implying, but that doesn't explain why there's zero passage to the kingdom." What an absurd comment; I clearly did not pick the right individual to ask.

The man turned to face me fully, and his grin transformed, massive canines protruding from his mouth. I quickly looked him over again, now seeing the subtle differences I should have picked up on. His ears were shorter and rounded with a slightly pointed tip. The tattoos on his arms were tribal; he was from one of the four main clans in the kingdom of Alun.

He was a werewolf.

"No need to be offended." His hearty laugh shook his belly, and he turned back to face the ticket booth. He was next. "Buy a ticket to Danu; you'll find a ship to Erebus at their trading post." The werewolf looked back at me, his eyes crimson red. "Don't tell anyone else your true destination and have a cover story prepared for when the military stops you on your way off the ship. Good luck, lass." He winked and left me standing dumbfounded.

"Next!" The shout startled me, and the attendant waved me over. The man had sauntered off, nowhere to be seen. I hesitantly approached the ticket booth and placed my hand on the concealed pouch of gold coins underneath my cloak. "How can I help you?"

"Two tickets to Danu, please. We want to depart on the soonest vessel available." The attendant behind the stall grumbled something under his breath and looked down at me. "State your name, reason for leaving, and the requested time."

Bless the vine. The awkward pause was beginning to lengthen, so I threw out the first name that popped into my head.

"Genevieve, daughter of Soren." This was one of the girls who had also participated in the rite of passage this season. I recalled her fiery-red hair and freckles, in the traditional shimmery gown. A slight pang in my chest had me momentarily placing a hand over my heart. I prayed to the vine that she was still alive after the attack.

"State your reason for leaving and the requested time." He scribbled something down onto a piece of paper attached to a clipboard.

"Right." I exhaled before continuing. "My friend and I are looking for special cooking herbs in Danu's trading post. We request three days, sir." I flushed at the lie, and I dug in my pack for the gold coins *Mãe* had gifted me the day of the ceremony.

"Three days?" His sharp blue eyes narrowed. "That's quite a long time for buying herbs."

I flexed my fingers in irritation underneath my cloak. This attendant was obnoxious.

"It's only one full day," I countered. "It takes a half day's travel, including the rest of today. Tomorrow would be one full day, and we head back from Danu's port the next day. There is not much time for shopping, sightseeing, and herbs."

He scoffed, stamping paperwork in front of him. I held my breath as a few seconds ticked by, and he replied, "That'll be six gold coins. And don't forget to check the list of banned herbs before returning. Your bags will be checked."

I sharply inhaled over the steep price as I dropped the coins onto the wooden counter.

The young man pushed the passes and tickets over, and without looking my way, he shouted, "Next!"

After the exchange, I walked away, holding the tickets and passes. I hadn't gotten far when the attendant announced, "Due to an ongoing situation, the ticket booths will now be closed until further notice." I froze as the crowd around me began to shout and complain. Guards began to fill the port, searching the area and checking faces.

I felt the color drain from my skin and ran through the angry, restless masses searching for Ornella.

A long white braid stood out amongst the disgruntled beings. Her eyes widened when she found me near the middle of the confusion before spying the two tickets in my hand. "What's going on?! Did you find us a way to Erebus?"

"Yes, and no. I'll explain later once we're on the ship." My words came out exasperated and in short breaths. "We need to catch one of the vessels departing now. I think the elders are onto us trying to skip town." My fingers intertwined with hers, and I pulled her toward the large ships down the dock.

"You're joking? Is that why the military is storming the grounds?" Ornella's voice climbed in pitch as we jogged to the docking area.

"Maybe not, but I don't want to stay to find out." The remaining boats were starting to set sail, casting off into the murky waters. This was not what I had expected to happen. I assumed we would simply find a boat to Erebus, and sail straight there. In the near distance, a large ferry was loading the last of its passengers. My pointed ears twitched, and I strained to hear what was being yelled by a crewmate.

"That's the one we need to board!"

We weaved in and out of the few lucky enough to secure tickets before the dock was shut down. Our feet pounded on the dock as we closed in on its location. I skidded to a halt, joining the line waiting to board.

My chest heaving, I leaned forward to try to catch my breath. Ornella was exasperated but not as winded as I was. The crewmember took our tickets and looked us over. "You two cut it close," he said before letting us pass onto the main deck.

"Too close." Ornella squeezed my hand.

The ferry was full of passengers, and the ground swayed beneath my feet before the boat's loud engine fired, jutting away from the docks. There was so much tension in my shoulders that they ached, and I opted for a free spot on the ledge to view the vast sea. As the ferry departed Alizeh, I studied the landscape of our kingdom from a distance. A deep ache radiated in my chest. We could no longer return to our small cottage. I would no longer stare at the moon through the crescent-shaped window *Mãe* had proudly carved herself. The sounds of *Mãe* singing under her breath and cooking in the kitchen as we pestered her for a taste were now just a distant memory. I was leaving behind my childhood, everything I once knew, along with our loving *mãe*.

The awareness that I would never hear the wondrous melody of her playing an instrument shattered my soul. Music had been her life's work. The overwhelming guilt weighed me down. I had only been concerned with inheriting her academy.

I clenched my jaw and dug my fingers into the vessel's side. My raven hair whipped violently in the wind, repeatedly striking me in the face.

If only I had drained the energy of that vile beast—the *Thereon*—before he had drawn his sword. I could have saved her and our family from being left in permanent shards.

I'm a coward.

Twisting to face Ornella, I exhaled and patted her shoulder.

"There's something that I need to tell you." And I relayed everything *Mãe* had warned me about several hours before she passed.

The *Ligação Mágica* was now a tool, and casting spells was forbidden. Only the *Creator* knows all who are watching and listening.

Chapter Ten

The gentle waves of green-and-yellow magic flowing out of the harbor and into the streets of Danu's trading post were the only recognizable comfort. Various species roamed the crowded sandy beaches, and the island was packed with unique tropical plants and colorful stone buildings. There was an unfamiliar aroma of a sweet fruit wafting through the salty air from the vendor booths nearby, and I licked my lips in hunger. This was the first time I had had an appetite since—I didn't dare finish the thought.

"We have two full days to find passage to Erebus before our time here expires." I patted my pocket containing the essential papers as I adjusted the weight of the straps from my pack. "Where should we start?"

"We'll need to find a place to rest for the evening." She shielded the moon's light from her eyes, scanning the nearby storefronts.

I caught sight of an inn close by, and we made our way to its entrance. I nearly slipped, unaccustomed to walking on soft sand. "There're surprisingly no guards around. No one checked our bags either." A small blessing in our current predicament.

The door creaked as we entered the cozy establishment. There was a small waiting area, a stuffy room with blue peeling paint on the walls cluttered with fragile sculptures and antiques. The scenery reminded me of the thrift shop back in our village.

Movement caught my eye as a goblin leaned around the corner. He had a stocky build with circular glasses nearly hanging off the bridge of his nose. The being grunted and ignored our presence completely. As my sister approached his counter, he tried to shoo us away with a wave of his hand.

"All of my rooms are occupied. A single bed in the attic is all that's left, but I doubt your kind would be interested." His sour attitude was enough for anger to heat my cheeks. The cranky goblin grumbled incoherently under his breath. "At this time, I will not be offering my amenities to anyone of the elven kind." He hopped down from his chair to leave the room.

"Wait!" Ornella's cry sliced through the hushed space, and I jumped from her abrupt shout. She quickly read his nametag before pleading, "Mr. Darvish, my sister and I would be more than happy to acquire your attic room." He examined us both through narrow eyes, his disdain for our presence apparent. "I know most elves from the city of Ascelin have . . . a peculiar taste, but we are from a village on the far outskirts of the Woodlands. We are vastly different from the elves you have met previously." My sister awkwardly cleared her throat.

Mr. Darvish adjusted the spectacles atop his pudgy nose and let out a long, deep sigh. "The elvish military made their rounds around my inn just last night, disturbing every single one of my guests. They were insulting and tried to force me to sign an agreement that if an elf uses my lodging, I will report back to them immediately." The irritable man uncrossed his arms and pulled a pair of rusted keys from his pants pocket. "That is why you cannot stay the night here; I do not want those guards on my property again."

My arms fell limp at my sides, and a cold sweat broke out on my forehead. An image of Elder Josias's face flashed across my vision; his cold, greedy stare was directed at my sister and me. Why it took me this long to comprehend, I did not know. Those in authority viewed us only as Alizeh's property and were determined to repossess their *Marked Ones*.

I clenched my jaw at being thought of only as an asset.

Ornella was suddenly at the man's feet, bowing while she pleaded. "Please, sir. Let us stay for one night. We will be gone by early morning. The attic space is more than enough." She locked eyes with him, her desperation clear in her watery emerald stare. "Our *mãe* recently passed, Mr. Darvish. We have no place to stay. All we ask is for one night, and we'll be out before you notice we were even here."

The old man grunted, pausing before tossing a large, rusted key our way. "Down the hallway and to the right, you'll find stairs that lead up to the attic. The cost is ten gold coins for the night. You must be gone by sunrise tomorrow and sneak out the side door. Do not let my other customers see or hear you; do you understand?"

Digging through my pack, I found my gold coins and handed the man his payment before Ornella could argue the price. We bowed to thank him for his kindness before tiptoeing over to the stairwell. The building smelled of peppermint and burning candles. As we silently climbed the steps, muffled voices seeped out of the cracks in the doorframes.

The attic was on the fifth floor, and cobwebs littered every nook and cranny. I slid the key into the lock—it required a bit of effort to force the entryway open. A cloud of dust covered us, and we had a fit of coughs as we stumbled into the enclosed room.

After opening the single window to let moonlight and hopefully a cool breeze into the stale area, I twisted to face Ornella. "That was some impressive begging," I said. More dust flew up into the air when she placed her bag onto the twin mattress.

"It was necessary, Sayah. If the military has been to all the nearby inns searching for elves, we can't risk being reported by anyone. I doubt Mr. Darvish will, but it's better to be out before the sun rises." Ornella began to unravel her braid, her hair raised and frizzy from the humidity.

"Care to tell me why you told Mr. Darvish we are not like the elves from Ascelin?" I shoved my hands into my pockets, leaning against an exposed beam. I had ignored the aches and pains catching up with me, but now that I was slightly more relaxed, my body complained of exhaustion.

Ornella rubbed the tired out of her eyes, and I could practically see the wheels turning as she formed a coherent answer. She sighed, and the dark circles under her eyes made me feel guilty for asking.

"You always stayed home when *Mãe* and I traveled to neighboring villages for performances; I would hear the latest gossip from her students," she began. Her emerald eyes looked through me as she recalled the memory. "It's better I tell you now, given our situation."

Her boots squeaked across the wooden floor as she paced. "Not everyone . . . likes elves. Many species believe us to be pompous, spoiled rotten hen eggs. And they have every right to believe that. The laws that keep us safe also make it difficult for other species and creatures to seek refuge in our kingdom."

Confusion was written along my features, so she divulged further. "I know what we were taught: Alizeh is a haven for all beings. But that is not the case. In the past several hundred years, our laws and military have made it near impossible to enter our borders if you did not bloom from our *Videira*. You have to be an elf to cross our borders. And elves are rarely allowed to leave for any permanent amount of time. It's not fair."

The room was silent; I went to sit on the bed beside her. "I believe you, but it's hard to grasp that we wouldn't let other species seek refuge," I answered. "Thanks for letting me know; I'll be careful when interacting with the locals." I tossed a towel to her that I had found in the lone dresser with a few toiletry items. They were the few objects not covered in dust.

"Go wash up; I saw a bathing room two floors down while we were climbing the stairs earlier. I'll clean and dry our clothes in the meantime." There was no way that Ornella wasn't desperate for a shower; she couldn't stand getting dirt underneath her nails, ironic for someone who loved to garden.

A halfhearted grin spread across her beautiful face, igniting the hope inside my heart for better days ahead.

"Thanks for letting me take the first bath."

After Ornella left to sneak down to the bathing quarters, the silence in the cramped attic was deafening.

The dark shadows playing at the corners of my consciousness made a good night's rest impossible. Nightmares penetrated my thoughts, and visions of horrid creatures cloaked in a black mist danced around their prey. Their scorching red eyes lusted after the power that lurked inside my veins. The bloodshot eyes surrounding me changed, shifting into scales. A pair of yellow eyes homed in on my presence, and I woke gasping for air as they loomed above me.

I tried to brush off the nightmare as we snuck out of Mr. Darvish's inn just before sunrise. Sweltering heat bounced off the sand and onto our skin as we strolled the sandy streets early in the morning. In Danu, hardly any trees provided coverage from the sun overhead. The diverse crowds of beings made the high temperature that much more intolerable. Sweat poured down my forehead as I peered into shop windows, looking for supplies we would need for our venture to Erebus.

The feeling of clean clothes put me at ease, even if it was the only pair I currently owned. I was intrigued by the variety of species that passed by on the sidewalks. But what was even more peculiar was that they intermingled with one another. An ogre leisurely strolled by, accompanied by the rare centaur. I watched in fascination as they passed, deep in conversation. Ornella nudged me and gave me a look, telling me I needed to stop staring.

We both passed by a less populated area a few blocks down. My vision homed in on an object that stopped me in my tracks. The faded pink building, with a large palm tree on its exterior, displayed multiple musical instruments beautifully by its storefront window. The most exquisite grand piano I had ever seen sat in the middle of its construction. It was in pristine condition, warm and rich brown, handcrafted from Alun's rare oak trees. I whipped my head to face Ornella, who already knew what I wanted.

"Go ahead; we can spare a few minutes." She gestured for me to walk inside the establishment.

I hesitantly entered, but once inside, I briskly walked to the piano's bench. Several other beings were inspecting instruments around me, and I glanced around to see if I had permission to play. The employee behind the counter nodded in approval while busy attending to customers.

The weight in my chest lifted as soon as my fingers delicately stroked the keys. I closed my eyes, picturing myself once more inside *Mãe's* academy. In my illusion, she was at her desk, shuffling through her different compositions. Her dark shade of blonde was vibrant in my memory, and she was completely immersed in her work. A satisfied smile danced along her lips, and her violet eyes lifted to mine in the silence, asking me to play.

I willingly complied.

The music flowed through my soul and weaved out for the world to hear and appreciate. My fingers played along to the familiar melody, its melancholy tune resonating and bouncing off the four walls. The rich notes tickled my ears, and I found myself content in its splendor. I did not care how I appeared to others at that moment. This song was for the woman who raised me and cared for me more than anyone else. Her love transcended all worlds; she continued to live inside my and my sister's hearts.

The sunlight on my face must have been *Mãe* smiling down from the heavens.

The bench shifted beneath me as someone joined me for a duet. Their sudden presence made me almost miss the following few notes, but I swiftly recovered. I was acutely aware that the musician beside me was not Ornella; I dare say they rivaled one of *Mãe's* best pupils back in our village. But they were no match for me. A smile lingered on my lips as the melody trickled to a soft end, the ethereal music lingering in the space long after my hands rested in my lap.

The composition was one of *Mãe's* favorites to play when no one had been watching—after her classes for the day at the academy had ended.

Nothing could have prepared me for who my duet partner was.

A man was inches away from me, our shoulders brushing.

And *bless the vine*, he was handsome. His russet eyes studied my features, the shadows beneath them only accentuating his tall, dark, and handsome demeanor.

"Who are you?" He shifted to face me directly, the question immediately stirring my heart, causing a flutter of butterflies in my chest.

I bit my lip, surprised at my immediate reaction to this stranger. His voice was distinctly raw, husky. "Who's asking?" I blinked hard several times, bringing myself back to reality. The man was pretty, but he was too close for comfort. I swiftly stood, narrowing my eyes at the beautiful creature before me.

The man smirked, standing an entire head taller than me. He brushed his long brunette hair behind his ears, and I examined their shape—short and pointed at the end. I finally looked away from his chiseled chin long enough to notice his muscular forearms; both had thick, black, inky swirls—tribal marks.

He was a werewolf. That explained the brazen personality.

"I'm curious how an elf knows one of my clan's hymns, that's all." The stranger waited patiently for an answer.

"Oh." My voice deflated. "My *mãe* used to travel often, and I'm sure she learned several different compositions during that time." After answering,

I twisted and bowed to the small crowd we had acquired there in the shop, their claps continuing even as Ornella and I left the establishment.

I felt the beautiful man's eyes lingering on my back as I exited the store. A rush of giggles nearly escaped my mouth, and I pretended to cough to cover the embarrassing sound.

"Well, that was fun." I stretched my arms and fingers, a smile threatening to reveal itself on my neutral face. I tipped my face to the sun and hummed as we returned to Danu's seaport.

There was nothing wrong with me.

I had never been attracted to anyone in our village; my heart was never tugged in a direction like Ornella's often would be. Boys would bring her flowers, which I thought was a silly gift. They wouldn't replant them in a pot, instead pulling daisies straight from the ground to gift my sister.

She would keep them alive, using her energy manipulation to help them thrive without a root system. Those flowers lasted much longer than the affections she felt for those who had plucked them for her.

Ornella and I were *Marked Ones*, so our build naturally differed slightly from our peers. We were taller and leaner. Most elves have a petite frame, just like our *mãe* had. The boys my age were shorter than me, their ears not as long. If I had been able to roam where I had pleased, my muscles would've been even more defined.

Needless to say, I had always assumed that I would never hold such affection for another, but today was a pleasant surprise.

I just was not attracted to the boys in my village. I was, however, attracted to men who could make my heart melt within a matter of seconds with hauntingly mysterious eyes. How primitive of me.

A sudden pain radiated from my ribcage; my sister elbowed me in the side while looking at one of the touristy maps she had snagged while we were at the inn.

"Goodness, Sayah, could you focus? We need to find passage to Erebus *today*, and you're daydreaming about that scary werewolf." I squinted at Ornella and genuinely smiled when I noticed her amusement. She refused to make eye contact with me, and I giggled.

Another pain ran through my body, but this time it was my chest. That was the first time I had laughed without *Mãe*. The realization brought me back to the present, and my smile faded.

As we approached the heart of Danu's trading post, the smell of fish and saltwater was pungent. My sister wrinkled her nose in disgust. It differed vastly from the tropical fruit scent that filled my senses at our arrival. We momentarily stopped walking to observe how business was conducted. The patrons here were lively and full of vigor, bartering prices and loudly disputing until an agreement was made. From the looks of it, that meant both parties had to be dissatisfied.

"We will need to keep our wits about us," I whispered into her ear. "Let's find us a boat heading to Erebus and pray to the vine that they do not charge us an arm and a leg for it." Our gold coins were waning fast and, based on the price of the inn last night, we would have just enough gold to make the quest to Erebus. We held hands as we headed into the fray.

Danu's trading post sold a diverse selection of goods, ranging from rare silks and fine jewelry to garbage disguised as unique satins and gemstones. It was the picture of inclusivity; I smiled and appreciated the varying walks of life all gathered into one boiling pot of chaos. Everyone had an equal opportunity to make a life's fortune in one stride—and have those unexpected earnings robbed by bandits in the next.

We weaved in and out of the tents, intent on finding a way to cross the Dark Waters safely. The sea was known for being an unforgiving beast, luring even the most experienced sailors to the depths of its endlessly growing watery graveyard.

A piercing wail erupted through the masses, followed by deathly quiet from the confused strangers.

"What was that?" Ornella's voice shook next to me. I pulled her into the shadows along the wall, placing a finger over her mouth. My breathing was terribly loud, and I did my best to calm my sputtering heartbeat. After several seconds of nothing, a few beings around us returned to minding their business and wagering prices with fellow patrons.

"We need to keep moving," my sister said, warily eyeing the crowd. Her illusion of safety had shattered. The *Ligação Mágica* was in a frenzy at our feet. Just mere seconds before, it had been calm ripples of green and gold.

I agreed, panicking as we picked up our pace to head away from where the scream had originated. The *Thereon* were near, and Ornella and I were their targets.

Another shriek filled the salty air directly before us on the main path this time. A decapitated head rolled from around the corner, and my eyes went wide.

A towering entity cloaked in black slowly crept around the bend, disregarding the masses of panic that resulted from the creature's obscene killing spree. Blood splattered the pathway as the beast ripped through the crowd, using his arms to tear innocent bystanders into pieces. He tossed their appendages aside, his movements like a tornado ripping through the countryside, leaving only destruction in his wake. This *Thereon* had once been an ogre, though its vibrant green skin was now a dull grey, consumed by the parasitic, dark magic that commanded both his mind and flesh.

The smell of death filled the air as a deafening roar escaped its mouth, the vibrations sending us tumbling backward on the blistering sand. The monster zeroed in on Ornella and me. He charged, the sickening thumps as his footsteps grew closer, sending shivers down my spine.

Ornella's face was etched with fear beside me; she dove to the side, narrowly avoiding the creature's grasp. It had clumsily barreled through me, knocking me to the ground in the process, my head snapping back and hitting against a blunt object on the sand. The sharp pain radiating from my temple had me stirring from my state of terror moments before.

I yanked my twin further out of the *Thereon*'s reach, and his bloodshot eyes snapped to mine. The anger radiating from his presence was palpable, and I could sense the wrath growing inside his being as he struggled to grab us; we frantically dodged his advances. The wooden stalls underneath the tents were no match for this *Thereon*'s jarring strength, and he easily smashed through all the objects we desperately sought refuge behind.

My vision suddenly changed, becoming notably vibrant and clear. I observed the tendrils of light emitting from the beings nearby inside the unfolding mayhem. The *Thereon* growled at us, and I perceived his aura was black, but he lacked the whisps of light. Nothing stemmed from his beastlike state; he was a shell without a soul.

I stood in a fighting stance, inserting myself between Ornella and the creature as I mentally prepared to fight with fists. My ears rang as the *Thereon* roared again, its drool spraying me in the face.

Unexpectedly, several dark figures appeared before me, blocking my vision, just as the *Thereon* tried to grab me with his meaty hands. I twisted around to face my sister and saw her entirely still in one of the cloaked figure's arms.

No. *No.* This could not be happening; not again.

I screamed, trying to claw my way across the burning sand to her limp body. I would *not* let her become another victim to the *Breeders of Thereon.* They would *not* have her.

A hand waved over my face as I desperately reached out to Ornella. My vision filled with radiant twinkling stars, and a dizzying calm fell over me.

The world turned dark, and I drifted into a peaceful slumber.

Chapter Eleven

The ground beneath me violently swayed as I came to, my eyes betraying me as my vision was still filled with glittering stars. I gradually remembered the events that transpired before falling asleep and reached out my hand to feel for the hot sand. Instead, I was met with a cold, damp surface.

"Ornella!" I cried, praying to the vine that she was still alive. I gasped, trying over and over to take full breaths, trembling on the solid ground. The last time I had seen her, she had been lifeless.

"Sayah, calm down! I am fine."

"Where are you? Why can't I see you?" I fumbled around the unknown area, searching for her touch.

"I'm right here." She took my hand and squeezed. "Wait for the effects of the fairy dust to wear off, and you'll be able to see me."

Fairy dust?

Silent tears painted my face; the relief was overwhelming. She was alive and shockingly uninjured. My hands were still shaking, and my body had yet to comprehend that we were momentarily safe. *How did we change locations, and how did the giant Thereon disappear?* Muffled sounds alerted me that we were not alone; I tensed at the unfamiliar voices.

My vision slowly faded from black to brown. The room was made of wooden planks from the ceiling to the walls and floor. A large oak desk sat across from me. I kneeled at Ornella's feet, and she stroked the top of my head to ease my worry. She was sitting on a narrow bed, its frame built directly into the wall. The queasy feeling in the pit of my gut grew in intensity as the ground beneath my figure swayed.

Astonished, I raised my brows; we were now on a vessel.

The door to the cabin creaked open, and a stranger walked in.

"You were going to fight a *Thereon* with only your two fists, were you?" He stroked his scruffy chin with a thoughtful expression. "Brave, but foolish."

The man leaned against a wooden post, observing us with a strange look that made me uneasy. "Glad to have you and your sister aboard, Sayah." His tone teetered on the verge of taunting.

Wait a minute. His russet eyes gleamed back at me as my mouth hung agape.

"You're the man from the duet." I raised my eyebrows once more. "What's going on? Where are we?"

I scanned him for weapons of any kind. He watched with an amused expression as I once again lingered on his square jawline, tanned skin, and tattoos. They consisted of intricate black-ink designs that disappeared underneath his shirt sleeves. The only change from the last time I saw him was that his long brown curls were now pulled back into a low ponytail.

Other than that, he was still the same tall drink of water.

"Women from Alizeh are not nearly as prudish as the rumors say," he answered, chuckling. "I'll explain more in a minute." Shouting from the deck above had the three of us pause briefly. "As soon as we have safely made it out of Danu's waters." The chiseled man turned to leave, but I wasn't satisfied.

"Stop," I said with the sternest tone I could muster. I was relieved when he actually paused. "I demand you tell me where we are and what your identity is." I tried to bat my eyelashes, but I instead blinked awkwardly several times while he watched from the doorway.

He temporarily looked up at the ceiling as if the answer was written somewhere on the wooden boards. I narrowed my eyes when I grasped he was trying not to laugh at my ridiculous attempt to woo him for answers. A smile stretched across his features, and his russet eyes held my gaze.

"I kidnapped you two for bait—*Thereon* bait."

My twin and I both gaped at the stunning werewolf, unable to think of a response.

Wait a minute; this meant he somehow knew we were *Marked Ones*. The blood drained from my face, and I squeezed Ornella's hand. Did he know because it was apparent the *Thereon* were after us? Or did my twin willingly relinquish this information?

I began to chew on my nails, debating whether I needed to go ahead and drain this eye candy of his energy and quickly escape or if we should listen to his side of things. I wouldn't mind hearing what he had to say—his voice consistently prompted my heart to skip several beats at its husky tone.

"There's no need to worry; I won't let anything happen to either of you." His grin widened, and fangs protruded out of his mouth. "Now that we have the proper lure, this will be quick and easy."

"Why do you want to capture one of those vile creatures? Are you mad?" I scoffed.

Ornella was quiet as she sat atop the berth, calculating. The mattress squeaked as she slightly swayed back and forth from the ship's movement.

"I wish to find a cure." The strange man's voice rang with an unwavering resolution. "We all do. We want to see if it is possible to turn a *Thereon* back into its former self." And with that, he shut and locked our only exit before his footsteps could be heard bounding up the cabin's stairway.

I was caught off guard by his answer and nearly melted into a puddle from the determination and passion that radiated from his character.

The commotion from the main deck above had quieted, and I joined my sister on the berth. "For kidnappers, at least they're easy on the eyes."

My joke was lost on Ornella as she groaned into the nearest pillow.

Chapter Twelve

A cure? I doubted that was possible. I paced back and forth, considering the idea, trying to remember the contents of the handwritten journal by the elf, Alizeh. Elves lived for hundreds of years, so the timeline was a bit hazy. Her lifespan had lasted over six thousand lunations—she had lived an extraordinary life. It was so remarkable that our kingdom had been named after her. That was back before the monarchy had fallen, and kings, queens, and the royal bloodline still existed. Now, the five kingdoms of Aksel all lived in peaceful harmony without a hierarchy.

Wouldn't she mention a cure somewhere in the text? Perhaps it had not been translated to *Xodó*. If the librarian had translated the passages for me, then there was also the chance she did not have enough time to finish the conversion. I rubbed my forehead deep in thought, watching Ornella doodle in the journal gifted to her by *Mãe*. Maybe I should use my own to record the current events, just as Alizeh had.

The truth can't be erased if no one knows it is being recorded.

"They saved us." She was beginning to sound like a broken record. There was no way that she would convince me we were safe. "The captain and his crew promised to feed and care for us if we helped them in their plans. This is better than having to try and fend for ourselves."

I clenched my jaw and flexed my fingers, exasperated. Ornella could be too trusting at times, willing to believe the thoughts and concerns of those around her. She was not at fault, though, for this behavior. My twin had been idolized by many; there had been those fascinated with her looks and powers. The simple-minded would spew word vomit to make her happy. This was her reality; it was all that she knew.

My reality had been vastly different.

"Those are just empty promises. We need to tread forward carefully." I gestured to the room around us. "Take a good look at where we are, Ornella. We are trapped inside a small room currently without food or water. And the biggest issue is we didn't have a *choice*. We didn't choose to board this boat or volunteer to be the bait for their schemes."

She snapped her journal shut. Her irritation with me was plain as day.

"They saved us, Sayah. They could have tried to capture the *Thereon* at Danu's trading post, but they chose our lives over their own desires. They've already proven that they're trustworthy."

I pursed my lips, trying to hold my tongue. Ornella had willingly shared our history and background with anyone who had ears and a few minutes to spare. I bet they knew what time of day I relieved myself in the chamber room. Unbelievable.

Arguing was getting us nowhere, so I kept my mouth shut and stared out the circular portside window. There wasn't much scenery; laps of water consistently smacked the glass, and the only thing visible every few seconds was the overcast sky as we sailed to an unknown location.

After the long, drawn-out silence, I side-glanced at my twin. She was playing with her locks of hair, a thoughtful expression cast about her features. I felt the guilt creeping in. Ornella was doing her best to make good out of our terrible situation. Her skin was already beginning to turn back to its peachy tones, and the dark circles under her eyes were fading. Whatever magic they had used on us, I will say, did wonders for our beauty rest. I'll give them that.

"Maybe it wasn't the best choice to be so open with strangers; I'm sorry. But you were still unconscious, and I woke up terrified. The crew was kind to me, and after hearing their plans, I decided I wanted to help them." Her emerald eyes met mine; they were clear with resolve. "If there's a way to cure those who've been turned into soulless beasts by their *Breeders*, then I choose to help however I can."

A silence filled the space between us, lingering.

Ornella never had the chance to make any decisions for herself back in our village, so I knew what this declaration meant to her.

I pressed my lips together, sighing as I accepted my fate to become the bait for the *Thereon*, only for my sister's sake. "I'll agree under certain conditions. If they are not met, we must be safely escorted back to land." I crossed my arms and tilted my chin slightly, waiting for a refusal.

Instead, her demeanor brightened, and she sat cross-legged on the berth humming. She doodled inside the pages of her journal. "Thank you, Sayah."

I curtly nodded in response, now staring at the locked door.

I declined to tell her she would not be risking herself. They would not endanger my sister's life; I refused to allow it, even if I was being selfish. This crew could have the purest souls and be willing to give their lives for the greater good of all five kingdoms. However, I was not a part of this plan, and I would always choose my sister's soul over a thousand others. I knew better than anyone that selfish desires are at a being's center, propelling them forward, regardless of their honest intentions.

It seemed a private conversation with the crew members was overdue. I smiled mischievously to myself at the thought of seeing that striking werewolf and hearing his irritation as I made him aware that I would be the sole bait for this scheme.

That evening, we were permitted the luxury of leaving the room and exploring the ship. I was accompanied by a werewolf, but not the heartthrob I had anticipated. I sighed and found myself scanning the area for any trace of him.

A few crew members scurried about on the main deck, tending to their assigned tasks. A sharp wind whipped about the deck, knocking various objects over. Out at sea was anything but refreshing; the salt burned my eyes and clung to my skin, layering me in a sticky film.

A man with sandy hair and a scar running diagonally up his left brow waited directly across from me. A calm and quiet storm brewed beneath his moody features. His tribal swirls along his arms were similar to those of the other man but not as intricate, and they stopped short at his biceps.

"Tell me your conditions, and we will meet them," he stated matter-of-factly.

"*Marked Ones* are scarce. What you are asking for is usually a hefty fee." I paused for dramatic effect, letting it sink in as I fibbed, acting like I had negotiated with someone other than the baker back in our village to buy his burnt pastries at half price. "Lucky for you, we do not need gold or treasures." Another half lie—we were starting to run out of gold coins inside our pouches. "If you want our help, we require your assistance as a means of travel."

"That's something that I can work with." He leaned in close. "Where is it that you wish to go?"

"Take my sister and I to Erebus," I said, crossing my arms, showing that I meant business.

"Erebus? What for?"

"I owe you no explanation." My eyes skimmed over the deck, and I found Ornella conversing with several other crew members. I wanted to ensure she was out of earshot when I said the next part. "If you promise to uphold your end of the deal, I will be your sole leverage to catch one of those ungodly creatures. But you must *promise* to keep this between you and me. My sister will not be used as bait. She cannot protect herself the way that I can. She's completely defenseless."

His golden eyes remained on my face as several seconds ticked by.

"Fine, but if I sail you to Erebus, you both will be treated as crew members." His devious smile made my stomach uneasy. "You want to eat, drink, and use our resources—then you will have to earn them. Both you and your sister will be treated as equals. Welcome to the crew."

He stuck out his hand, covered in calluses and old scars. At least it seemed like he would be doing his part in sailing the ship too.

Unsure of how to react, I slowly shook my head, refusing his hand out of politeness. It was almost jarring to witness someone willingly offer me their acceptance. Especially since the entire crew had been warned of my powers and still seemed unafraid of my touch.

He retracted his arm, understanding in his golden irises.

"The woman I am trying to save—the reason I have joined this escapade—is a *Marked One* too." His pat on my back was gentle as he passed by to head to the ship's stern.

"Remember to be kind to yourself, Sayah. Your skin bleeds the same red at the end of the day as the rest of us. Treat yourself as such." The sound of his steps dissipated into the ocean's lively waves, splashing against the wooden planks.

A knot tied itself in the pit of my otherwise hollow stomach.

I was unexpectedly lonely.

Chapter Thirteen

The vast sea was indeed a treacherous place. My grievances with the werewolf and his company were long forgotten as several moons passed overhead, and I embraced my new role as a crew member. Instinct pushed me to the brink of survival, and cohesive thoughts were no longer a luxury that I could afford. My body moved long after the point of exhaustion, desperate to keep us afloat. The dark waters surrounding us were angry, trying their best to capsize our vessel. I was drenched from head to toe; blisters formed on my hands from the constant battle I held with the unrelenting winds on our battered masts and torn sails.

I leaned against the railing for a quick breather.

The aching muscles in my forearms and back were nowhere near as painful as the pulsing headache that now continuously plagued me.

My eyes naturally shifted to the doorway on the main deck; behind it was a stairwell leading to the cabin where my sister and I had initially woken up.

Ornella was in there now, safe from the elements. Our presence was needed on this massive ship. I refused to let my twin get her hands dirty and help with anything related to sailing. She had found her place just as well within the crew, given one of the most critical roles.

The crewmembers had kept their word and given Ornella the task of tending to the injured or wounded. After the sun had disappeared behind the horizon, she also handed out our single meal for the day. She was unknowingly protected from the dangers that the rest of us would endure; she was safe from being captured by the *Thereon*.

The hunky werewolf that I was keenly aware of at all times was the ship's master and the one the crew heavily relied on for answers. He had been kept busy, keeping the *Thereon's* trailing ship nearby with breadcrumbs of our existence without letting them get within reach.

It was one long game of cat and mouse.

There was nothing but sea in all directions, a watery graveyard for the vessels that never reached their desired destinations. We had encountered pirates only once, and it was brief and short-lived. This small crew of misfits knew their way around a knife and sword; the real threat to our lives was the unforgiving ocean we now embarked across.

Tonight was the night we would gather inside our cabin to discuss strategy; we would finally be taking a short break from manning the sails.

My heart skipped a beat, searching the galley for the ogress. Pots and pans could be heard clattering about, and I paused, gathering the courage to turn the corner.

"Hey," I said rather cheerfully to the woman busy cooking the crew's supper.

Enid barely looked my way as she tossed ingredients into a bowl. Her shoulder-length brunette hair had been pulled into a ponytail, and she hummed quietly. You could tell from how her body swayed she was at home here in the kitchen. Her movements were always confident when adding spices and chopping meat and vegetables.

"If you're just going to stand there, might as well help me." She tossed an apron in my direction, and I stumbled while catching it. The ogress did not laugh, much to my relief. She just stood with her hands on her hips, expectantly. "Wash your hands and get out the dishes and silverware."

I nodded, glad that she had not sent me away. She was the only woman aboard the ship besides my sister and I, and a prickly fairy named Kazumi.

After scrubbing the dirt and grime off my hands in the sink, I dried them with a towel before pulling the plates out of the cabinetry. I counted seven plates and set them on the cramped counter space.

"What is it that you wish to ask me," Enid said, pulling me from my thoughts.

Hesitating, I kept my hands busy, pretending to inspect the dishware. "I know this is a ridiculous request," I stammered, unable to meet her stare. "But would you be willing to teach my sister how to cook?"

After several seconds, I met her warm brown eyes.

"Hmm." She continued with the recipe, taste-testing her mouthwatering concoction. "You're asking me for your sister? Why does she not ask me herself?" A giant scoop of scalloped potatoes plopped onto the dish next to me.

"She would never ask herself," I started, but quickly explained further. "Before our rite of passage, Ornella had been eager to learn how to cook. But now, with our mãe no longer with us . . ." I cleared the lump in my throat. "I'm afraid that she'll never get the opportunity to. And I really think this would be good for her here, in the kitchen."

She had cried herself to sleep every day since Mãe had passed. And now she was stuck inside our small quarters all day. I felt responsible and wanted to give her something to look forward to.

Enid had finished plating our supper, and she exhaled, her expression full of joy as she inspected her work. "All right, I'll ask her to help me starting tomorrow," the ogress decided.

A grin played along the edge of my features, but I bit my lip to try and play it cool. "Thank you, Enid. I can't tell you how much I appreciate you." I bowed to her, and she bobbed her head with two plates in her hand.

"Go and let the others know that supper is ready; I do not feel like shouting at everyone," she replied, and that seemed like her way of acknowledging my thanks. Her humming bounced off the walls as I headed to the main deck, my face beaming.

On my way to the bridge, I practically ran into Brom, Enid's brother.

"Take this, elvish girl." The burly ogre handed me a flask of water.

His size and height would be enough to have any adversary cowering in terror, but his warm chocolate eyes and jolly laugh immediately put me at ease. At mealtimes, I gravitated towards Brom and his sister. They were the only other siblings aboard this floating coffin, and Ornella and I found their presence comforting.

I chugged several mouthfuls of water and tossed the container back. "Thank you." I gave a slight nod in his direction. "I think I've had enough water to last me a lifetime in the few moons I've been aboard." Brom grinned, a knowing look etched across his face. "Is the sea always so violent?"

"Depends." He groaned, stretching his arms up above his head, yawning.

That was another reason I had come to like Brom in such a short period; while others usually complained and grumbled about our circumstances, he managed to harbor a joyful attitude.

"Enid says that supper's ready." I patted his arm, as he was too tall for me to reach his shoulder.

"Fantastic." Brom patted his belly, eyes now awake and alert. The man could eat an entire week's worth of food for me in one sitting. "What's on the menu?" he called after me as I jogged to my destination.

"Steamed vegetables, scalloped potatoes, and stuffed chicken!" I shouted back in his direction.

His face lit up when I mentioned the stuffed chicken, and I smiled. I saved the best for last on purpose. I reached the bridge and poked my head around several crates to make the announcement.

"Supper's ready!" The three inside the bridge jumped at my message, and I winked before heading back to the cabin to tell Ornella. Kazumi had been fluttering around Silas, the werewolf with sandy hair and the scar going across his left eye. He chuckled and waved as I quickly came and left.

The man with the russet eyes and impish grin's name was Nox. The mere thought of him made my heart erratic and my cheeks flush. He was the shipmaster—the one in charge of this motley crew of misfits.

Our cabin door swung open with a slight push, and I happened upon Ornella reorganizing the medical herbs.

"Oh, hey!" She laid the tray carefully on the berth and faced me eagerly. "Has the sea calmed yet?"

"Yes, and it's time for supper! Let me check my appearance before we head to the galley." I flittered my hands about the large desk until I found the handheld mirror stashed in one of its drawers. I laid it on the wooden surface, fixing my mane. I left my raven hair half down, with the top half braided back into a tight bun. "Can I borrow that lipstick you have in your pack?" She always had a small makeup stash on hand, regardless of the activity.

"You look fine, Sayah." I could hear my twin rolling her eyes in her tone, but she handed me the mauve-colored, matte lipstick, a neutral shade she used almost daily.

"I want to look pretty, not fine," I answered, sticking out my tongue. Examining my appearance in the mirror, a content smile surfaced as I was pleased with my quick work. My lips were plump, and my board-straight hair was tangle-free, with the waterfall braid adding a softness to my sharp features. Thick black lashes accentuated my grey eyes. "I'll have to buy a different shade of lipstick when we get to Erebus. That way, we can share."

I smiled at Ornella, a sudden wave of gratitude overcoming me. "Thank you. I mean it."

Her emerald eyes crinkled in response, reminding me of how Mãe's used to when she was happy. My twin grabbed my wrist and pulled me out the cabin door. "I love you too," she answered. "But I can't wait another minute for something to eat and fresh air, so I'm leaving for supper whether you join me or not!"

As we walked arm in arm, our upbeat voices melded into one harmonious sound that I never wanted to forget.

We paused out on the main deck to witness the sunlight begin to cast a warm glow across the ocean, and for the first time since being on the ship, the Ligação Mágica revealed its gold-and-green colors—twinkling like stars just beneath the water's surface.

A feeling of relief filled my being. Ornella and I were facing the sea in a moment of silence. My breathing slowed, and my eyes glazed over, staring at the now tranquil water stretching as far as the eye could see.

I felt a level of understanding of the mysterious sea before me.

At times, my gift flowed calmly in my veins, entirely in sync with my mind and soul. Then, there were occasions when my gift was angry, spilling over and out of my being into the ground and those around me.

Some fear the ocean and its massive power. Some accept it for what it is and love the vast waters and the treasures it holds.

The ocean and I were the same in that way.

"Finally," Silas said from next to me. He had approached while I was lost in thought. "We can take a break from manning the ship and discuss our plans." The smell of Enid's cooking lingered on his garments. He must've had his supper already. My stomach growled in hunger, the pain breaking my stare.

"How will we be the bait for the *Thereon*, exactly? Will it put us in danger?" Out of the corner of my eye, I noticed Nox noiselessly conversing with Kazumi. He somehow knew I was directing my interrogation at him, and I tilted my head in question, asking. His moody eyes held mine for several seconds before heading to the bridge.

I wished to follow the handsome man, but food was more important.

I tugged at Ornella, with whom I was still locked arms, before adding to Silas. "I'm going to go and scarf down our plate before Brom is tempted to eat it."

He chuckled before whispering between Ornella and me, "Better hurry then. You would not be the first to lose your supper to a hungry ogre, and you most certainly won't be the last."

We both gasped, sprinting toward our meal. Silas's laughter followed us across the ship and into the deck below. By the time we got to the galley,

Enid was smacking Brom's hands from touching the last two plates. Her icy glare made us both flinch.

"You're lucky I kept his grubby hands off your food." Enid pushed our dishes down the island, and we simultaneously caught them before they slid off the countertop. "You"—she pointed at Brom, who was now sulking a few paces down—"go wash the dishes. It's your turn."

He nodded, embarrassed about almost devouring our plates just a moment before. "I'm sorry to the both of you." He choked out the apology and stuck his hands in the sink's sudsy water. "It is hard to control myself when my stomach is thinking for me."

"It's okay, Brom," I said, rather chipper. "If I ever have any leftovers, you can have them. One plate is not enough for a male ogre anyway."

He paused, scrubbing a plate, and twisted so that he could see me. "Do you mean that?"

I shrugged, chewing on a piece of chicken. "Of course. I usually don't finish my plate anyway. Elves have petite stomachs, you know." After taking a couple of bites of each item, I gingerly pushed the food in his direction. "See, I'm already full."

Brom hesitated at first but went up to my plate after a momentary pause and scooped all the potatoes, vegetables, and chicken into his mouth in one fell swoop. My jaw nearly touched the ground at witnessing such an event. He pushed back his short brown hair, smiling sheepishly.

"Did you even chew?" I exclaimed before leaning over in a fit full of laughter. Brom and Ornella joined in; the amusement was contagious. From the corner of the galley, I saw Enid crack a smile.

The ogre wiped a few tears from his eyes, still grinning. "No, ogres don't typically chew. Our stomachs are hardy; we can digest bones."

My sister paused mid-chew; her brows knit together in concern. "Not elf bones, right?"

She usually elbowed me in the side for saying something insensitive, but this time, my elbow jabbed her ribs while I glared at her.

"Ouch!" Ornella hissed at me. "I was joking, sort of!"

"We do not eat the bones of other main species," Enid's sharp tone cut across the kitchen like a knife blade directed solely at her. "You, with the white hair"—the ogress briefly pointed at Ornella with her fork while leaning over the countertop on her elbows—"what's your name?"

"Or-Ornella," she stammered, her face flushed as she spun her utensil in what was left of her potatoes.

Enid cleared her throat. "Ornella, you'll be helping me in the kitchen from now on."

It took my sister several seconds to register her response before slowly lifting her head. My twin's emerald eyes were shining with delight, her shock evident.

"Really? I can help?" The giddiness in her tone pulled at my heartstrings.

"Yes, but let me warn you, you'll be put to work. Working in the galley is strenuous." Enid flexed her biceps, a mischievous smile playing across her lips as she challenged my sister. "Do you think you can handle it?"

Ornella, who had never once been questioned about her abilities, was clearly offended. She strode over to Enid, her white braid bouncing as she moved. She held out her hand, placing it over her heart as she spoke. "I promise, Enid. I can handle being in the kitchen with you." Her head dipped as she fully bowed, wholly committed to the arbitrary task of being most likely the new dishwasher.

The ogress looked uncomfortable, her usual calm and collected demeanor squandered by my sister's show of dedication and passion to whatever she set her mind to.

"Yes, well"—Enid pulled at her shirt collar, her cheeks red—"I'll see you bright and early tomorrow morning." Her face was flustered as she headed out the narrow hallway. "You all should make haste. I bet Nox is seething about how long it's taking us to get to the bridge."

Ornella immediately pushed her plate to Brom. "Finish this."

He nodded, swallowed the food whole, and washed the last dish.

We ran to catch up with Enid and the others, making our way to the main deck.

"That was nice of you to give Brom your food. Mãe would've approved," she alleged as we walked up the few steps to the main bridge.

Everyone besides Brom was there, waiting.

Nox whistled, and everyone snapped to attention. The playful banter, the ease with which we had enjoyed each other's company, was gone. Reality had crept back into the room with us. The crew members were silent, their expressions grave.

"Our ship is currently sailing out of the Arching Depths, and we will circle Alun, passing between the giant's territory and the Unknown." His voice was hushed, barely above a whisper. Kazumi muttered under her breath, audibly displeased.

The Unknown was the Uncharted Waters, the part of the cold-hearted sea surrounded by a thick fog. Unfamiliar and mysterious, no one had yet returned from what was supposed to be an ominous graveyard of vessels and poor souls.

"The *Thereon* are gaining on us, so we will make landfall within the next full moon to prepare to engage with them. So far, I've detected only one ship following, which works in our favor." He pulled out a map, following the route that he anticipated our vessel would make with his index finger. "Our target destination is the Isles of Cadogan." The ship's master paused, carefully surveying the room.

At this revelation, the room erupted into several sharp breaths and gasps. I raised my eyebrows and looked at Ornella next to me, whose fear was plainly visible in her features.

"Have you lost your mind, Nox? We will be greatly outmatched without the ability to cast magic," Enid retorted, and I studied how her appearance and complexion matched Brom's. They both had warm brown eyes, but there was a hardness inside hers, a bitter cold that came with being the responsible sibling. "I will not step a single foot on that cursed soil." She tightly crossed her arms, and her gaze fell upon her brother, who had just entered the room, daring him to counter.

Brom's massive size comprised nearly half of the space, but he was the least threatening. He sighed and shrugged his shoulders at their ship's master. "You heard my sister." The large ogre leaned against the wall, looking around at the rest of the crew, waiting for something he deemed interesting to captivate his attention.

"The both of you can wait back at the ship then," Nox responded, a sly grin playing along the edges of his mouth. "I know our other attempts at catching a *Thereon* did not go as planned, but now that we have the proper bait, I'm confident we will succeed."

My eyes flickered toward the werewolf at the mention of his bait. "Why are you trying to find a cure?" I needed to know. "Why should my sister and I risk our lives needlessly?"

The small cabin went silent as I waited for an explanation.

Before anyone dared to speak, the small rose-colored fairy fluttered inches from my face. I had never seen a fairy up close before; they also originated from the kingdom of Alizeh. Not much is known about their kind, only that they bloom from an enchanting plant inside the woodland forest. However, fairies were unlike elves in any other aspect; they did not openly share their rituals or history with other species. All that was known was that they were notorious for holding grudges and would curse you for anything they deemed unsightly.

I held in my shock at the sight of her mouth, which was filled with teeth shaped like shards of glass. I could only imagine what a bite from a fairy would do to your skin. Her face was beautiful, but the black, beady eyes alongside her jagged teeth masked whatever beauty remained.

She was absolutely terrifying.

"Needlessly?" The fairy hissed and spit into my face. "Do you think we chose to have our homes destroyed by the *Thereon*? Our family members captured and tortured?" Her voice was high-pitched and raspy, and I instinctually recoiled from her.

"Those murdered by the *Thereon* deserve to be avenged; the same goes for those who were turned into the horrid creatures, not of their own free will. So, you and your sister can put your lives on the line for all the innocent souls that were so needlessly taken." She fell silent, not budging an inch as her words penetrated my cold demeanor.

"I'm sorry." My apology fell flat, and remorse tightened its grip on my chest. The fairy flew up to Nox and sat on his shoulder; her harsh eyes never left mine.

"So stubborn and naïve." Her wings angrily fluttered in response. "We should only involve her sister; she's at least pleasant."

I studied his face, the feeling of dejection overwhelming. The werewolf stayed silent, impartial to the plea conveyed in my eyes.

"Pleasant or not, both of the girls are necessary for my strategy to work." He searched each of his crew members' faces with a solemn but determined expression. "For those whose lives were lost, and family members that were taken. This time, we will capture a *Thereon* and be closer to finding their weaknesses. Any unanswered questions will finally come to a conclusion."

Nox's stare rested upon my sister and me. He gestured to us from across the bridge.

"The *Marked Ones* will use their gifted powers to assure our victory."

The murmurs of approval were evident as I crossed my arms in refusal but stayed silent. It was Ornella who voiced her concern.

"I have a lot of practice and patience using my gift; Sayah does not." She looked around the room, her emerald eyes full of sympathy. "I understand that you want our help, and you shall receive it"—my sister cleared her throat—"but Sayah has practiced her entire life on doing exactly the opposite of what you are asking her to do. Our family has sacrificed a lot to make that happen. The elders and priests in our village hesitated to let her be present for her rite-of-passage ceremony for fear of draining the energy from the Videira and those in attendance. Only recently did they show interest in teaching Sayah how to control her gift so that she could join the military ranks. I don't think this is a good idea."

All the focus was directed toward me as tears stung my eyes, and my breaths were short spurts of air. My twin did not have to speak about me as if I were a burden in front of everyone.

Nox stepped forward, and I averted my eyes; they were glued to the wooden floorboards. With a gentle confidence, he closed the distance between us and lifted my chin with his index finger so that I was forced to meet his gaze. My heart betrayed me, stammering from his touch.

I steadied my breathing and held in the embarrassment, forcing my face to stay neutral, even inches away from his.

"It looks like we will be spending quite some time together." His soft grin caused a blush to rise to my ears and chest. "In the next few moons, I'll teach you how to use your powers safely. You'll master control."

My lips were sealed tight, the power churning beneath my skin beginning to boil. I was not a silly, naïve, and stubborn child. If they insisted on defining me, I'd handwrite the definition for them.

I, Sayah, daughter of Aster, was a *Marked One*, a sister, pianist, jokester, and most importantly, lover of hot tea served early in the morning.

Nox's russet eyes were piercing, and I was fuming mad that he was my sparring partner.

Chapter Fourteen

The following day, Nox met me on the main deck just after sunrise. Ornella had left our cabin right at the same time I did, as she was meeting Enid in the galley. After hearing her opinion of my abilities with the rest of the company, I hardly talked to my sister that morning. She apologized but said it needed to be addressed. My lovely twin was entirely against me practicing my gift and said there was not enough time to hone my skill confidently against the *Thereon*.

I knew that I would forgive her before sunset; I detested being angry with her.

Ornella was trying to protect me like I was trying my best not to let her be involved with any of the scheming. I agreed with her that there was too little time to master my control over my powers; however, after seeing Kazumi up close, I was not about to go against the rest of our company.

That spiteful fairy would hold a grudge against me if she didn't already.

The arrogant werewolf was already waiting for me, stretching his limbs and looking across the endless ocean. His shirt sleeves were rolled up, and I took a quick peek at his muscular biceps and forearms before hating myself for staring.

"Start stretching, or you'll hate yourself later," Nox said as he jogged lightly in place.

I stood there dumbfounded, watching this man's exercise routine.

"Um, excuse me." I tapped his shoulder. "Why do I need to do—whatever this is that you're doing again?" I gestured to his ridiculous body movements. I coughed loudly to try and conceal my laughter. "You're teaching me how to use my powers, not martial arts."

Today, my attitude matched my appearance. I had braided my hair tightly back into my usual hairstyle. There was not a hint of makeup on my face. The only thing I wore was my disdained expression and an icy glare.

He abruptly stopped stretching and bent his body in various contorted positions. Nox was in front of me, and then instantly, he had vanished.

"Where did y—" My head whipped back as my feet were no longer on the ground, and I was in the air, screaming.

Just before my skull contacted the hard surface, Nox cradled my head, holding my body in his arms with my face just inches away from his. His russet eyes were glorious in the morning sun, and my breath caught temporarily at his closeness.

His breath was in my ear, his husky voice sending shivers down my spine. "You are learning basic defensive tactics *and* how to control your powers." He placed me gently on the ground. "Sayah, you have zero ways to protect yourself. Your sister at least can use her powers, though she's more equipped for assisting those on the front lines."

His frown deepened as he thoroughly examined my body. My gaze lingered on his full lips and chiseled chin until he started jabbing his fingers into my biceps, ruining my fun.

"Hey, quit poking me!" I whined, smacking at his hands. I never thought I'd say this, but I actually wanted him to stop touching me.

He stepped away, breathing in a large inhale of air while flexing his jaw. Nox shook his head, making a clicking noise with his mouth as if he disapproved of something.

"You have zero muscle and no idea how to use your gift. There's no way we're starting with even the basic movements." A mat had been laid out on the main deck, and I started to sweat when it became evident that it was for me. "We're going to build you from the ground up, my precious jewel."

I cringed at his nickname for me, which made him snicker before crossing his arms.

"Every day, I want you out here, on the mat. You'll do push-ups, sit-ups, crunches, whatever I tell you to do." His voice was starting to sound unappealing as he forced me onto the mat.

"For how long do I need to do each exercise?" My hand hovered over my eyes as I checked the sun's location. It was still early morning, the sun just rising over the horizon.

"Until you are physically able to—no." He waved me over to the mat to get started. "Until I tell you to stop. Now start with push-ups; let's go."

"Can't I stretch first?" I wildly looked around the deck for someone to save me from this devilishly handsome tyrant.

"You had your chance already; you'll find out today what happens when you don't stretch properly." Nox leaned down, his long waves tickling my face, as he whispered, "No one is going to save you, Sayah. You're going to have to learn how to save yourself."

That was the start of my intense training schedule and the first day I began trying to avoid Nox as if he were a plague.

Every muscle and fiber in my body ached; stretching before the strenuous workouts and ice baths for my sore muscles were the only things that helped soothe the throbbing in my arms and legs. There was nothing to ease the agony in my bones; however, Nox was determined to completely break me of my stubborn attitude. He never said it, but his cold demeanor and harsh schedule kept me continuously on my toes. Only fourteen moons had passed overhead, and I was already numb to any feeling that wasn't physical pain. The man kept my mind so busy and overworked that I didn't have time to think about how much I hated this training and how much I was beginning to hate him.

Begging my sister to let me join her and Enid in the galley was a lost cause; they both seemed to enjoy each other's company, and Ornella kept assuring me that this was good for me as she squeezed my biceps, impressed with my progress.

I kept going and showed up at every training session with Nox. Silas and Kazumi were busy steering the ship and watching for the *Thereon*, who would suddenly appear at our heels. We had narrowly avoided their ship on several different accounts, all thanks to Kazumi's fairy dust. I quickly understood how vital her presence was on the ship, even if I wasn't fond of the spiteful fairy.

I waited out on the mat on the main deck under the moonlight. Today was the first day off from exercising, and my body was grateful for even a tiny break. Nox had told me to meet him here tonight to finally begin discussing my powers and how they worked.

He casually strolled out from the shadows, his hands in his jogger pockets. His shirt was barely a shirt—it was sleeveless and ripped down the sides. Perfectly chiseled abs peeked out as he went to sit on the mat, leaning back to get a good view of the thousands of stars twinkling across the sky.

I went to sit beside him, cross-legged, hugging my knees.

His body tensed next to me, and I rolled my eyes. "I won't look at your abs if you promise not to jab my bicep a thousand times." My chin rested on my knees as he heartily laughed, and I turned to face the other way to conceal my smile.

"I know it sucks, but the vigorous training is worth it; trust me."

Suddenly interested, I turned my view to the side to see his expression. Nox's face was peaceful, soaking in the light reflecting off the moon. Even with the shadows cast across him, anyone would be able to tell that he was beautiful.

"Why are you so mean to me, Nox?" I inquired so softly that it was barely audible over the constant flow of the ocean waves and the accompanying wind.

I hadn't thought he had heard me until his face was right before mine, his russet irises radiant in the dark.

"Because I want you to be able to protect yourself in any given situation." He flashed his arms, the swirling tattoos now glowing. "Werewolves are taught from an early age that to be on top, you must be the strongest."

"Is that how you get your tattoos? By being the strongest?"

He eyed me warily, and his shoulders tensed at the subject. "Yes and no. The technical term for my tattoos is tribal markings. You earn them with every fight that you win. And when you lose, a marking gets transferred to the winner on the next full moon."

The moon in the sky was almost complete now, and I looked back at his forearms, where he sat with his palms facing up in his lap.

"How many tribal markings do you have?" I blushed as I grasped that it was an intimate question. "Sorry, you don't have to answer."

Nox chuckled. "No, it's fine." He pulled off his flimsy shirt to reveal that the black swirls traveled up his arms, covering his chest and over the entirety of his back. They were all glowing, shining brightly as my eyes glanced back and forth between his pectoral muscles and the intricate design.

Instinctually, I reached out to touch his chest out of curiosity.

Our eyes met, and I felt connected to his soul underneath the moonlight, my heart beating rapidly at this odd sensation. His russet eyes had a depth to them that I had never noticed in any other being before, and his lips were now close enough to brush against mine.

There was a noise of either Brom or Silas laughing near the stern of the ship, causing me to snap out of my daze. Abruptly aware of my actions, I pulled my hand away, embarrassed.

But Nox didn't flinch away. Instead, he grabbed my hand and placed it on his chest. The glow emitting from his markings began to form into tiny orbs of light, twirling up and following the intricate design of his tribal swirls. I gasped at the ethereal display. It was precisely what stars would look like if they could dance.

His russet eyes were shocked as he began to absorb every feature of my face.

"Has that ever happened before?" I bit my lip nervously.

There was a meaningful pause, and I wanted more than anything to know what he was thinking in that instant.

"No, it hasn't." His fingers delicately stroked my cheek, the skin beneath his touch now burning.

"Are you not afraid of me?" It didn't make sense that he did not shy away, even if my powers made me naturally pull at the beings' energy close to me.

"No." His tone was serious as he delicately brushed a hair behind my ear before answering. "Have you not noticed? You're not siphoning my energy now. I only push you past your breaking point because you need to be strong in order to survive with a target always on your back."

He was right—the power that had been leaking out of my core had subsided.

The stars above us then twinkled, and I couldn't help but believe this was *Mãe's* way of agreeing with him.

Nox exhaled audibly. There was something tragic about the helpless look in his russet eyes when his vision slid over to where I sat beside him. "I simply want you to live, Sayah." His few words moved my fragile heart, and overtaken by his declaration, I leaned forward and gently kissed his cheek. It was a sign of endearment for elves, but I blushed, realizing this might not be the case for his species.

His skin was warm beneath my lips, the sensation of direct contact causing my heart to race. The surprising scent of cinnamon lingered from an unknown source, filling my lungs. I pulled away, embarrassed to meet his gaze. I was thankful it was nighttime, as the dark atmosphere camouflaged my expression.

"What do you know about your gifted powers?" Nox inquired, keeping the conversation going without letting there be an awkward pause.

"When I make contact with something that is filled with life—the power that I have been so graciously gifted—sucks the energy out of whatever it is that I am touching. And since my blooming, it is apparent to those around me that my emotions are tied to my gift."

After several seconds had passed, I cautiously peeked at Nox, who was deep in thought. He began to speak, revealing a part of his past.

His brown curls moved like silk as he ran his fingers through his thick mane. "My sister is a *Marked One*. She taught me everything I know about these five kingdoms and the *Ligação Mágica*."

"Where is she?" As soon as the question had escaped my thoughts, I wanted to take it back. Nox's face deflated, and he stared into the distance for some time before answering.

"The *Thereon* took her."

I took a sharp inhale of breath, and naturally squeezed his hand. "Nox, I'm so sorry." It made perfect sense why he was adamant about defeating the *Breeders of Thereon* by finding a cure. Not much was known about the vile beasts, and he feared that his sister had been captured and possibly turned into a horrid creature.

He interrupted my thoughts, letting go of my grasp.

"Wait right here." I watched his figure vanish into the shadows, only to appear shortly after holding a mysterious object. "Hold out your hands."

I complied, eager to see what he had brought back.

"First, I want you to tell me what you know of our *Ligação Mágica*." He poured seawater into my hand, helping me cup it inside my palm. His finger twirled inside the water, and I watched in fascination as the gold-and-green magic lifted from the salty liquid and danced between our palms.

My laughter caused the synchronized magic to bounce between our hands, swirling briefly above our heads, before rejoining the rest of the wavelengths inside the ocean.

"Amazing." I marveled at the discovery. "I did not know that you could touch the land's magic, let alone hold it in your grasp." A memory quite suddenly came forth, and I remembered the enchanting magic during my rite-of-passage formality. "During my blooming ritual on the ceremony grounds, I could touch the magic as it was pulled into the *Videira*."

He nodded, accepting my answer, and we both released our hands. The water fell to the wooden boards beneath us.

"You can touch the *Ligação Mágica* if you are synchronized with its properties." His gaze fell upon me, lingering. "Why do you think that is, Sayah? What exactly *is* the land's magic?"

Hearing him say my name sent another blush throughout my cheeks and ears, and I twisted back to the ocean.

I searched the vast waters for an answer. Honestly, I felt a bit embarrassed that I had never questioned why or how the magic of the kingdoms worked around me. All I knew was that they tethered the lands and all living things to one another.

Oh, and that people can abuse the magic system to spy on you and figure out your location if you cast spells.

After I had been quiet for several moments, he answered for me. "Think of magic as a tangible lifeline to everyone and everything. We all can synchronize with one another. Even with the consciousness that created our oceans and kingdoms."

My eyes scanned the vast waters, now enamored with the gold-and-green ripples flowing alongside the currents.

A physical lifeline. One that connects me directly to the *Creator*.

"What is the purpose of being connected with all other life? There are certain lives I would rather not be linked to."

His abrupt laughter startled me, and Nox rested his arms on the top of the vessel's siding.

"The purpose is not for our own convenience; it is for our *Creator's*. Believe me, there are those I wish not to be tied to. But that is not our decision to make."

"My *mãe* told me not to cast spells—or synchronize with the waves of magic. She said that our elders and priests were spying on us because we are *Marked Ones*. They were watching my sister's every move."

"There's a way to combat that." He grabbed my hand, catching me off guard. "I can teach you and your sister how to protect yourselves. It is something that the four main clans do to protect our kindred."

"How is that possible?"

"All *Marked Ones* have a deeper connection to the lifeline established by our *Creator*. It will be easier for you to comprehend simply because of your gifts. Watch this." His tribal tattoos flashed, and tendrils of light encompassed his being as he stood beside me.

He gestured first to the familiar green-and-gold magic swirling beneath the water's depths. "We can all see the *Ligação Mágica*, but you have the gift to see our lifelines to that magic, the very essence of our souls: our *Gavinhas*," Nox said, summarizing his explanation. The light in his eyes as he spoke made me hopeful.

"They are called *Gavinhas*." I felt a lightness in my chest as one of my many questions had been answered. My eyelids closed, and I envisioned my own before me. I had yet to try and take a look at my wavelengths connecting me to the vine.

When I blinked to reveal their bright light—I frowned.

The *Gavinhas* encompassing my aura were a solid onyx. The black whisps visibly moved outside my vibrant energy barrier, a bothersome reminder of how different I was from everyone else.

"My tendrils of light are a shiny onyx color," I said, my voice deflated.

"That is not unusual for a *Marked One*," He shifted his weight so that he was now looking toward the kingdom of Adara. "My sister's *Gavinha's* are blue."

"What is her name?" I requested gingerly.

The question caused a fond smile to spread along his features, and he met my gaze with a certain softness that hadn't been there before. "Her name is Tabitha."

Nox and I finally had something we could relate to and shared: we loved our siblings.

"Tabitha, how beautiful." I let the name roll off my tongue. "What are her gifted powers? This is my first time hearing of another *Marked One*. Ornella and I are currently the only gifted ones in Alizeh."

"Her powers are lunar manipulation." His chin tilted upward as he examined the moon. "My sister has always been adored by our clan, even though she does not originate from our own flesh and blood. Her presence is vital to our success."

"What is lunar manipulation?" I reddened, facing the sea. "Sorry for all of the questions. It's just—hearing of someone that understands what it's like to be different—is comforting."

From what Nox had revealed so far, Tabitha sounded similar to Ornella. Everyone loved my sibling for her gifts; the same could not be said for me.

"Remember how I told you that werewolves earn their tribal markings? Before the staged fights with our rival clans, Tabitha would use her lunar manipulation to give us the strength of the full moon, regardless of its current phase in the lunar cycle."

My eyes traveled over the tribal swirls while I considered what this meant.

"Did any of the other clans have an issue with this? My first thought was how livid everyone else must be that your clan had an immediate advantage." I could imagine how this would cause rifts between the peaceful agreements that have been put in place. After the monarchy fell, the four clans' territory and leaders reached a peaceful agreement relatively quickly.

That had been before a *Marked One* with lunar manipulation resided inside Alun.

"That's a discussion for another time—but the short answer is yes, all other clans find it unfair. That is why my clan, The Fangs of the Fallen, is both feared and envied. But less about me, more about your powers." Nox winked before tying his hair up off his shoulders.

"And what you and your sister have been gifted—I believe it is more complex than energy manipulation." He ran his sturdy hands along the ship's railing, clearly debating something.

"Ornella and I have been able to see these tendrils of light since the day of our rite of passage." At this, he whipped his head back in my direction, now intrigued. "It was as if we became one with the *Videira,* and I haven't felt the same since."

"If I were to guess, I would say those were your powers fully awakening." He exhaled, stroking his stubbly chin. "I don't have all the answers, as my sister was still trying to understand them herself. But my clan is well-versed in the wavelengths of your soul, the tendrils of light. Not only are they your soul, Sayah, but they hold the essence of who we were in past lives and who we are now. They are the key to reincarnating in the future. Without our *Gavinhas*, our ability to pass from this world to the next dies. That is why it is such a tragedy to be transformed into a *Thereon*; that poor being has lost their soul and the chance ever to redeem themselves in the next life. They cease to exist completely."

An overwhelming state of grief temporarily clung to my core, for the creatures who had now lost their souls for eternity. But I could not forgive the ones who had mercilessly taken so many innocent lives in their mindless rampage of terror.

"When someone synchronizes with you using the land's magic, it is directly through your *Gavinhas*. The tendrils of light are specific and unique to that individual. You can place protective spells on your wavelengths, making it more difficult for those on the outside to find you."

"Are you able to see your *Gavinhas*?" His tendrils were brighter than most; the essence of his soul was powerful. When he one day passed from this world to a new one, Nox would be reincarnated into someone just as brilliant. I was sure of this.

"No, I wish I could; Tabitha is the one who helped me place the protective spell on my wavelengths along with the others in our clan."

He walked the few paces between us, grabbing my hand and leading us to the middle of the main deck. The others were either asleep in their beds or playing a game of cards in the galley. I had overheard Brom and Silas discussing Kazumi's love for poker nights when the storms overhead had been relentless.

"But you can place the spell on your individual *Gavinhas*, Sayah. And I understand how the spell works. We can do it together." He held up his arms, his callused palms rough against my newly blistered hands. "The spell that we will cast is *Escudo das Almas*. Its purpose is to act as a shield to prying eyes."

"You will be placing a false memory inside your tendrils. For the viewer to believe that the events are current without revealing your location or any vital information, ensure the setting is nondescript. Do not include anything of interest or anyone you care about. Those well-versed in synchronizing with the *Ligação Mágica* will be able to spot the lies, but they won't see your current self either." He flexed his jaw in concentration. "Sayah, think of a false memory that you'd like to plant inside your tendrils of light; this is where my presence is essential. I will also embed a memory inside yours that is my own. This further confuses the one secretly spying and prevents them from finding your current self easily."

I started to inhale gradually, and only when my lungs were bursting with air did I exhale. Instinctually, my body began to repeat the calm-breathing sequence, and I kept my eyes closed until I was sure my mind was clear, and my heart was steady.

"I'm ready to begin," I answered, rolling my neck back and forth.

Instead of answering, Nox began to hum. The vibrations of his low notes made the air around us tingle, and after a few flashes, I opened my eyes to witness the land's green-and-gold magic swirling around the two of us in an enchanting vortex.

I squeezed my eyelids shut, afraid that somehow witnessing the spell take place would make the protection on my *Gavinhas* ineffective.

"Start to imagine the memories you're embedding as your armor." Nox's voice was entrancing, barely above a whisper.

A library popped into my mind, and I purposefully did not recall the titles of any of the works of literature. My hand reached for a random novel on the shelf directly in front of me, and I strolled leisurely to a bland wooden table with a lamp as its only decor. I sat at its long bench, turning on the orange light, casting a warm glow about the musty room. Slowly peeling back the novel's cover, I could feel a content smile playing on the edge of my lips.

An ink pen appeared beside the open book, and I picked up the feathery utensil and began to write on the novel's blank pages. My eyes crept along the sentence, fully absorbing every word.

It's not nice to synchronize with another being's memories without permission, Elder Josias.

My hands slammed the old piece of literature in my face, temporarily blinding me with dust particles.

When I felt the memory cling to my onyx tendrils, I finally opened my eyes.

Nox was staring at me, his russet irises mischievously playful.

I was about to speak when I saw the image of a large vineyard in the middle of summer flash across my mind. A tall young woman stood in front of me, bent over laughing. Her skin was a gorgeous ebony, with tight curls of strawberry-blonde. Short fangs revealed themselves as her amusement continued. I called her name, and she leaned over, picking up something off the earthy floor.

Her startling blue eyes instantly met mine as she threw a handful of grass and dirt in my face. Inside the false memory, I stumbled to the ground in surprise, wiping my face with dirt. My face beamed as the beautiful woman leaned over me, her white gown tickling my legs. I could almost feel her breath in my ear as she whispered a secret.

It's not nice to spy on a woman's soul, you wicked monster.

I pursed my lips to keep from laughing as Nox's false memory now attached itself to my *Gavinhas*. A lively smile remained on his lips, and he raised his brows, the hum still emitting from deep in his throat.

He followed my lead, and we clasped our hands together, fingers intertwining, creating the friction needed to cast a spell.

"Escudo das Almas!" We pronounced in unison, and the vortex of the land's magic swirled around us aggressively for only a moment before disappearing into the ocean again.

We paused, our hands still entangled as our wild laughter filled the night sky.

"That was absolutely brilliant!" Nox exclaimed through several chuckles. He beamed at me, and my heart fluttered at his admiration. "When I redo my memories, I'm leaving a note for those trying to synchronize with me without permission."

"I can help you do it now if you'd like." I grasped his callused hand, and he gently squeezed it before shaking his head.

"It's getting late; we need some rest before continuing our lessons," he said, stretching his arms and rotating his shoulder blades. The dark circles around his eyes were more pronounced, and I was suddenly aware that casting such a spell was quite draining. My aura had dimmed, which was a rare occurrence.

"I'll work with you on a few defensive tactics in the morning. I would love to teach you everything I know, but in our short time frame, I want to show you how to defend yourself against someone larger than you."

"That works for me, sparring partner." I returned his earlier wink before bowing and heading to the cabin, where I prayed to the vine that Ornella was soundly asleep. Nox's laughter followed me down the narrow stairway, elevating my giddy attitude as I pinched my cheeks. They hurt from smiling so hard.

I creaked open the door, sneaking into the dimly lit room. Shadows were cast about the wooden walls, the only bit of light streaming in from the miniature round window. The soft sounds of Ornella's sobs emanated from underneath the blankets as I stood staring at the berth.

My elation dissipated instantly.

Chapter Fifteen

I experienced my first peaceful sleep on board the vessel thanks to the false memory that Nox embedded into my *Gavinhas*. The beautiful woman had laughed with me, pulling me along the vineyard's rows as we passed by luxurious, ripe fruits hanging precariously, ready for harvesting. My feet were bare as we ran along the ground's fertile soil, her piercing blue eyes meeting mine as she ensured I was still behind her. I did not know who she was, yet I felt I had lived a thousand lives with her. Everything about the dream was vivid, and I was entranced by the warmth it brought to my soul.

When I woke that morning to Ornella brushing her hair up into a high ponytail beside me on the berth, I wished to stay in my state of slumber. The happiness was intoxicating, and I was sad that the dream had ended so abruptly.

"How are things going in the galley?" I yawned and stretched my limbs.

Ornella smiled to herself before answering. "The cooking lessons are going well—great even. Enid is not only a talented chef, but she explains things in a way that I understand." She briefly checked her face in the hand mirror, content with her appearance. "I love how patient she is, and that she knows I'm not going to do things perfect on my first few attempts."

I sat up, nodding.

Ornella had been held to such high expectations back in our village that she often felt the sting of dejection when others realized that she was, in fact, not perfect. The friendships she had made were only surface-level; they were fascinated with her looks and gifted powers. But as soon as they discovered something about her that tainted their image of what she should be, they suddenly became busy with other peers, never making time for Ornella.

Seeing others make my sister wilt while she was forced to appear happy and tend to their needs crushed my soul. *Mãe* would always want to have a *heart-to-heart* with me for this, but I occasionally used my powers on those who wronged my sister.

I would slowly drain them of their energy for a few moons time. The girls would fall asleep during their chores and be scolded by their parents. Ornella did not appreciate me doing that, and I would be punished severely, but I did it anyway. The fear that the elders tried to instill in me could not keep me from defending my sister on my terms.

And after a little while, they got the message.

The girls in the neighborhood stopped pestering Ornella as if she were purely meant for their entertainment, to show off her abilities.

Hearing my sister sing praises of the ogress made me appreciate Enid even more because she treated her with the same kindness and understanding given to everyone else.

"Good, I'm happy that you're happy." I lazily grinned, noticing the color returning to her cheeks. She had always been sun-kissed from spending her time outside; the pale, washed-out tones did not suit her.

Ornella fixed her posture and smoothed out her clothes. "There's something for you on the desk; Enid gave us a matching set." Her eyes darted to a black cloth sitting on its wooden exterior, and I jumped out of the covers to have a look.

I held up a fitted black shirt, the material thin and sturdy. Alongside it was a pair of leggings of the same quality and new undergarments.

A wave of emotion overcame me as I was caught off guard; I had never received a gift from a friend. Ornella studied me, her smile content with my reaction.

She quickly spun in a circle, holding her arms up. "Ta-da! What do you think?" I had somehow missed her outfit change; the new clothes molded to her effortlessly—she looked ready to tackle the galley with Enid.

I smirked, raising a brow. "Where did she find us new outfits?" I sniffed my current shirt, pretending to wince from the smell. "Do we stink that bad?" I cackled as my sister rolled her eyes.

"This is one of Nox's vessels used by his clan for importing and exporting goods out of Alun. His family keeps extra clothes in the cargo holds for emergency purposes. That is what Enid told me anyway."

At the sound of his name, I was suddenly alert.

"Nox's ships?" My eyes went wide, my head spinning. "He has multiple, as in more than one? How is that possible?"

Ornella had walked the few paces to the door while peeking out at the sun through our small window. "I'm already running late, Sayah. Why don't you ask him yourself? And shouldn't you be out on the main deck already?" She gave a small wave before disappearing down the corridor and up the narrow stairway. "See you for supper; I'll be cooking alone for the first time!" Her excitement was evident, her voice echoing off the wooden planks.

Bless the vine, Ornella was right. I was late.

I changed into my new clothes as hastily as possible. They were snug without being overly revealing, and it was obvious that they were made to endure intense weather conditions and the outdoors. After redoing my braid, I looked at my reflection in the mirror.

My skin had always been pale—mainly because I enjoyed spending time indoors reading tales of lore and sipping hot tea out of the same chipped mug. It had been my daily routine back in the Woodlands, which brought me immense peace. So much of our lives had been out of our control, and this was the little ray of sunshine that I often had for myself.

Today, my skin was flushed, the rosy color highlighting my cheekbones and the tips of my pointed ears. My eyes, though dull, appeared happy. My sudden awareness that I was alone caused a rush of emotions to bubble to the surface. Placing the mirror down, I ran out the cabin door and up the stairway before I had time to acknowledge those feelings.

Times like these were when I missed *Mãe* the most, and waves of guilt consumed me for experiencing a brief moment of happiness without her.

She should be here with us too.

As I approached Nox and Silas on the main deck, I forced myself to think of other things. Their tense demeanor and serious expressions contrasted with the clear morning sky.

"Is something wrong?" I asked softly, gauging the situation.

"You're late." Nox frowned, his russet eyes intensely staring out into the horizon. His jaw flexed as he side-eyed me, crossing his arms, his gaze lingering. "The new attire suits you."

Silas twisted away from the sea to face me now. Dark shadows were beneath his golden irises, and he pushed back his sandy hair in exasperation.

"The giants, Nox. Three are currently on the shoreline, pacing back and forth." He gripped the siding, his forearms tense as he relayed the next bit of information. "And worse, we seemed to have entered their fight with the *Thereon* sailing directly behind us."

Giants? I stumbled over to the starboard side and gasped at the view.

The shape of Alun's beach was visible in the broad daylight. Two giants stood on the sand, their grimaces visible from a distance.

I choked back a scream at the massive giant wading through the ocean's current, waist-deep, approaching our vessel.

"Why do they feel threatened by us?"

"Giants usually are docile beings, but they are incredibly territorial. The idea was to sneak past their waters unnoticed, but the ship filled with *Thereon* made that impossible," Silas answered. The other threat was now approaching adjacent to the giant. Black sails were accompanied by a group of vile creatures reacting impatiently as they loomed nearby.

"How did the *Thereon* alert them from this far out at sea?" It did not make sense that the giants would hear or see their ships; their stealth was on another level.

Nox gently patted my back, directing me to look back at the coastline. "It's the same way I've been monitoring their distance from our ship: through the *Ligação Mágica*."

I felt silly for not noticing sooner.

The swirls of green and gold were once again distressed; they moved in a jagged disarray up the beach and into the great cliffs and mountains of Alun, where the species resided.

I flipped around, ready to run down the galley to warn Ornella and Enid of the alarming threat near our vessel. Nox grabbed my wrist, pulling me close with one arm and gripping the ship's side.

"What are you doing?" Even under attack, the man could still send shivers of pleasure down my spine with just a gentle touch. My face and neck reddened at his tight grip around my waist. "Don't we need to warn the others? Where're Brom and Kazumi?"

I hardly ever saw that spritely little fairy. But that was because she was permanently stationed at the bridge, where I rarely was.

"They are exactly where I need them to be." Nox focused on the giant, lurking dangerously close to striking distance. The *Thereon* ship had begun to sail toward ours, no longer focused solely on the giant.

"Should I give the signal?" Silas asked with urgency. But the ship's master stayed quiet, letting both opponents approach. "Nox, come on! I can smell him; he's so close! The signal?" His eyes narrowed, his mouth twitching with disapproval.

And a few seconds after Silas had said it, I nearly collapsed in Nox's one-armed grip.

The smell.

His appearance was jarring, but the stench that encroached on the ship made me want to vomit. The giant was covered in moss, and birds circled above his enormous head, their nests embedded in his matted hair. Bugs and creatures alike began to move up his body to escape the water, their nests now submerged in the salty waves.

"Now!" Silas yelled across the deck to those I assumed were Brom and Kazumi, and a thunderous crash rang in my ears. A luminescent magic appeared at the ship's hull, our vessel nearly shooting through the water. We had just evaded the giant as his arms crashed into the rippling waves.

Now I knew why his grip was so tight around my waist. The jolt had forced almost everyone to tumble to the wooden floorboards below, except for Nox and me. He held me upright, ensuring I did not end up against any of the ship's masts. The waves rocked around us, the salty water splashing up onto the main deck.

Only after the ship had settled did he release me to sprint to the hull, where the explosion of magic had originated.

"Are you both all right down there?" His voice was tense as he impatiently awaited his companions' reply.

There was a slight pause, and everyone was silent. Unease began to creep in when Brom finally answered, "Yeah, we're great. That was the biggest blast yet!" The sound of the ogre's excitement made Nox roll his eyes and rub his forehead, but relief was apparent in everyone.

"Next time, use less explosives and more fairy dust! We're trying to escape our demise, not be the cause of it!" he hollered down at the two, and we were met with a roar of laughter.

"Whose demise? And why are Brom and Kazumi playing with what is left of the explosives?" Enid joined us, followed by my doe-eyed sister, who was covered in flour.

"Did you end up covered in ingredients before or after we shot across the water?" I winked at Enid, who smiled knowingly, and Ornella's glare was razor-sharp as she crossed her arms and kept silent.

Silas came down to the main deck from the bridge, his petrified face sobering to us all.

"I—I've never in all my moons witnessed something so soul-wrenching." His voice quivered, and he ran his hands through his mane warily, pointing back to where we had scarcely escaped being crushed by a giant.

In the brief pause, Brom's footsteps could be heard as the wooden boards beneath his feet groaned under his weight as he approached. The ogre appeared before us, with Kazumi fluttering obnoxiously close behind.

"What's wrong?" Her shrilled rasp sliced through the ominous silence, piercing the air with her bluntness as she went to sit atop Silas's shoulder. Her soft-pink hair made her appear like a blushing rose, but upon closer inspection, I knew better than to pick that flower. It had thorns, sharp and vicious.

A monstrous wail filled the stagnant air, and the vibrations tested our vessel's integrity as we momentarily lost our footing. The crew ran to the starboard side to see what caused such a stir.

My eyes widened in shock as I began comprehending the scene before me. Time seemed to pause as the constant flow of wind surrounding the ocean had all but disappeared. Saltwater still clung to my skin and created a burning sensation in my vision as I watched helplessly. The giant angrily threw his arms in the air, pulling violently at his clothes and skin in panic. He thrashed above the ocean's surface, baring his teeth as if he had suddenly gone mad. A *Thereon's* vessel with black sails appeared directly beside the creature, mainly submerged in water. Another ship was not far behind, barely visible inside an enchanted mist.

Nox had been wrong about there being only one vessel following us; my nerves were shot at the dreadful discovery.

His roar of anger turned into shrieks of pain as what looked like large ants crawled out of the black vessel and onto the giant, swarming his figure.

The magic beneath the sea's exterior jerked violently in response.

"The *Thereon* have taken their next victim." Kazumi's piercing voice behind my head caused me to quiver.

"Victim?" I inhaled and squinted at the black silhouettes overpowering the giant as he thrashed, desperate to remove the soulless creatures from his body.

He was only trying to defend his territory; he would lose his soul permanently if no one acted. It was a fate worse than death—one that even the most revered of beings could not escape.

Heat began to rise to my face, and I narrowed my focus on the group of *Thereon* clinging to the giant's body. A deep-red color began to stain the being's tattered clothes, spilling out and mixing with the salty water. The soulless beasts attacked ferociously, their teeth like sharpened knives digging deeper into his skin. They were unyielding and relentless, the black mist encompassing each beast unfazed by the giant's desperate grasp as he managed to throw several into the ocean below. But it wouldn't be enough to stop their attack. He was outnumbered, and the two other giants on the shore fell to their knees in sobs.

They had wished to enter the water to save their companion, but he would wail and move farther out to sea as if to say, *I'll drown before I let you face the same fate as me.*

I squeezed my hands into fists at my sides, my jaw clenched tight. The power pulsed beneath my skin in response.

"We need to do *something*," I said aloud to no one in particular, pacing back and forth with my hands on my head. But the stretch of silence grew;

the ringing in my ears grew louder and the pace of my heartbeat quickened as I abruptly halted in front of the crew.

Still, no one answered, not a soul.

They all hesitated, wearing the same conflicted expression—even Ornella.

My shoulders tensed, and I turned my heel in frustration, away from everyone. I clenched my jaw before walking briskly toward the stern. If no one wanted to help aid the giant, I refused to watch a moment longer.

The rage growing inside me caused my powers to stir, awakening the beast within. Tendrils of light encompassing each individual became apparent, and a loud crack had me instinctively turn my head back to where the giant wrestled for his life. He squirmed in the murky sea; his head and neck fell back onto the *Thereon's* vessel. His strength was fading, and the glow from his tendrils flickered outside his aura.

Small objects began to fall from the massive being in his torment. They were various shades of earthy tones, plopping into the sea rapidly. My ears twitched as they picked up on odd cries before the sound would vanish, growing eerily quiet. I gasped, the color draining from my face as I recognized the pelt of a fox floating out to sea. The forest animals that had once found protection in the safety of the giant's build now descended to their watery grave.

The magic tethering the kingdoms together was in a complete rage beneath the choppy waves, clearly affected by the *Thereon's* presence. It resembled how I felt: anger at the monsters who attacked the giant and anger at myself for not finding a way to help.

A bystander to evil is just as corrupt as the one inflicting pain on their victim.

"Isn't there anything that we can do?" I choked on my words, tears pulling in the corners of my eyes. I gripped the siding of the vessel, my fingernails digging into the wood.

Nox was now beside me; his expression was grave.

"This is why I want you to train," He crossed his arms, his russet eyes stern. "The *Thereon* are capturing an adult male giant, Sayah. *In record time*, I might add."

Any reply that I might have quipped back to him had sunk to the pit of my stomach. The giant was no longer fighting and had stopped resisting. It lay motionless with its head on the ship, its haggard breaths audible even from our distance.

Enid swiftly sprinted toward us, the alarm in her tone evident. "The *Thereon* have only made a side stop; they will be on us like bloodhounds with a fresh sent if we don't start moving." The crew had already begun sailing our escape route in haste, and they did not wait for Nox's approval.

He nodded in agreement to the ogress and uncrossed his arms as he prepared for our immediate departure. The sounds of his footsteps grew quiet as I was now left alone.

The wind had once again started, and I could hear the clamor of the crew members as they hustled about the main deck.

But I remained frozen, unable to turn away from the atrocity that awaited both Ornella and me.

The giant had already lost his battle. Dozens of *Thereon* surrounded his face, now blocking the view of the creature's deadpan stare, void of hope.

I saw a reflection of my future in the giant's eyes.

Sayah, you're a coward, my soul whispered. The power inside of me buzzed in agreement.

My body lurched forward into the vessel as the weight beneath my feet unexpectedly shifted.

The ship moved rapidly across the water with Kazumi's assistance. Fairies had their own set of magical properties but with limitations. Their fairy dust was powerful but brief. Our current situation required her to diminish the rest of her magic for the time being to allow us our escape.

The giant's skin began to turn sickly grey, and his eyes, now transfixed on our vessel as we raced away, faded to a bloodthirsty red. Even at the growing distance, I could see the parasitic magic form around his still figure.

In his soul's last moments, he pulled the massive vessel down into ocean, disappearing underneath the surface. *Thereon* howled and shrieked, jumping off their ship in large numbers. The ominous quiet remained, as pieces of wood now littered the water next to their one remaining ship.

Suddenly, the giant gradually resurfaced, staring in the direction of the two giants on Alun's shore. The tendrils of light surrounding him snapped, and a piercing wave of despair shook my core at witnessing the death of his soul. He had lost his connection with this world and would cease to exist in another once his heart stopped beating. The black aura surrounding him was now nothing more than a dark object as our ship fled for safety.

Silent tears painted my cheeks, and I wiped them away with the sleeve of my shirt and pushed off the siding, forcing myself to go and help the others with a newfound urgency.

My hands pulsed in pain from finally releasing my grip; my power once again trickled out of my figure. I knew what I needed to do.

A haunting thought repetitively threatened to break my mental wall as I made my way to the cabin, my body shaking at the loss of control.

You could have at least tried to save the giant, Sayah.

I knew it was impossible to do on my own. But I didn't even try.

Memories that my younger self had buried long ago began to swarm my mind. Images of my peers from back in Alizeh observed me with a deadpan stare as the weight of my bully's words inflicted a pain that cut deeper than any blade could.

Those who stayed quiet in the corner, watching horror unfold without so much as a movement of action.

And I was just as horrid as them.

I shut the door to my room behind me, shucking off my shoes and crawling beneath the sheets of our cot. The thin fabric did nothing to shut the rest of the world out as I wrestled with the pain inside my chest and the ringing in my ears until I dozed off.

Though even in my sleep, a single thought remained.

Because of me, the giant was soulless; now a Thereon.

Chapter Sixteen

I had it all wrong; it wasn't a heart of stone I had needed; it was a hardened physique built for combat.

Every muscle and fiber in my body ached, but training with Nox was essential. After witnessing what the *Thereon* were truly capable of, I no longer complained about the pain.

The image of the giant's *Gavinhas* snapping replayed in my mind as I took another blow and fell onto the mat. My heart was made of burning flames, lit by the anger that I hadn't been able to do anything to stop those vile beasts. As we escaped into the distance, shrieks and wails of despair sounded from Alun's shore. The other two giants had witnessed their beloved turn into a monster.

And there was no cure, no way to turn them back to who they once were.

My thoughts were with what Nox wanted to accomplish, which seemed dauntingly impossible as I failed to put him into a chokehold, and he threw me back down to the mat repeatedly.

Several moons had passed since then, and we quickly approached the Isles of Cadogan. The crew wanted the confrontation with the *Thereon* to be at this location to avoid involving innocent lives. Without the *Ligação*

Mágica to help us, we would be at a disadvantage. Silas had said there was a way around that, and it involved pulling from the ancient magic imbued around Cadell's Chamber. The risk was high, but I only cared about whether or not my sister was safe in the process.

The *Breeders of Thereon* ought to pay for the souls they've eliminated.

And the destruction to our kingdoms that they've singlehandedly created.

"Let's move on to your energy manipulation; you're clearly not focused. You're doing worse than when you first started, and almost an entire lunation has passed," Nox said.

I exhaled, rolling my eyes when his head was turned in the other direction.

"I saw that."

"How!" I whipped back around in disbelief, only to find him smirking. His mass of brown waves was tied up, and his figure was mesmerizing, the sun behind him creating a warm glow around his silhouette.

"Because I have eyes in the back of my head. Also, you're extremely predictable." The hunky werewolf chuckled as my glare lingered on his massive biceps.

Teasing him, I pointed my chin to the sky with a smug expression and put my hands on my hips. "If anyone is predictable around here, it's you, *Captain*. You wake up at the same time each morning; you drink your coffee, and after our lessons—you check the sails, the entire ship really, before heading to the bridge to talk to Silas about the *Thereon's* current location. And then you eat supper before taking the first shift while everyone else sleeps." I felt the sun on my skin, and my eyes closed. "It's rather repetitive and dull, wouldn't you say?"

My question was met with silence, the only noise the peaceful sounds of the waves lapping against the ship.

The wind abruptly knocked out of me, and I opened my eyes wide in surprise. Nox held me against his chest, and I felt his heart pounding beneath his warm skin. Those delectable russet eyes of his were inches from mine, and gold flecks swirled inside their vast depth.

He leaned down, whispering, "When I sail you to Erebus, I'll show you how unpredictable I can be." His heated breath tingled in my ear, and he set me down gingerly on the mat. It wasn't often that he teased me back, but it sent my heart into a frenzy that lasted for days on end. He straightened, taking a moment to gently caress my cheek with his index finger before pulling away. "But for now, I have to be predictable. Keeping this boat afloat and those who occupy it out of harm's way is of the utmost importance. It's what keeps *you* safe, Sayah."

Nox walked to the other side of the main deck, waiting. It took me several seconds to fully gather myself as I tried to keep a neutral face and my feet steady. But my heart was beating feverishly inside my chest, and his mischievous smile made me believe that my suspicions were correct—he could hear it.

"Let's get started then." Was all I could manage without another blush rising to my cheeks. We had practiced this daily since the *Thereon* had made themselves known on Alun's shore, and there had been no improvement.

Control did not come naturally to me. I felt I was only made of spontaneous chaos, ignited by the most minor inconveniences.

Letting go of my grasp on my power was not the issue; it was reigning it in afterward.

Regardless of my past failures, I stepped toward him confidently, placing my hand on his bicep like I had done many times. Closing my eyes, I pictured my power as if it were a tangible extension of me, just as Nox had suggested. Eager to be released, the vines flowed out of my body as a soft stream of swirling black.

I allowed them to encompass his aura. His sharp intake of air made my eyes flare open; waves of guilt flooded my chest, and I rapidly let go of the source of his energy.

He pulled his arm from my grip, and I lowered my head, waiting for his words of disapproval. But no confrontations came. He was quiet. I meekly looked up between my lashes, and his usual brooding eyes were full of sympathy.

"When was the last time you cried?" He spoke softly as if he were coaxing a bird with an injured wing.

"Why are you asking me that?" I inhaled sharply, hugging my arms into my chest. "I always cry; I'm sure you're aware."

Nox gingerly approached me and held my hands. "Those were angry tears, Sayah. When was the last time you released your grief?"

I pulled away from his touch, wanting this conversation to be over. "Right after *Mãe* died." My memory went hazy. All I could recall were the trees and nature around me, wilting as if I were a disease quickly spreading throughout the kingdom.

He strolled to the training mat and patted his hand on its cushioned surface, asking me to join him.

I released a massive breath, and I obeyed his wishes. We enjoyed each other's company for several minutes without words, instead feeling the salty wind that I was growing accustomed to tickling my exposed skin, the sun peaking in and out of the clouds every so often. I was beginning to drift into a state of tranquility when his husky voice brought me back to reality.

"From what I've seen, you cannot control your powers because you do not have control of your emotions. It's not that your feelings control your gift; rather, they overflow inside you, seeping through the cracks of the foundation of who you are. That is why you're lacking control." Nox observed me as I lay out on the mat, feeling overwhelmed and exhausted. "So, let's talk it through, Sayah. Tell me your most vulnerable thoughts so you can take the next step to moving forward."

An awkward laugh escaped my mouth as I held my hands over my head to shield them from the sun.

"It's not that simple, Nox. There are just too many emotions bubbling up inside of me, and I'm unsure where to begin."

"Then start at the very beginning, and we can work our way from there."

I sighed, thinking. "Let's see . . ." I paused briefly, trying to summarize my childhood. "My entire village was scared of my touch, as they should be." I winked in his direction and continued. "Ornella was always favored, which honestly didn't bother me because I think she had it worse. She was held to such high expectations, while I had hardly any, other than to keep to myself and not cause trouble."

"Which I'm assuming was rather difficult for you." He snickered and I grinned in reply.

"Only occasionally." I sheepishly turned my face away and carried on. "Music became my life's purpose, and I was set to inherit *Mãe's* academy after our rite of passage. Every elf is given a purpose within our community, and I thought surely this was mine. But then, right after the ceremony,

Elder Josias informed me that I would be training in the military and that I was to leave immediately following the end of the ceremony for Ascelin. I was devasted."

Tears welled in my eyes, and I brushed them away with the back of my hand. "All I ever wanted was to be our village's music teacher and take over *Mãe's* legacy, which she had to fight for. She was a single parent, which is rare in the elf species. Typically, the *Videira* only sends a *Meir* to couples with a lamp on their door, signifying they are willing to care for a child. *Mãe* had been blessed with two infants without any of the usual protocols. And we turned out to be *Marked Ones*, who are highly coveted."

I shrugged, my face impartial. "That's just how it was, and after several years of other elves complaining, they eventually accepted it."

"What happened? How did you and Ornella end up in Danu?" His question was innocent, but it felt like the words were shards of glass piercing my heart, digging into a wound that refused to heal.

"We—" A lump formed in my throat, making speaking difficult. Nox was alert as I suddenly sat up, pulling my knees into my chest and squeezing my legs as I held myself together. My face was turned to the other side, silent tears spilling down my cheeks.

Nox's hand was on my back, gently moving in a circular motion. His touch was soothing, and the anxiety that had gripped my voice slowly began to release its hold on my vocal cords. After several minutes, I proceeded with the retelling of that horrid night—of *Mãe's* death.

"The night of our rite of passage . . . During our ritual, something odd occurred. When blessed by our sacred vine, a giant light shot out of the sentient being, and the ground shook like an earthquake. But it only lasted a few moments, and everyone was pleased with those results as my sister and I are *Marked Ones*. We had our traditional celebratory meal, and the *Meirs* arrived, followed by those newly chosen by the *Videira* to be parents. Everything was proceeding as expected. And then, in the woods, all of the animals went quiet. And out came several creatures cloaked in black. They did not act rabid like some other *Thereon* I've seen, which is quite odd."

His arm moved to my arm, and I paused.

"I am not trying to interrupt, but there is a reason for that. How beings are turned into *Thereon* is still unknown. However, once someone is turned, their thinking process is compromised. Brom says it takes around one complete lunation before they've lost their ability to think coherently." Nox nodded for me to continue.

"There's something I don't understand . . . what do the *Thereon* want? What is their purpose now that they've lost their *Gavinhas*? Are they not technically dead?" The questions began to spill out of my mouth, one after the other.

Nox removed his hand from my back and scratched his chin as he thought.

"They are a living corpse is the best way to put it. *Thereon*, they are no longer who they once were; the essence of their soul and ability to reincarnate has been relinquished. Craving something that only their *Breeders* can provide; what that is, no one is sure. So, the dirty work is accomplished for their masters in exchange for something." His voice hitched, and his eyes gleamed with a subtle determination. "And in two moons time, we will find out what exactly that is."

He nudged me with his shoulder, patiently waiting to hear what else had happened.

"After our military warned them to stay off our ceremony grounds, they attacked. And nothing could get through their impenetrable black shield of dark magic. Not swords, arrows, fists, not a single weapon touched them. And we all helplessly watched as many lost their lives on what was supposed to be a joyous occasion. *Mãe* had sprinted to where the infants were being kept, to protect them. Ornella stayed behind to help give energy to the injured, and I went after *Mãe* to assist her."

I rubbed my neck as the anxiety made it hard to breathe. I inhaled and slowly exhaled, now determined to finish.

"Nobody was there when I went to the tents off the grounds. It took me a bit, but what *Mãe* had mentioned earlier gave me the idea to use the *Ligação Mágica* to find her. So, I did exactly that. And then"—I paused, working up the courage to push through—"I found her. A man who I thought was a *Thereon* was standing over her, but now I know that he had the same parasitic magic as one, but his *Gavinhas* were still intact, and he could speak."

I remembered now, clear as day. His eyes had been multicolored; one of his right eyes was green, and the left a golden hue.

Violent tears began to pour, and I clenched my jaw in rage. "I threw myself at his feet and begged him not to hurt her. I told him I was the one he was looking for, but he didn't believe me." Now, through choked sobs, I managed to say, "And then he stabbed her."

The boiling anger transformed into grief, and I let it flow out of me like a raging river. Nox held me in his tight embrace, stroking my hair. My face was pressed against his chest, and he cradled me for some time afterward. I wasn't sure how long we sat on the main deck out in the open, but he didn't seem to mind.

This time, it was not my powers that had come undone. It was all the pent-up emotion I had held inside, desperate for a release. I mourned for *Mãe* and our family, for the life we would no longer have together.

And I mourned for little Sayah; the girl deemed a monster from the moment she bloomed. The child, that everyone looked at in disgust, who was labeled weird and odd. I mourned for me, forced to watch life happen in the shadows, desperately wanting to enter the light where everyone else was.

Because I had deserved love too.

Ornella cooked supper that night and waited nervously beside the island countertop in the galley to gauge everyone's reactions. We waited patiently as the smell of turkey and vegetables wafted beneath our noses causing several stomachs to grumble audibly. The entire crew was inside the kitchen area this time; we all would eat our last meal together before arriving at the Isles of Cadogan. The name sent shivers down my spine as I choked down an extremely dry piece of turkey leg. Everyone was gloomy about our arrival tomorrow, or it could be my sister's dreadful attempt at cooking.

From the way Brom slowly finished his plate, I think it was the latter.

Enid was Ornella's support system; she practically clung to the ogress's apron in tears. "I told you it wasn't good enough to eat," my sister whined, her emerald eyes defeated.

"Even the best chefs in all the five kingdoms had to start somewhere." Her brown eyes were large and kind, as she assured Ornella, but a switch flipped when she scrutinized the rest of the crew. They were deadly daggers, skimming the room to prepare the reveal of who would be on dish duty tonight by how much of their plate was clean. Enid's shirt sleeves had been rolled up, and she looked ready to pounce on anyone who commented negatively about their meal.

To my astonishment, Silas smiled contently and ate his entire plate in under a minute.

"That was delicious, Ornella, thank you." The werewolf patted her back in encouragement, receiving a look of approval from Enid before exiting the room.

His face had turned green just as he rounded the corner, and I grinned.

I cleared my throat, ready to deploy my escape plan; I smirked at Brom, and I patted my face with a napkin, cleaning it of crumbs.

"Oh, bless the vine, I'm stuffed." I grabbed my stomach, pretending it ached, and pushed the overcooked turkey leg and burnt vegetables in his direction. "Brom, you said you need more than one plate to get your fill, and I promised to share." My voice was an octave too high, and the ogre glowered at me as I fluttered my eyelashes to appear sweeter than the pastries, I used to eat.

Just thinking about the delicious gooey filling inside the warm baked bread had my mouth watering. My stomach growled loudly.

Coughing did not completely cover the sound, and he snickered. "Sayah, don't be shy on my account. I know that you've been not finishing your meals for my sake. Your act of kindness and generosity is truly touching."

Oh no. I felt dread wash over my expression as I pursed my lips tightly.

Brom gestured widely to our two plates as he continued. "So, tonight, as it is our last night together before we reach the isles, I will share my food with you." The conniving ogre scooted his plate and my own in front of me. "Out of kindness." He bowed to me and lifted his gaze before winking.

A shrill laugh pierced the room, causing me to jump and nearly tumble sideways into Nox. The ghost of the ship had finally made her appearance.

Kazumi had an evil smile dancing across her lips as she addressed me. "Nice try, elvish girl. But you'll have to be more conniving than that to make Brom, of all beings, eat something that he doesn't want to." Her translucent wings fluttered inches from my ear as she stood on my shoulder.

My entire body tensed, terrified of what might happen next. I've had a little debate going on with myself about whether or not I would prefer the wrath of a *Thereon* or Kazumi. She whispered in my ear, and I nearly fainted.

For this instance, I'm going to choose a *Thereon*. The fairy was more frightening.

"If we live to see another day after tomorrow, I'll let you join our next poker night." Her cackle echoed in my ear. Kazumi flew in front of my line of sight; my eyes transfixed with her black swirling orbs of terror.

"Kazumi, that's enough." It was Nox coming to my rescue. I raised my brows in disbelief as his plate was also clean. "We will see you bright and early in the morning." He pointedly glared at his acquaintance. She backed away from me, but not before revealing her sharp, pointed teeth.

The fairy disappeared.

My head turned this way and that to scan the room for the spritely fairy, but she was indeed gone. The feisty woman could vanish at a moment's notice.

The galley had almost cleared out, and Ornella's face drooped. She sauntered over to Brom, almost comically dragging her feet. My twin took off her apron, which was smothered in food. "Is it that bad, Brom? Enid said that ogres eat practically anything." Her shoulders sagged when he didn't answer for a few moments.

It was Enid who saved the day, coming over to elbow her brother in the side rather forcefully. "Brom isn't feeling well; he gets anxious before battles—or having to do physical labor of any kind." Enid rolled her eyes dramatically and turned to stare at him directly. I smiled because even though I could only see the back of her head, I knew from the look on the large man's face that he was in trouble. Brom paled, and he instantly changed his reaction.

"Ornella, your food is absolutely delicious!" he said, scarfing down the food and swallowing it whole. "I was trying to be kind to Sayah, but if she isn't hungry, it will fill this ogre's stomach with joy." He had finished my plate with his, and I bowed to him graciously when only he was watching. "That was satisfying!" Patting and rubbing his belly, the ogre winced and darted from the room.

Needing the lavatory, no doubt.

A pleased expression settled on both my sister's face and Enid's.

I walked over to the sink and filled it with warm, sudsy water. "I've got this; you two go on ahead and enjoy the moonlight and fresh air. You've both been stuck down here all day."

Ornella's behavior changed instantaneously.

Her emerald eyes were bright as she dragged Enid toward the main deck. "That sounds like a wonderful idea; thank you, Sayah, for cleaning up!" I waved as they disappeared in the narrow corridors.

Enid's head popped back into the room, her green cheeks a bit rosy. "Yes, thank you, Sayah." Her eyes were full of appreciation. I smiled knowingly and nodded. Her shoulder-length hair was down, and she had a happy glow about her.

"Your hair looks lovely tonight, dear." I blew some of the soap suds from the sink in her direction, and she laughed heartily before trailing after my twin. The remaining bubbles floating in the air popped.

I was now by myself. My grin immediately fell, along with my mask of happiness.

I stared into space for several minutes, leaning on the sink in front of the dirty dishwater. Nox must have left at some point when Enid scolded Brom and me for bickering over who should eat Ornella's supper.

A dull ringing in my ears was the only noise to pierce the quiet that invaded the space, and my thoughts were blank. There was an ache inside my chest from the emotional wound that had been ripped open earlier.

For most of my existence, I had convinced myself that I preferred my company to others. But I felt the burden of the vacant room now.

I was shocked when an absurd thought crossed my mind: I might even prefer Kazumi's presence over the quiet. Laughter from the main deck echoed down to the galley, and I rushed to pull the drain on the dishwater, heading up to meet the others.

Alone with my thoughts is not a place that I desired to stay in.

Chapter Seventeen

My dream began with me sitting in nothing but darkness. The shadows resembled the ones contained in the narrow passageways back in the Woodlands, so I felt at peace. However, this quiet was unfamiliar because the constant ringing in my ears had abruptly ceased. A faint cry sparked my interest, and I strained, listening.

And then it was close: a woman's plea begging for someone to help her. I followed the sound until it faded completely.

I felt her—a soul tethered to mine.

Instinctually, I looked over my shoulder, and the woman was now inches behind me. She lay in a crumpled heap on the floor, defeated. Her sobs were of someone who grieved another, and my heart ached knowing the same pain. I approached cautiously, sat on the floor, and rubbed her back to calm her.

Her cries instantly stopped.

"Who's there?" She backed away, tense. She began to pull on the chains around her wrists. "I can hear your breathing and feel your touch. Now answer me; who are you?" Her skin was covered in filth, and her curls were untamed and matted with debris.

Rusted bars appeared around us, and I gradually gathered that we were inside a cage.

"Are you okay?" I gingerly touched her arm.

The strange woman gasped, now desperately trying to find my location. "Please save me." A spark of hope ignited in her eyes as she heard my question echo into the darkness. "He's going to devour us all; we need to escape." Falling back down to her knees, her head hung in defeat.

There were several beats of silence before she began speaking to herself.

"I must be going crazy." She exhaled, gripping the iron bars containing us both. "I can't believe I just spoke to a voice inside my head."

"Your head? This is *my* dream, so it would be my consciousness you're inside." I laughed with sincerity as she pounced backward in fear, tripping over her chains. "Oh, I'm sorry." I reached for her and fell backward with a gasp when I recognized her eyes.

Her irises were a startling blue.

"Tabitha?" I whispered in disbelief.

The woman sat up on her knees eagerly. "Yes, that's me! Oh, bless the moon above; my prayers were answered!" Her body shook joyfully, tears streaming down her beautiful, high cheekbones. "Are you here to help me?"

I paused, unsure of how to respond.

"I—I'm not exactly here—wherever this is." I rubbed my forehead, deep in thought.

She paced around her circular prison, thinking. Her blue eyes darted around the space, and Tabitha urgently asked, "What is your name?"

My response was immediate. "Sayah, daughter of Aster. Child of the *Videira*."

"An elf?" Her shock was apparent as her pacing momentarily paused. "How do you know me, Sayah?"

"Technically, I don't know you," I answered, a bit embarrassed, while biting my nails. "But Nox, your brother, is with me. He embedded a memory of you inside my *Gavinhas*. That is how I know who you are."

Tabitha lurched towards me, grasping at nothing but air.

"Nox?! He's alive?" Her relief was evident; another wave of emotion crashed down on the poor woman as she fell to the floor with her hands over her heart. "Oh, thank you, thank you." She rocked back and forth, smiling contently. "That was a gift in itself; thank you, Sayah, for telling me," Tabitha whispered.

I observed her soundlessly for an extended time as she relaxed.

"Will you stay with me?" Her voice was suddenly anxious. "I've been alone for a long time."

"Of course, I will stay," I replied, embracing her with a side hug, as *Mãe* used to when she consoled Ornella and me as children. "Nox is coming to rescue you. He has a ship and a plan."

Tabitha's blue eyes were so close that I could see the few golden freckles shimmering beneath them and along the bridge of her nose. "You're stunning," I said, examining her unique features as she giggled. What species are you?"

Her eyes widened, and she was silent for several beats as the tension around us grew.

"That's okay; you don't have to answer, Tabitha." I cleared my throat. In the silence, I started to sing to her a comforting lullaby from my childhood.

And as she drifted to sleep inside the cage, I slowly came to.

My head pulsed with a migraine, and I desperately wished for some hot tea. Several moons had passed since I had my routine cup of happiness in the early morning to wake me.

Ornella was next to me in our small berth beneath the covers. She groaned, smacking me in the head with her pillow.

"Hey, what was that for!" I tumbled out of the bed, away from my sister's range of motion.

"Sayah, are you serious?" She frowned, pulling the covers back over her body. Tufts of her hair poked out from beneath the sheets.

"You wouldn't stop sleep-talking the entire night!"

"Really?" I scratched my head, confused. "What did I say?"

"It was a bunch of incoherent gibberish." Her tone was soft as she stated, "And you repeatedly sang the lullaby that *Mãe* used to sing to us as kids . . . when we were sad."

Ornella's waves of white were a crazy mess from a sleepless night, and she jumped out of bed and surprised me by holding my face in her delicate grasp. "Are you okay, Sayah? Do you need to talk about it?"

Gently pulling her hands down, I reassured her. "I'm all right. The odd thing is, I don't remember dreaming at all."

"Oh well." She exhaled and searched her bag for her brush. "Let's not focus on last night. Today is vital, Sayah. We help the crew capture a *Thereon*, and they can start working on a cure."

"And then we travel to Erebus," I added, excitement building.

She was right, like always. Today's success was critical in moving forward.

A thick fog rolled in, blanketing the sea with an eerie silence. Our ship was approaching the Isles of Cadogan, where the dreadful Cadell's Chamber housed thousands of felons in its stone walls imbued with ancient magic. Behind the isles, the haunting border of a hazy mist stretched across the open waters, where the Unknown was now visible. The uncharted sea, the unexplored depths of our world. What mysteries must lie behind the ominous border faded from my mind as we began to focus on today's task: capturing a *Thereon*.

The entire crew was up on the main deck, and the haze made it challenging to see everyone's location, though they were just a few feet away. I shifted my feet and strained my shoulders. I was hyperaware of Kazumi, a pinkish-dull glow moving about the crew members. Every time she came within a few paces, I could hear her haunting laughter echo along the main deck.

The spritely fairy's teasing was problematic. I didn't hear a lick of what Silas had just relayed about the details of our plan.

"Listen carefully." Nox leaned forward, still handsome as ever. He used his knee to rest his elbow as he spoke. "We will be entering from the back of where Cadell's Chamber is located. From what I have researched, there should be no guards of any kind."

The gorgeous man's attire was similar to mine today. He wore the same black, fitted shirt and pants, which suited him better. I had only begun to marvel at his pectoral muscles when a flash of pink startled me.

Kazumi flew forward, her wings fluttering at a rapid pace. She nearly snorted at the idea of using caution. "Of course, there's no need for guards on the Isles of Cadogan. One, the magic used is of an ancient spell only known by the first *Marked Ones*." Her voice was a raspy whisper. "But more importantly, if we get too close to the prison walls, we will be sucked inside and permanently stuck with its lovely inhabitants."

Everyone who resides inside the five kingdoms of Aksel has heard the rumors. Once inside the chamber walls, there is no way out. No one knows what waits inside, and the isles are said to be cursed without the land's magic to connect the barren soil to our *Creator*.

But that was just nonsense. The elderly women in my village often gossiped and repeated the same tales, so I knew that it was likely false.

"Well done scouting ahead for us this morning." Nox's hands rested on top of a barrel as he wore a grin speaking to Silas. For someone who could possibly meet the *Creator*—or worse—because of the *Thereon*, he seemed almost jubilant.

"Today is a pivotal moment for all of us here." Nox began his pep talk. "We will move forward as planned, and with the assistance from Sayah and Ornella, we can obtain information imperative in stopping the *Thereon* and their attacks on our kingdoms. And we can plan to invade Mount Auberon in Adara, where all the other *Marked Ones* are being held." There was a serious gleam in his russet irises as he was briefly applauded.

All? As in . . . my twin and I are the only two left? That was news to me. Unease began to creep up my arms, making the hairs on my neck stand. Why was I suspicious that the crew was withholding information?

Enid approached me after the short pep talk, her eyes full of concern.

"Protect Ornella and yourself above anyone else; you both are more valuable than all the treasure hoarded in Mount Auberon." Her eyebrows raised slightly at the sight of my disbelief. "I'm not trying to flatter you, Sayah. There are hardly any *Marked Ones* that haven't been captured."

The color drained from my already-pale skin, but my face remained neutral to her comment.

"Are you sure of this? I know gifted ones are rare, but my sister and I can't be the only two left unharmed. Why hasn't anyone said anything until now?" I inquired while picking at my cuticles.

The mere idea of the grimy hands of a *Thereon* gripping my skin like a leech made my mouth run dry. I couldn't imagine what it must be like to be captured by a foul creature led by a desire so strong all other capabilities to think freely have disappeared.

"We didn't want you two to get a big head," Enid smirked temporarily before sympathy filled her warm chocolate eyes. "Nobody wanted to scare either of you. There's already pressure. Don't worry about minor details."

I barked a laugh and shook my head, my response oozing with sarcasm. "Ah, yes, minor details." I saluted Enid and turned my heel to walk back to our cabin briskly.

This new piece of information was enlightening. As events clicked in my mind, an unsettling feeling deep inside my stomach grew.

Elder Josias ordered me to join the military because the kingdom of Alizeh wanted to protect what was theirs; their biases toward me no longer mattered. Not to mention the burdensome military presence on the ceremony grounds.

I nearly crumbled to the floorboards in shock, the realization causing me to be immobile outside of our cabin's entryway.

They knew. Bless the vine and all things sacred.

Those conniving priests and elders knew of the *Thereon's* presence in Alizeh and did not take the proper actions to defend our kind. How shocking that they had risked the newly bloomed infants. Not a single soul had been warned; hundreds of lives could have been protected. If my memory served me correctly, not even the soldiers had been notified of the vile creatures. I wondered what they could have been told, what deceptions and lies had been spread. Only those in power knew the severity of the threat, and they did *nothing*.

I clenched my hands at the boiling rage inside of me because of the simple reality—the lost lives could have been avoided if Ornella and I had not attended the rite of passage.

The events of that night all at once flooded my memory, causing my head to spin.

The bright flash of light emitting from the *Videira* alerted those far and wide of our existence and precise location. How quickly the *Thereon* appeared at the ceremony grounds, prepared to kidnap Ornella and me.

Bile began to rise to the top of my throat at the absurdity.

They had already been there, inside of Alizeh. The *Thereon* were hot on our trail, and we made it easy for them to find us.

A cold sweat blanketed my body as my fingers trembled to open our cabin door.

Ornella and I were the last two *Marked Ones* safe inside the five king-doms.

And nobody had wanted us to find out.

"You don't look so good." Ornella examined me; concern etched along her features. Her hair was pulled back from her face, and she was surprisingly calm for our current situation.

"I'm fine," I retorted, pulling at the straps of my pack, annoyed by their weight.

Our vessel was anchored relatively close to Cadell's Chamber. The entire crew and I had taken the dinghy up to the beach. The *Ligação Mágica* beneath the water's exterior curled at the end of its reach, slowly fading until disappearing entirely. We had jam-packed that tiny boat, and I tried to calm myself now that we had made landfall.

The aisles of Cadogan appeared precisely as I had pictured them. They were filled with giant black boulders, and the sand was ash-colored. There was no greenery, no sign of life other than the occasional bird perched upon a jagged rock. My focus was scattered between the desolate islands, void of nature, and Cadell's Chamber. The green-and-yellow magic that tethered the five kingdoms together nipped at the shoreline but did not break the water's surface. It was evident that the help from our *Creator* would not be found here.

Ornella was just a step behind me, and I could practically feel how anxious she was. Her excitement to help must have worn off now that plans were being made. Nox asked if she would take his binoculars and be the designated lookout.

The massive chamber made of stone and steel was intimidating. Its walls were higher than those of the buildings in Ascelin. A magical current was embedded into the welded steel, glowing with a blueish hue. I had not witnessed magic with that vibrancy before, and although it was enchanting, I could feel the warning rooted into its spell. There was an ominous pull in its ancient origins, daring me to touch the stone that would have me sucked into its prison for eternity.

The mere thought of being stuck inside its concrete walls without a hint of sunlight sent a shiver down my spine. Our crew was on full alert, scanning the unknown terrain. Who knew what evil lurked in its bleak shadows or if the *Thereon* were lurking, waiting somewhere hidden in the cracks and crevasses.

"Yes, this will do." Nox pointed to an area near the chamber, between the maze of giant boulders. "We should start, they are not far behind."

"Sayah, you ready?" Silas inquired from up ahead, using a foreign liquid metal to build a trap by pulling the magical current away from the chamber walls. As I approached, the enclosed circle flared a brilliant white, burning like a hot iron rod in the sand.

"What is that?" The question lingered on my lips, my eyes entranced by the unfamiliar substance.

"A conduit for the magic," Silas answered as he stepped back from his work, slowly walking around the circle, inspecting his work for discrepancies. "We need a physical channel for the magic to consistently flow through to create the trap. This type of conduit is becoming more well-known. Think of the city of Ascelin; your kind is using it to power the buildings with the help of the *Ligação Mágica*. Not that I agree with that." He mumbled the last bit, now turning toward the chamber.

I now inspected Cadell's Chamber closely. The mighty stone walls were encompassed with reflective metal, hiding beneath the mysterious electric blue currents crackling up and down the prison's surface.

Kazumi now flew close to the chamber walls, and I inhaled as she paused for several beats. It was excruciating to witness; the ancient magic was trying to absorb her into the chamber's black abyss. She somehow managed to take a piece of the defensive spell, though it fought her violently, causing her veins to swell beneath her skin in the struggle. Sweat dripped down her forehead as she released the magic, and it spread like wildfire to become a condensed sphere encased in cobalt-like flames flickering along the hardened metal.

I finally exhaled just in time to notice Brom and Ornella jogging back to us; their expressions were full of worry.

"They're already here." My sister's lip quivered, and she touched her face in concern.

Brom's tense shoulders relaxed at seeing the trap already put in place. "Everything's set, yeah? The *Thereon's* ship is already unloading its ghastly beasts onto the beach. We only have a few moments."

We all ran into place, my sister and I standing on a ledge above the trap. The plan was to have one of the bloodthirsty creatures come directly at me, and I would jump out of the way as it fell directly into the circle of fiery ancient magic. From the shore, the trap was not visible. But if anyone walked around the boulders and rocks we were perched upon, it would be clear as day.

I prayed to the vine that *Thereon* were not intelligent; otherwise, this plan was iffy at best. The only thing we had going for us was their overpowering greed and desire to capture Ornella and me.

Nox held out his hand, helping me steady and climb on top of the landmass; Ornella was at the bottom, watching, her brows knit together in worry.

"If you're up here with me, jumping out of the way will be difficult," I called down to her, but my focus was on the shoreline. Nox had been right; only one ship besides our own was there; its ominous black sails whipping in the wind were all visible, though we were shrouded in a deep fog. I stretched my shoulders, preparing. My sparring lessons were not lessons at all; they were more instructions to teach me how to get out of the way quickly. I had not had enough time to learn the proper skills to fight with a sword or arrow. A dagger was tucked away in my boot, but that was my only weapon besides my gifted abilities. My pack was now with my sister, who would be waiting off to the side with Brom to protect her. I felt content knowing that as I studied his massive figure, which was made of pure muscle. Enid was with Kazumi, crouched behind a boulder, quietly conversing. They were tasked with knocking out the *Thereon* using fairy dust and carrying it aboard our vessel for studying and safekeeping.

The *Thereon* would become a necessary tool in discovering a cure. Now, all we needed was for this not-so-elaborate plan to work.

I fixated on the noises coming from the shoreline moving in our direction. Screeches and shrieks echoed up the sandy path, and my breathing became haggard as anger and fear boiled beneath my skin. The haunting noises were of the small army of *Thereon* headed our way, and I slowly exhaled to keep calm. Separating feelings from power was essential, and my grey eyes flew open with determination. My surroundings were clear and vibrant, even inside the foggy, bleak landscape. The tendrils of light encasing each being were once again visible, as were their auras.

Chapter Eighteen

Black silhouettes slowly crept from the shadows along the jagged rocks; the *Thereon* had arrived. All but myself hid between several large boulders near Cadell's Chamber. This was my first time absorbing their appearance into memory. The *Thereon* were vastly different sizes, and I did not doubt they had all been other species at one point. But they now shared the same bloodlust-filled eyes that craved power, their skin a greyish hue from their physical metamorphosis, and the parasitic dark magic ran up and down their bodies, constantly moving and seemingly never satisfied with just one host.

They growled and lunged like rabid dogs. I ignored their response, enduring their bared teeth and snarls inches from my feet as they homed in on my figure from above. Nox's russet eyes met mine as he hid behind the boulder adjacent to mine, telling me to prepare to jump.

A high-pitched whistle sounded through the mist, the screeching ringing long after the noise ended. I had cringed in pain, my hands protecting my ears.

The *Thereon* went quiet, slowly parting beneath me, forming an opening. Out from the shadows, one of the soulless beasts came forth, his demeanor more relaxed than that of his companions. The inconspicuous figure stepped out from the mist and into the light; his silver *Gavinhas* a dead giveaway to his identity.

Like Ornella, the man had flowing white hair to his waist. The parasitic magic ebbed and flowed off his pale skin, content with its master. A permanent smile was twisted into his features; his arched nose was sharp, like the tip of a blade. The multicolored eyes that met mine were just as I remembered from the day *Mãe* was slain; his right eye was green, while his left was golden.

My focus shifted solely to my enemy, oblivious to anyone else in the vicinity. Heat rose to my face, and my powers ferociously twisted in a craze centered at the core of my being. I barred my teeth, an animalistic sound ripping from the back of my throat. Flickers of red lined my vision while images of *Mãe* being stabbed through her abdomen flooded my thoughts. Her cry of pain was still fresh inside my ears, a haunting noise that would stay with me until it was my time to pass from this world to the next. Pure hatred began to burn violently in the crevasses of what was left of my shattered heart, and luck had finally presented itself to me with an opportunity: to avenge the death of the one I had cherished most in all my existence.

His soul was mine and Ornella's to judge, and I would be the one to make him pay for his crimes against my family and elven kind.

Power seeped from my fingertips, pouring out of my soul. It was startlingly visible; the black whisps the same color and vibrancy now as my *Gavinhas.* They flowed along the boulders and rocks in my vicinity, and I faintly heard the gasps of the crewmembers as they witnessed my slow transformation.

"I think we might have crossed paths before, perhaps?" He leaned forward, clearly relishing our encounter. The man's temperament was odd; it was as though he was talking to an old friend, not someone's life he had destroyed. "I suppose *I should* have listened to you back in Alizeh." He wiped a bit of sand from his clothing and appeared to be wearing a white robe beneath the black that encompassed him.

He took another step forward and exhaled. "It's not often that I am wrong, but I am delighted to learn of your and your sister's existence. And here I thought, only one *Marked One* was announced that day. It now makes sense why your vine burned so feverishly. The *Thereon* alerted me to her presence shortly after you both had disappeared."

My face paled, and I side-eyed where Ornella was now, hiding a reasonable distance away with Brom as her guard.

"Such perfect timing, killing two birds with one stone." The man's steely glare snapped to my sister's location; heat flushed my cheeks.

The black whisps of my power began to seep out of my figure as a tangible smoke; I was more than willing to siphon all the energy nearby. My rage was burning brighter than my voice of reason, which was now but a soft whisper in the crevasses of my mind.

I blindly extended my hand to the man I hated more than all the *Breeders of Thereon* and their abominations of experimental creations. His smile twisted into a sinister expression as if this was precisely what he wanted to happen.

Nox and Silas stepped out of the shadows. The *Thereon* snarled, drool dripping off their chins. Their distorted features twisted in pain and agony, no longer the intelligent beings they had once been. They waited impatiently for the man who clearly controlled them to give the orders to attack.

But his hand went up, silencing them all at once. He raised a brow to the two werewolves. "What is it that you desire? I will make it happen in exchange for the two *Marked Ones*. There is no need to play this trivial game when we already know the outcome." He side-glanced at the soulless beasts, disgusted by their presence. "I do not wish to lose any more of his creations, and I'm sure you would prefer not to lose more of your crewmembers, is that right?" His wicked grin had both Nox's and Silas's fangs protruding, the words sharper than any blade could have been.

Nox's tribal markings glowed, and the usually nonexistent claws were fully displayed. My body was frozen, unable to move. The weight on my shoulders was immensely heavy, and it was as if I was suspended in time. My hatred for the stranger contorted my features.

It was the feisty fairy who broke the tension.

"Nox." Her voice was unexpectedly loud and sharp, carrying across the space between them. "I do not wish to lose someone else." Her translucent wings fluttered erratically, and her expression was pained. "Let us make a trade. Our plans have been thwarted."

Shocked, I stumbled forward, catching myself on my hands and knees before I could fall off the boulder entirely. Pain shot through my hands, cut on the jagged rocks.

He was conflicted, his attention darting between Kazumi and me, unable to decide.

The stranger before us shifted his weight and crossed his arms, growing impatient. "As fun as it is to experience your faces twisting and turning in agony, I'm going to decide for you if you are so incompetent you cannot make a simple decision."

Kazumi flew closer to the man, his silver *Gavinhas* close enough for her to touch. "We will make a trade, then." She pointed directly at me, her black beady eyes the only sign of her guilt, as they pleaded for forgiveness. "You take only one *Marked One* and, in exchange, give us one of your *Thereon*."

My jaw dropped open wide at her words. Her betrayal nearly knocked the wind out of my lungs.

But the man laughed hysterically as he wiped a fake tear from his eye. "You see, *this* is precisely why I typically do not do exchanges or take orders from others. They never go how you intend them to." His multicolored eyes gleamed even through the mist and parasitic magic as his gaze met mine. "Maybe I should have taken your deal, though, dear. That pathetically weak woman would still be alive if I had, and I would have captured you effortlessly."

The instant the words escaped his thin lips, all I could see was red.

A scream ruptured from my throat as I tumbled forward directly at the murderer. I zeroed in on my prey, unwilling to let him escape. Even if it cost me my soul, I was willing to take him with me into the darkest abyss.

He held an object up in the air, causing the *Thereon* around us to become feral. Howls and shrieks pierced my ears as their bloodthirsty eyes surrounded me even inside my tunnel vision. The soulless creatures' auras were full of black energy, and I could have easily siphoned their strength. But they were not my target, and I wanted to use every ounce of my abilities on his wretched existence.

The moment my feet touched the blackened sand, our crew clashed with the horde of *Thereon*.

My boots slipped on the sand, searching for traction. The man stood only a few paces away, but the look on his face behind his parasitic mask was as though he had already defeated me.

My body lurched into the air, and I clumsily rolled across the sand until I hit a nearby boulder with a sickening thud. I screamed as my head whipped back and pain erupted through my skull. The immediate ache in my spine made it difficult to focus on the irritation rising in my chest as my target casually strolled to me, unaffected by the chaos.

"You truly are just a child; I almost feel bad for you." His words carried over the sounds of roars and metal hitting a blunt object. I briefly looked at the surrounding scene, only to discover that the crew's attacks were unsuccessful. My skin drained of what little color I had as I took in the scene before me. It was a losing battle, mirroring the night of my ceremony.

Nothing was working. Nox and Silas were on defense; their sharp claws could not move through the *Thereon's* impenetrable shield of parasitic armor. It constantly moved about their body, deflecting jabs and swings of anyone who dared to inflict damage. This gave the vile beasts the perfect opportunity to go on the offensive, as they moved at near lightning speed, slicing the skin on the werewolves, who were highly skilled in battle.

It became apparent that if I did not help my friends and drain the *Thereon's* energy, heads could soon roll across the sand.

Still dizzy from the impact, I struggled to stand. I had made the wrong choice yet again.

The man read my expression, peacefully content with his findings. "Ah, yes, dear, your friends will now lose their lives because of *you* and your immature reactions. I suppose that you'll be a witness to their deaths too."

I tried to run around him in the fog, but he easily tripped me, and I fell into the sand.

The stranger chuckled, leaning forward to whisper into my ear. "If you haven't learned how to control that *gift* of yours and your anger by now, I'm afraid there's nothing to be done for your friends."

Underestimating my pure resolve and strength would be his ultimate undoing.

I seized the opportunity, and without moving a single muscle, with my head still bowed to the sand and debris below, I grasped at the man's *Gavinhas* using my power. The black tendrils shot out from my fingertips and across the short distance, homing in on their target.

He gasped, and to my surprise, the tendrils of black curled around his silver whisps—the essence of his soul. I witnessed for the first time his wicked smile recoil into a frown, his multicolored eyes bulging from his head in shock.

"You little—" He choked, attacking me as I began to drain him of his soul. Nox had taught me basic defense, but I knew little to nothing about how to defend against someone using a weapon who was trained to kill. The *Thereon* were swift, but nothing compared to this calculated and conniving man before me.

I did my best to escape his blows, rolling in the blackened sand. The gritty substance was in every crack and crevasse of my clothes, mixing with my sweat as pure panic rushed down my spine. His sword was just inches away from meeting my flesh at each strike. Before long, his blade met my skin with a scorching pain.

My focus remained on his footing, watching intently as he was about to swing, his feet betraying where the next attack would come from. This is what Nox had taught me, and it proved to be a vital skill. I was still on all fours inside the mist, crawling backward and occasionally getting knocked to the side as a *Thereon* bulldozed straight through me.

I did not lessen my grip on his *Gavinhas* during the pandemonium, still relentlessly holding his soul hostage.

His panicked movements became more erratic with each passing second. He had managed to push me near Cadell's Chamber, growing dangerously close to the ancient magic embedded into the stone walls. I could feel its ominous pull, threatening to secure my being inside its eternal prison.

The man's movements began to slow, and fear was present when I met his eyes through the dark magic encompassing him. He sheathed his sword, panting as his opaque skin became translucent. The aura around his flickering silver *Gavinhas* was all but gone, and I came to the startling awareness that I possessed the power to diminish a being's soul.

I was no different than a *Thereon*.

I pushed the thought away, though, as his dark magic, a thick black poison branching off from their host extended, trying to grab hold of my throat. If I were unconscious, I would no longer be able to drain him of his soul. But doing this was also overwhelmingly exhausting. Draining a soul was nothing like draining a being's aura.

In his last moments of desperation, the stranger pushed me into the ancient magic; I screamed as I was pulled into what I thought was death. The pain was excruciating and did not relinquish its grasp on me.

He chuckled in relief as my body contorted in pain, now stuck inside the trap we had set to catch a *Thereon*.

"For a moment, I thought I would actually die." The man wiped the sweat from his forehead and leaned over in evident exhaustion. My head felt as though it were about to burst as his silver *Gavinhas* recovered rapidly, no longer flickering as they had moments ago. I fought against the pain, against the magic that tortured me inside and out to stay conscious. His arms crossed; he faced me with a narrowed, scrutinizing glare. "That is the last time you or anyone has the upper hand on me."

I could hardly hear a word he said as I writhed in agony.

A cry nearby caught my attention, sending shivers of fear down my spine. Ornella's shriek was enough to momentarily pull me out of the pain, and I reached out of the circle of blue fiery magic containing me.

My extended hand did not go for the man's throat just mere inches away, but rather the shiny object he had held up in the air earlier, now located in his robe's inner pocket. I felt like my skin would melt off my bones, but I successfully obtained the mysterious item, screaming in the process.

He took a step back, concern casting over his features.

I gripped what appeared to be a vial containing a thick black liquid. I tucked the mysterious contents inside my pocket, securing it for later inspection. Another wave of pain had me crying out in discomfort, and I fell to my knees, gasping in pain. The still mist surrounding us made the man pause, and we searched the haze for a reason for the change in atmosphere.

The *Thereon* were slowly disappearing.

I twitched, my veins pulsing as I tried to focus on the events occurring around me now that I was inside an inferno of unending misfortune.

Enid was nearly backed up against the chamber, the bluish electrical current protruding from the prison walls striking the ogress several times. Her face contorted in pain with each whip from the spell as it began to grasp her figure to pull her inside the prison against her will. The usual glow on her green skin was dull and vacant; she was a bloody mess, as the *Thereon* had managed to bite deep into her flesh.

My heart rate spiked as three black figures surrounded her in the mist.

"Enid!" I choked on her name as I collapsed inside the circular blue inferno that consumed me. The ancient spell was not meant for a soul to endure repetitively; it was meant only as a barrier to keep beings from escaping their judgment. Paralyzed by fear, I watched as the last visible *Thereon* dove at her, shrieking in delight. Nox appeared out of the vaporous fumes, pushing the soulless beasts forward with all his might as Enid dove out of the way.

Their blackened figures crashed into the chamber, shrieking. The dark magic cloaking their form was in a frenzy before they vanished; the prison was a monster of its own accord, devouring them whole.

A wave of relief briefly consumed me before I crumpled to the sand.

The sound of bones rupturing passed through the still air. Nox was on top of the wicked man, aggressively striking at his face. But the parasitic magic was a solid shield, and he had only landed one blow on the man's jaw before his dark magic came to his defense.

I whimpered in pain, my eyes heavy from exhaustion. My body wanted to give up the fight to live, but my soul fought vigorously to keep me planted in this world.

"Sayah!" Nox's voice sounded alarmingly far away.

"She is going to die." The wicked man's voice was a whisper, expressing an almost tender regret. "So, what will it be, mutt? Will you take me hostage or save her?"

There was a second pause before I heard a torturous scream from up close, my eyes unable to open. Something pulled me out of the ring of torture. I landed with a thud, and I recognized Nox's voice, screaming in agony.

"How could this have happened!" Ornella sobbed from above my battered frame. "No need to worry, Sayah. I'm here to help." She gently brushed my back with the palm of her hand in a soothing motion.

But I could not feel peace; the alarming feeling of dread helped me slowly pull myself onto my elbows, there in the sand. I pointed at Nox, still screaming in pain. "Him," I desperately cried. "Help him first."

My plea was met with only silence, and I could still hear Nox's voice contorting in pain. I somehow rolled over onto my back, wincing. Ornella's hands hovered over me as she tried to pour energy into me.

"No!" I shoved her hands away from my chest, gasping. My eyes finally met her emerald ones, swirling with worry. "Please, Sister. Help him first, for me."

She hesitated above me. Her long white hair cascaded over me, shielding me from the sun's rays peeking through the thick fog. In an instant, warmth and light were on my face, and Nox's cries began to lessen.

My mind began to relax now that it was finally quiet. Several others were above me now, but I ignored their muddled words.

I was just relieved to be free from the eternal agony.

Chapter Nineteen

My appendages still twitched as if bolts of lightning coursed through them. After helping Nox, my sister immediately returned to my aid. Kazumi used what was left of her fairy dust to heal the werewolf's arm from the damage inflicted by the hazardous ancient magic. His skin had begun to melt off his bones. Still, with everyone else's help and his rejuvenation capabilities, the only evidence left of what had occurred were permanent scars covering his right forearm. His tribal markings had been contorted, now branding his tanned skin with white swirls.

After fully comprehending what he had done for me, I couldn't take my eyes off the man. Nox had knowingly let the malicious criminal escape and used all his strength to fight through the near-indestructible spell to pull me out of its everlasting grasp.

Even in a dire state, my heart's pace quickened at every glance in my direction.

Our ship was covered in flames when we returned to investigate the aftermath. All we could do was stand and watch as our only means of hope sank to the bottom of the Dark Waters. What was left of our vessel, the *Thereon's* ship, and the mysterious man who wielded the parasitic magic were gone. My stomach did multiple flips, as we were an easy target, stranded on the Isles of Cadogan. I knew he would return with twice as many soulless beasts as before.

We wordlessly traveled across the shoreline and headed south. The silence we now experienced was void of any feeling. We were wounded and exhausted.

Brom was ahead of me, carrying Ornella's and my packs. He was just out of earshot, and I was trying to eavesdrop when Kazumi appeared before me, frowning as she perched on my left shoulder.

"You look terrible." The rose-colored fairy clicked her tongue on the roof of her mouth, the tips of her pink hair close enough to tickle my jaw.

I didn't respond, and I tightened my fists to keep myself from flicking her off my shoulder.

"I was never going to trade you for information, Sayah." Her raspy whisper sent shivers of displeasure down my skin.

Snorting, I rolled my eyes. "My *mãe* used to say that words were the deadliest kind of poison. I think I understand what she meant, having experienced that pain firsthand," I countered before pretending to yawn and stretching my arms so she would be forced to fly off my shoulder.

Kazumi was inches from my eyes, forcing me to focus solely on her. "We were out of options, elvish girl. Something had to be done, and I never intended to let him leave the isles with you. None of us would have let that happen." She pushed her chin out, her expression dissatisfied, as her beady eyes bore into mine. "But *somebody* lost control of their temper, causing the situation to get out of hand immediately."

The repetition of her wings fluttering near my ears reminded me of a noisy bumblebee—a bumblebee with sharp needle teeth and the ability to remove my intestines within seconds.

"And explain the trap to me," I croaked at her, my bones groaning in protest as we slowly moved along the sand. "You were going to capture the *Thereon*, and then what? Because whatever you were planning to use to remove the creature, you could have done so for me."

There was a moment's pause before she answered.

"We were trying to kill it, Sayah. Initially, Enid and I were to make sure it was dead before remelting the conduit to break the circle momentarily to remove the carcass and take it aboard the ship for further evaluation." Her voice was like sharp needles poking at my patience. "Next time, think with your head and not your feelings."

There was nothing I could say at that moment because the feisty, aggravating little ball of pink buzzing circles around my head was right. Things could have gone differently if I hadn't reacted the way I had. I observed the shoreline, watching as everyone continued on, bruises and all. Their footprints faded with every passing tide, and I fixated on the imprints until they had vanished completely.

I wouldn't forgive myself if something happened to them—even Kazumi.

"I'm sorry." My late apology blended into the sounds of the ocean making contact with the shore. The fog was not as thick on the outskirts of the islands; my vision and thoughts, reflecting that fact, were no longer deep within the haze. "I wasn't always this way." My head bobbed, and I turned to see if Kazumi was still there.

To my surprise, she was, her expression hard as she faced forward. "Events happened out of your control, and you had to adapt." Her figure was weaving up and down, and I realized she was tired but continued to be with me, knowing that I was not too fond of her physical contact. "I don't blame you for acting the way you did. I would've done the same if I was given the opportunity."

And for the first time, I witnessed tears in her beady eyes, tears of anger.

"Oh, come here," I flipped my braid onto my left shoulder, allowing her a place to rest. I oh so carefully plucked Kazumi out of the air, her expression astonished as I gently placed her to perch near my collarbone. "I know you're tired; don't argue."

After a few brief pauses, a quiet giggle escaped her tiny frame, and we continued heading south in the midday sun, content to be alive, soaking in every inhale of fresh air into my lungs.

By evening, we had unpredictably traveled to the edge of the first island and located a good place to camp for the night. Without the convenience of the *Ligação Mágica* to help us light a fire, we were exposed to the elements.

But that didn't stop Brom from trying, as he held two pieces of wet twigs that had washed up on the shore.

"*Fogoe*!" He grunted, slapping the sorry excuses for pieces of wood together until they snapped.

"Brom, please." Silas pushed his sandy hair back between his fingers, resting his palm on his forehead as he sat uncomfortably on a rock. "You can't cast a spell without the magic present."

It felt as if I was watching a scene unfold between a parent and their stubborn child.

"At least I'm trying something!" The large ogre huffed, pouting, and parked himself on the sand, his back against the cave's opening. We were doing our best to rest in the small sanctuary.

Ornella had hardly spoken. Using our abilities made us feel weak for short lengths of time. A rush of guilt came over me, as I realized the only reason I could stand was because she had filled my aura back up with energy. She was resting beside Enid. The stab of jealousy from seeing the two of them together surprised me. I turned away to look out at the moon and stars as a distraction.

Nox was out near the sea, his form a dark shadowy figure pacing back and forth along the sand. I had been unable to approach him, still forming the right words in my mind. A simple thank you did not seem sufficient.

"Go and talk to him." Enid's voice had me blushing, caught in my stare. If this had been an ordinary situation, I would have approached him by now, but something about what had transpired in the latest events had me holding back.

"I'm not sure I know how to or what to say." My boots shifted in the sand as I deliberated. Either I would end up having to talk about my feelings with her or be forced to face Nox and express to him that I was sorry for scarring his beautiful, bronzed skin.

"You'll figure it out." Her soft smile buried the guilt even further into my chest.

I nodded, turning my heel to join Nox out on the shore because I couldn't handle the expression in Enid's warm chocolate eyes any longer.

The fog from earlier had finally lifted, but the deserted islands still appeared bleak with hardly any vegetation. I approached him cautiously, well aware how tense his demeanor was as he paced alongside the shoreline.

"You know, you really took my breath away today, Nox," I said casually as he paused, stiff, his russet irises glowing brightly in the shadows of the night.

"How so?" He began his cadence again, repeatedly moving back and forth.

"I'm having difficulty conversing with you because you chose to save me over your goals. And I wasn't prepared for you to do that." It was my turn to pace as he was forced into hearing my confession. "How am I supposed to go on living, knowing that your arm was mutilated by those ancient flames, leaving scars on your hard-earned tribal markings." Tears began to fall from my face, sinking into the sand with dull thuds. "I know how much they mean to you and your species, Nox. You went through so much to earn them. It's all my fault; this isn't how you treat the person you fancy."

He stopped moving and turned wholly to face me, his back to the ocean.

"Fancy?" A mischievous grin etched his features as he walked a few paces inland before plopping down on the sandy earth. "Come sit; I have something to tell you."

I reluctantly went to sit beside him when a wave of grief unexpectedly came over me. This reminded me of when *Mãe* and I used to sit together on the bench in the garden. Her simple presence was calming, even after a hard day.

My lip quivered as I missed everything about her, from her violet eyes to her dark-blonde waves. I missed the scent of her soap when she leaned in to comfort me and the wafting smell of her delicious cooking making its way to our bedroom as she hummed contently. All five kingdoms in Aksel would miss her pure, raw talent, as she could evoke the most intricate emotions from one's soul without a single word. There would never be a single being who could play the piano like she could.

"Silas' scar, I'm the one who gave it to him," Nox said calmly. His abrupt admission caught me off guard, and I turned to raise my brows at him. "Believe it or not, I used to be what I consider one of the worst types of beings; the scum of the earth."

I couldn't help but roll my eyes, turning to the side to study his features. His eyes were momentarily cold; the shadows beneath them told me there was truth to his claim. An image of Silas briefly flashed in my mind; his scar above his left eye was old and faded. It hardly crossed my mind when I thought of the intelligent and thoughtful werewolf.

"What happened? Was it an accident?" I inquired, mainly because I knew he wanted me to.

"No accident. I attacked him when we were young, just before I was of age, eagerly ready to fight with the other clans in the duels." He cleared his throat, and his jaw flexed at the recall of the memory. "Silas is older than me by several lunations. I was jealous that he had already turned one hundred and seventy lunations and could enter the arena."

The sullen werewolf shook his head, regret heavy in the air between us.

"But Silas did not want to fight; he had zero interest in what werewolves were bred for. War and battle. One day, behind my family's vineyard, I found him harvesting the crops instead of with all the other young men at sparring practice." He paused, his gaze lingering on my face. The guilt was still there, etched in his features. It was something that he had carried with him, the remorse forever embedded into his soul. "I forced him to fight me, to try and make 'an example' of him. Only, he didn't fight back. He flat-out refused. By the end of it, the poor kid was a bloody mess. I stood there, huffing and puffing, furious with him. I screamed in his face, calling him all sorts of names. But Silas was wordless, staring at me with pity."

Nox stroked the stubble on his chin, sighing. "I demanded to know why he rejected our heritage and culture. And I'll never forget what he said; his words were an omen I should've taken seriously." He tilted his face to the moon, closing his eyes as he repeated Silas's words.

"My life is a never-ending duel that I'm continually losing."

Silas's words repeated in my thoughts as I carefully considered. "How did you respond?"

"I didn't." His hands dug deep into the blackened sand beneath us as he clenched the grit in his grasp. "I stood there like a gaping idiot as he got up and disappeared. Not soon after that, I got my wish. When I was of age, I entered the sparring grounds, excited to meet my first opponent. But out walked another young man with fear in his eyes, and the words Silas had said to me popped into my mind. Deep in my gut, I knew that something was off.

"We fought, and I easily won. But it didn't feel victorious like I assumed it would. I couldn't help but stare at the kid. His old man was livid. The fight was over, but the boy went home more terrified than when sparring with me. That's when I began to slowly figure things out, that there was an uneven shift of power hiding in the shadows of our clan's way of life that I hadn't been exposed to before. I come from a well-off family because my dad is the feared leader of The Fangs of the Fallen, and up until that point in my life, I had been ignorantly oblivious to everyone else's pain and suffering."

The raw emotion in his eyes, the unbearable guilt, flashed across his features before he returned to a neutral expression. "My tribal markings only show how many duals I've won. What's hidden from view is the prejudiced customs of our kind; many fall through the cracks, unable to obtain respect as an individual simply because someone else is stronger or more aggressive. They mean hardly anything to me besides being a security blanket when I return home. No one challenges me anymore."

He extended his right arm completely, examining the white scars on his forearm with a grin. "This right here; this is a badge of honor. I saved someone's life to earn these scars."

I gasped audibly. My heart threatened to stop beating. There, beneath the moon, Nox's eyes twinkled brighter than any stars could have.

"Silas forgave me for my past long before I was able to forgive myself." He stood, extending his hand out to help me to my feet. His russet eyes were kind, causing a feeling of warmth to blanket my skin, even with the slight breeze tickling me. "Today was filled with mistakes, Sayah. Don't take the burden of this failure alone."

We strolled back inland to the small cavern behind the many boulders, the dire situation returning me to my senses. There was nothing I could say to ease his burden, even after all he had done to alleviate my concern. I tried to shove my hands into my pockets to sulk, but a blunt object was in the way.

The spark in my step returned, and I confidently reached for Nox's hand.

His shocked face was a treat, and I pulled on the collar of his shirt, bringing his face down to meet mine, savoring that his full lips were centimeters away. "Who said that today was a failure?" I bit down on my lip in anticipation and handed him the mysterious vial of liquid—stolen from the man controlling the *Thereon's* movements.

Nox froze, staring at the dark liquid in his hand in fascination. "Sayah, what is this?" I could tell by the look on his face that he knew but wanted my confirmation.

"It's the object that man held up in the air to control the *Thereon*." I had backed a few feet away from him to watch the fire return into his eyes, the drive and will to find a way to keep pushing forward. "It is what those vile, soulless creatures crave now more than anything else. We may not have caught a *Thereon* yet, but we will. And we'll be ready."

Jogging the rest of the way back to the others, I couldn't help but smile, knowing we would shake off this hopelessness.

We would all survive the Isles of Cadogan and live to tell the tale. Bless the vine, our entire crew, still recouping from the fight, could use a bit of good news. The blackened liquid sloshed inside the clear vial as Nox held it up in the air with pride for the others to see as we approached.

Whatever its contents were, it was our saving grace.

Chapter Twenty

The entire crew and I stood in a ring formation inside the cavern. The vial filled with a black liquid in the center of the crew was placed on a rock as we gawked. Everyone had different theories of what it contained, causing various arguments. There was one thing in particular, however, that we all unanimously agreed upon.

We should *not* open it.

As I scratched my chin, pondering, a blunt force whacked me in the back of the head, causing me to tumble forward on my knees.

"You mean to tell me, Sayah, that you've had this in your pocket the entire day without letting anyone know? Are you kidding?" Kazumi's nagging voice was in my ear, angry.

Ornella quipped before I could respond, "That sounds exactly like something my sister would do." My glare snapped to her, but the light fading back into her eyes kept my mouth shut. She was beginning to perk up, the color returning to my twin's cheeks. Her emerald eyes met mine, and she openly smiled.

Oh, great, so she was enjoying me being punished by someone other than her.

I sharply twisted my head to meet the fairy's scowl, narrowing my eyes. "Oh, I'm sorry; I forgot that I'm not allowed to forget things, even in critical situations when I could have died, Kazumi." I let the sarcasm drip from my mouth, and she flew to Brom's shoulder, still annoyed.

Crossing my arms, I mouthed the words; *I could have died* to taunt the little fiend. That feisty lady was seriously no joke. *Her personality could be so fickle,* I thought to myself as my stomach growled in hunger. *Ah, wait a minute, that must be it.*

I smiled knowingly at Kazumi. She was *hangry.*

Silas waved his hand in the air, quieting my thoughts. He was enthralled by the mysterious item, and his gold eyes whirred with excitement as he left the circle to pace. You could almost see the wheels turning inside his mind, thinking.

"Nox, come take a walk with me." My eye candy stood up, leaving us to bicker amongst ourselves as they went to have a private conversation.

"Great, the two most civil of us left the room; now we're in trouble," I sneered.

Kazumi huffed at my comment, her wings fluttering in annoyance.

"What do you think it is?" Brom considered. He winced as his stomach rumbled loud enough for everyone to hear. Enid warned us that if he went too long without a meal, he would become a monster worse than the *Thereon*.

"Nothing that you can eat." My eyes widened at Kazumi's harsh comment, and Enid jumped to her feet, leaving Ornella's side to defend her brother.

"Wipe that smirk off your face before I do it for you," the ogress growled. "One hit from me, and you'll be splattered against the wall, you annoying pest."

Kazumi shot across the floor and spit at Enid's feet, turning the argument into a brawl. Brom stood, putting himself between Enid and Kazumi to the best of his abilities, but it wasn't an easy task. The ogress tried to slap the fairy out of the air, but the palm of her hand accidentally landed directly on Brom's cheek. He stumbled backward from the impact, yelling as he fell to the cavern's hard surface.

"Sheesh! Ouch!" Brom stood, rubbing his backside. "Can you both calm yourselves? One, everyone is hungry, Kazumi. Don't think I didn't hear your stomach a few minutes ago." He raised a brow at his sister while massaging his temples. "And two, Enid, how many more times will you erupt and go hostile when she makes a snarky comment? Every other word that comes out of her mouth is cruel."

Enid frowned, turning to join Ornella back on the wall. My sister and I shrugged in unison, unsure how to react.

"What's going on?" Silas exclaimed from the cave's mouth.

Nox walked in, his eyes immediately darting around the floor. "Where's the vial?"

Time stood still as we all fell to our knees and searched the cold hard surface of the cavern below. I felt between the cracks and crevasses of the floor, as did the others. Our bickering had stopped, and the silence that took its place loomed over us. There was no sign of it, and there was only a slight sense of relief that at least the tube was still intact because there was no sign of broken glass. Shortly after the quest began, a groan rippled from Brom's mouth. His hands were clasped together behind his head as he started to sob in despair.

"I'm so sorry," he wailed, holding up his massive-sized shoe.

A black, tar-like substance slowly dripped off his foot onto the ground. A putrid smell filled our noses, and we all gagged as we escaped through the cave's opening.

My heart sank to the pit of my stomach. Brom wasn't to blame, but it felt as though our own stupidity had destroyed our only success. We stood out underneath the stars, exposed to the cool breeze that snaked its way along the blackened sand.

There were several beats when our hesitation paralyzed our movements. What was left to show of our hard work and weeks of planning and preparing had been squished beneath Brom's foot. There were no words for the devastating loss. The crew was back to square one, and I felt partly responsible for today's failure. Not only would we come up empty-handed, but we were stranded. Standing there in the sand, our crew no longer had an idea of hope or what direction we should now take. We were trapped on the islands without a means of departure.

The crew stared listlessly at the mouth of the cave until Kazumi flew off alone, no doubt needing time to vent before she exploded in fury. I did not want to endure her wrath.

Silas was the first to move, letting out a big exhale before approaching the distressed ogre.

"Well, I was going to suggest we open it and pour out a small amount to examine its components in a somewhat controlled environment anyway. That's what I went off to discuss with Nox about. Don't worry yourself too much, Brom. Go thoroughly rinse your shoe off in the ocean and be careful of any glass stuck to the bottom of your foot." He patted Brom's shoulder, his eyes understanding and kind.

I felt a pang of empathy for the sandy-haired werewolf. What he must have endured in their clan, defying what he felt was against his morals, is heartbreaking. He was the kind of man who showed grace to those who did not deserve it. I was deep in thought when Nox walked up to me in all his glory. It was nighttime, but I could still view every inch of his muscles protruding from his shirt.

"You can't have him; he's already mated to my sister." He began to observe Silas with me, his russet eyes glancing in my direction every few seconds, his jaw and shoulders tense.

I smiled deviously before spinning to face him.

"Oh, really?" I sighed, feigning disappointment. "He seems like such a sweet and kind-hearted person, based on what you told me." I tucked the loose hair from my braid behind my ear and bobbed my head.

There were a few beats of silence, and my mood fell. We no longer had a place to sleep, away from the elements. I was worried for Ornella, who was still exhausted from gifting us all energy while simultaneously draining her own. Emotion overcame me as I realized how grateful I was to have her. She, Enid, and the pink dot of light down the way that must have been Kazumi, were all perched on a large boulder, basking in the starlight.

"Nox, what will we do now?" I whispered, staring out at the vast ocean. The seriousness of the situation started to set in, and I creased my brows. "We have no means of escape, and the *Thereon* will return. Oh, and we only have the food in our packs, which won't last us but a few days." I twisted to look inland and squinted at the cave's entrance, spotting my bag leaning against its stone exterior.

I went to retrieve my belongings from the mouth of the cave and a sudden secure grip on my wrist spun me directly into Nox's firm chest. From beneath my eyelashes, I flicked my gaze up to his.

He leaned forward into my hair and sharply inhaled, focusing solely on me. Even in the moonlight with shadows cast over his features, I could feel his mood shift, now stagnant in the air.

"I borrowed you temporarily to mask the horrid smell; I hope you don't mind. It was difficult to think coherently with that scent stuck in my nose." His rough laugh caused my breath to hitch; my thoughts were hazy in his presence.

"I have trouble forming a rational thought when I smell your scent; it smells of cinnamon," I absently stated, now relaxed by his nearness.

There in the dark, his movements were fluid and silent. Nox's arm flexed against my body, and his palm pressed against the small of my back, setting my heart ablaze with desire.

His figure had always towered above me, but tonight, I was aware of how intense he could be. Leaning down to whisper into my ear, his soft brown curls tickled my chin. "I'll find a way, Sayah. I'll get you and Ornella to Erebus."

His russet eyes were vibrant in the dark, full of promise. His determination alone sent a spark of hope through my recently dwindling resolve.

With his thumb, he ever so gently lifted my chin and brushed his lips against mine, the taste of him intoxicating. I reassured him with my hands, intertwining my fingers into the back of his mane as I pulled him into me. My kiss was ravenous; I had fantasized about this moment from the instant I encountered him there on the piano bench in Danu. The way his lips caressed mine, I could sense his overwhelming desire and emotion. His callused hands held my face, the intensity between us growing.

The sudden chatter of voices nearby startled us both, shattering the moment and leaving me with overwhelming waves of disappointment.

He purred in my ear, "How was that for spontaneous, my jewel? I can't wait to show you Erebus; it's enchanting."

"Jewel?" I inquired, my face still flushed and heart racing. "Sticking with that pet name? You're not going to call me *darling* or *sweetheart*?"

"Heavens, no," he playfully crooned in my ear. "You're far too precious for such a usual nickname." He twisted us both slightly, facing the shimmering ocean's water in the moonlight. "You're the rarest of treasures, and your soul is so delicately perceptible, swirling inside those gemstone eyes. That is why you're *my* jewel."

His possessiveness was exhilarating, a dopamine rush of an all-consuming craving. I wondered if my remark about Silas had brought out a sense of jealousy inside him. I bit my lip to hide my genuine smile. We stood in each other's embrace, staring at the sea's dark depths, the shimmering liquid in the moonlight only adding to the romantic atmosphere.

"That was quite spontaneous." I batted my eyelashes, and he chuckled. "I guess I'm all right being stuck on even the Isles of Cadogan if it means you'll keep me company."

I winked in his direction before walking toward Brom and Silas, who were having an intense discussion on the shoreline.

"I'm telling you, Silas, somethings not right about this place." Brom glanced around in suspicion, narrowing his eyes at every shadow amongst the rocky terrain.

"You're just spooked because you broke the vial accidentally; there's nothing here but us."

"No, you're wrong; I saw something move!" The ogre bellowed and pointed behind his sister, which contained nothing but a dark, desolate landscape. "I went to look for a different cave or somewhere to camp out, and out of the corner of my eye, one of the boulders shifted!"

It was evident that Silas was losing his patience, running his fingers through his hair to calm himself.

"Let's go check it out then. Finding this landscape sustainable would be difficult for any species. The *Ligação Mágica* is absent, furthering my deductive reasoning that the isles are nearly uninhabitable." The two began to walk inland, with Nox and I trailing behind them as we passed the others on top of the large boulder.

"What's going on?" Enid shouted at us.

"We're out exploring for other forms of life; care to join?" Nox half-heartedly yelled from beside me as we ventured farther inland.

"No thanks, we're good here," Enid replied, turning back to hear my sister's laugh beside her. Kazumi whispered things in Ornella's ear, and I had no doubt they were absolutely scandalous. She hardly ever laughed so freely, and her taste in jokes was shockingly unrefined.

Which is ironic for a girl who usually thrives on perfectionism.

A sudden yell came from ahead of us, sounding like Silas's voice. Alarmed, Nox and I began to move as fast as we could through the narrow passageways to see what was the matter.

"Silas, you all right?" Nox called out as he deliberately placed himself in front of me.

There was no answer. The deafening quiet was ominous as we walked out unprotected into a surprising change in landscape. The boulders were gone, as was the blackened sand mixed with earth. Instead, there was an area of flat land, with a few sparse areas of vegetation poking through the soil.

The hairs on my arms and neck stood on end as I spotted our friends ahead. They were frozen, paralyzed where they had fallen to the ground, their eyes wide with fear.

A large creature crouched before them, fangs protruding as it bared its teeth at the two men at its mercy. An unearthly growl ripped from its throat; it seemed to think our crew mates were a threat. Smoke swelled in the beast's mouth, its skin reflecting the moonlight. As it moved forward, I froze, recognizing the scales and serpentine-like tail from a distance.

"It's a *dragon*," I exclaimed, recognizing the familiar curvature of the creatures' spine, its blue scales sparkling like gold underneath the sunlight.

A different massive head whipped around from behind the boulders, followed by several others with yellow gleaming eyes, all hissing in irritation. The largest one stood, shaking its stiff limbs from a long slumber. The wings along its scaly back opened and closed, letting moonlight seep through the translucent membrane.

A horde of dragons now stood before me. I thought of the dagger still tucked away in my boot, thankful I had something to protect myself. My body was still drained from the encounter with the *Thereon* earlier, my bones and muscles twitching occasionally.

However, it's not as if we would stand a chance against even a single dragon.

"I thought that all dragons were bound to the soil of Adara," Enid murmured under her breath next to me. She was in a defensive position, her eyes homed in on her brother. My sister and Kazumi were nowhere to be seen, and I could only pray Enid did the right thing by telling Ornella to hide.

"Apparently not." Nox's tone was sharp. His fists were clenched as he fought the urge to release his claws.

The dragon's scales began to shimmer, transforming from the dull camouflage to vibrant sapphire, onyx, and jade hues. A smaller dragon emerged, its yellow-slitted eyes staring straight into my soul.

"It wreaks of *him* and his corrupted flesh," the dragon said, the fumes spilling out of its mouth and nostrils, surrounding Brom and Silas in a cloud of smoke.

They were speaking in Reinos—I did not know that dragons knew the kingdoms most recently elected dialect.

Several other dragons emerged from the shadows, forming a ring around our two friends. They began to sniff the air, the dragons' eyes flickering with recognition as they snarled and nipped at Brom.

There was a low rumble, and another dragon stepped forth, the color of the sea containing a bright sapphire hue to its scales, and it was twice the size of the dragon that spoke.

"Their *Gavinhas* are still intact, so they are not his creations." She snorted, sticking her tongue out in disgust. "They carry his foul smell." The dragon flicked her tale in a feline-like manner. "Tell me, green one—why does your stench smell of a *Breeder of Thereon*? Have you been to Adara?" she purred, and an underlying threat could be heard in her venomous tone.

"No, no, I haven't." Brom shrunk back, sweat dripping down his clammy skin. This was the first time I had witnessed the ogre truly cower in fear.

"Then explain if you wish to survive to see another day," the sapphire dragon spat.

The brief pause in the air was chilling; Silas caught on quicker than Brom and began to speak for him as the ogre was tongue-tied in fright.

"The *Thereon* chased us here, onto the Isles of Cadogan. We escaped by pushing them into Cadell's Chamber—"

The dragon's tail suddenly swiped Silas, tossing him several feet back. He grunted as he rolled, wincing from the air being knocked out of his lungs.

"*Quiet*! You dare to speak out of turn?" She nipped the air, her claws extending in frustration.

Brom gulped, his short hair clumping to his forehead from sweat. He adjusted his posture and began to speak with his eyes at the dragon's feet. "A—a vial. I broke it with my shoe, and the black liquid spilled everywhere."

Her head turned slightly to the side as she considered. She moved closer to Silas, making Nox tense next to me.

"You," she snapped. "The *Thereon*, are they gone?"

"Yes." The werewolf hesitated. "But they will return."

All the dragons in the vicinity's heads snapped in his direction at the news, growling and hissing.

"Why did you lead them straight to us, boy?" The anger in her words was backed by short bursts of flames, shooting across Silas's head. Fire began to erupt from all directions, the heat scorching the nearby boulders and sand. The dragon with blue scales stepped forward, her serpentine eyes narrowing. "You and your companions will burn until you're nothing but ash."

A ball of scorching hot flames grew inside her mouth and pointed directly at Silas. Nox was already moving toward his friend, and I screamed.

There was no time; not even Nox, who sprinted toward his friend without fear, would reach him before dissipating into cinders.

I faced the sapphire-scaled dragon head-on; power simmered inside my veins, and I unleashed it upon the irritable dragon. Her aura was a massive bright light, glowing in pure strength.

The fire inside her mouth immediately vanished, and her attention snapped directly to me. She prowled across the earth, hunched and eyes fixated on me.

She paused only a few paces away, inhaling the air around me.

"You're a *Marked One*, yes?" Her eyes darted to a boulder behind me and shifted back to mine. "There's two of you?" A clicking noise came inside her mouth as she curiously leaned around me to view my twin.

My face paled as Ornella was forced to leave the shadows along with Kazumi.

A smaller jade dragon moved next to the other; disappointment layered in his gravelly voice. "I wanted to eat one." A short chortle sound came from his mouth, and I think it was a laugh.

The blue one nipped at his neck, now angry at the remark.

"Fraener, can't you smell their scent? Two have the mark of power flowing through their veins." She lowered her massive head, and her yellow eyes glimmered with interest as her demeanor entirely changed. "And what brings you all to the isles? We have not witnessed a *Marked One* in several centuries."

I seemed to have lost my voice, shocked by her friendly behavior. She flashed her teeth briefly, and the moonlight accentuated her vibrant scales. This dragon was peculiar.

"My sister and I, along with our companions"—I gestured to the rest of the company, which dragons of various sizes now surrounded—"The *Thereon* have left us stranded here after attempting to capture my sister and me." I waited patiently for her response, not foolish enough to ask the many questions running through my mind.

The horde made low grumbling noises deep from within their throats, communicating amongst their kind in an unknown dialect.

"Yes, I can sense the mark of power runs deep in their veins," a giant, clay-colored dragon grumbled, poking its head into the middle of the conversation. The hints of orange in its face reminded me of burning wood. "It would be unfortunate if Bakunax acquired these two for his growing collection. Perhaps we should have them for supper." He chuckled, and it echoed within his large frame. His head alone was the size of the dragon named Fraener, who agreed that we would make a nice meal.

"That kind of talk got us in this predicament in the first place, Terragorn." A puff of fire suddenly left the sapphire dragon's mouth, aimed directly at the massive creature. She sat on the rocky earth, no longer in a defensive position. "Look at what became of him; he did not respect nature's hierarchy, and that corrupted beast will now pay a hefty price."

"What do you mean?" Ornella's voice was just above a whisper; she dared to question a dragon out of turn.

I hesitated, instinctively moving closer to her side to do what I could to protect her at a moment's notice. She luckily was deemed worthy of a response, the dragon's tails twitching in amusement, much like a playful housecat.

"Bakunax was a dragon long before his soul was corrupted, transforming him into a Breeder *of Thereon*. His heart has been completely overtaken with greed; his blood runs black, tainted by his desire for power." Her eyes flickered and were transfixed on the ocean as she recalled a memory. "This is a result of what happens when our kind gives in to our deadly sins; not all of us do. Many dragons hoard treasure, which is just the beginning of the insatiable hunger to possess everything, including that which they cannot control: the *Marked Ones*." Her tongue clicked, and she glanced now at our group.

"It is a fatal flaw in our design; we are dominant creatures, but some of us can be easily swayed. The beginning of our end, if you will. And Bakunax is far beyond that point." Her head swiveled, and the sapphire dragon's talons came too close for comfort as she moved towards the sea. "He needs to be taken care of. We should have eliminated him far before the treaty was written in stone."

I racked my brain for information regarding the official agreement between the five kingdoms. Still, all that I could muster was that several centuries ago, to keep dragons from rampaging and wreaking havoc, the monarchs of each kingdom came together for a truce and formed a proposal. Each kingdom gave Adara a hefty sum of its gold and treasures. In exchange, dragons were prohibited from roaming outside Adara, or so I thought.

But here, standing in front of me, was a small horde of dragons. I counted a dozen or so fully grown and four hatchlings. That particular period was also before the rulers of these lands had fallen. History had been erased, and just as time eroded our memory, the outcome was the same for our kingdoms.

They were only kingdoms in name now, with long-forgotten sovereigns.

I met the sapphire dragon's stare—her reptilian eyes were filled with wisdom, and they were somewhat intimidating. "What liquid was inside the vial that Brom stepped on?"

Our entire crew held their breath, anticipating the reveal.

She became agitated, her tail twitching as she shifted her feet, claws digging into the earth. "It is the blood of the original *Breeder*—Bakunax." Several sneers could be heard from the dragons encircling us, smoke simmering from their mouths in irritation.

"Dragon's blood?" Enid inquired, captivated by every word. "Why are the *Thereon* drawn to that?" She was still in her defensive stance, with her hands ready to unsheathe the two daggers at her hips if need be.

"Because it is from which they were created," Fraener snapped. He inched closer to the ogress; his jade-colored scales were radiant in the starlight. "It is not the blood of a dragon, but of a *Breeder*. Bakunax creates his *Thereon* by corrupting their souls with his blood, severing the species' *Gavinhas*. They are bound to the blasphemous liquid, with an insatiable craving for the grotesque concoction."

Breeders of Thereon's blood. The answer we desperately desired was disgusting. My stomach grew queasy at the thought.

"Wait a minute—Bakunax has been corrupted for several centuries? Why are we now just seeing the *Thereon*?" Nox spoke, and Fraener nipped at his feet, annoyed with his lack of manners.

"Do not share our history with him, Obsydora. I don't trust those who are not blessed. He could easily become a *Thereon* and betray us to his *Breeder*." The jade dragon blew a puff of smoke at Nox as a warning.

The one called Obsydora scrutinized Nox, and whatever she found, she believed him trustworthy enough to converse with. "The history contained in your fat leather-bound books lies." She blinked and drew close to him, eager to relay the truth hidden by our ancestors, or so she preached. "There were no rampages or killing of any sort. Our kind had managed to live peacefully between all Aksel's kingdoms."

She snarled, her anger seeping out of her scales.

"A single dragon instigated the chaos that would lead to more than half our kind being cut off from the ancient *Creator* and its magic. Bakunax was the first to turn, and others followed suit."

A warmer breeze suddenly tickled my arms, and I looked around the beach as the sunrise began to crest the horizon. I was so entranced with her insight that the night had evaded me. My gaze fell back to Obsydora, who watched the hatchlings play alongside the shoreline.

"He consumed a *Marked One*, discovering that he could absorb their power. The monster immediately hunted only those gifted from their birth or creation. His entire mindset devoured the idea that particular beings' power could be transferred directly to him. This unfortunate discovery caused several other dragons' hearts to turn black from pure desire."

Her head bobbed as she flexed her translucent wings in the morning light.

"The few began to pursue this craving solely, and the kingdoms feared for everyone's safety. The monarchs banished Bakunax and his following to Mount Auberon using strong magic unbeknownst to most. The treaty is just a fable told by those who wish to keep the blindfolds on those who would rather live in blissful ignorance."

Bless the vine. My sneaking suspicion was correct. The elves were being lied to. Ornella reached out and squeezed my hand, seeking reassurance. This news would be the most difficult for her to bear, knowing that those who adored the ground she walked on had fed her fabrications of the truth her entire existence.

"The reality is that dragons can travel anywhere they please, and there's not a single thing anyone can do to keep us from doing exactly that." Her serpentine eyes gleamed mischievously. "We stay out of sight simply out of kindness. But we can do so no longer." Obsydora looked to Terragorn, and he solemnly bowed his head.

"Bakunax is not only corrupting other species, but peaceful dragons with his tainted blood to join him in his quest for power. It is straight blasphemy. He may be bound to Adara, but his soulless creations are not. He found a way around the ancient spell, a loophole. You see the few of us who have escaped his wrath. A few other hordes are hiding in different locations. It was agreed upon to spread out and protect the rest of our hatchlings by concealing our existence before our species goes extinct."

Silas stepped forward, having recovered from the near attack. His expression was solemn yet understanding. Several dragons' heads snapped in his direction, blatantly scrutinizing his character.

"He hasn't consumed all *Marked Ones*, has he?" The words left his mouth like a confession, and he patiently waited for a response. His golden eyes stood out amongst the morning shadows and were full of emotion.

Obsydora once again made a clicking noise with her mouth, and she shook her head.

"They are kept in iron cages hanging from his despair fortress. The rusted bars are protected with the same spell used on Cadell's Chamber; there's no use in trying to save those trapped behind them." Her ethereal voice grew wary, sending goosebumps down my arms. "Bakunax is planning a ritual of some sort; he will strategically devour all of the power of the *Marked Ones* at once. As to why, I wish I knew."

Fraener interrupted, his anger getting the better of him. "That is why the vile beast created *Thereon* in the first place. He plays off others' weaknesses and promises them unlimited power. For how much I hate him and don't want to admit it, Bakunax is cunning. I have never seen a dragon with his ability to adapt to every circumstance. A formidable opponent."

The horde of dragons began to dispute something in their tongue; the rumbling sounds deep inside their throats echoed across the sand and waves. Terragorn, the largest by far, nipped at Fraener in a fury.

"You *dare* refer to Bakunax as one of our kind; he lost that privilege long ago," the orange dragon bellowed at Fraener, who hissed and ran to hide behind several boulders farther inland. "He is wicked and not of this world, and if any of you so as much follow in his footsteps, I will dismember you accordingly." The dragon bared his massive canines for us all to see. "I do not eat rotten carcasses."

"Ogres don't taste good, or so I hear." Brom chuckled anxiously, shifting his weight on the sand. He was hinting at what we all wanted to know: what the dragons planned to do with us now that their presence had been revealed.

Terragorn and a few other dragons barked a laugh, and he lowered his gaze to the burly ogre. "Our diets are strictly fish and the occasional whale.

Depends on what we find while we are out for a swim. We will not eat you, but I would be careful around the hatchlings. They can be curious."

We laughed nervously, and I eyed the four hatchlings on the blackened sand. Their scales' coloring was a bland ashen hue to match the surrounding landscape. When dragons hatch, their scales first take on the shade of the surrounding nature before they shed, their actual shades gradually revealing themselves with each transformation.

"Can you—will you—fly us to the kingdom of Erebus?" Ornella unexpectedly pleaded, kneeling on the ground as she bowed and lowered her head. "The *Thereon* burned our vessel; it has sunk to the bottom of the sea. We have lost everything."

"What do you think we are, pack mules?" Obsydora shook her head in distaste, upset by my sister's request. The others bordering us mimicked her reaction, and my body tensed.

I placed myself before my sister and bowed directly to Obsydora as I spoke. "We did not mean to disturb you and your kindred." My eyes were cast downward in respect, and I paused to clear my throat. "The *Thereon* will be back, and it will not be safe for us to be on these islands." I lifted my head, baring my soul for her to search. "Please help us. You do not have to, but your entire species is kind enough to stay in the shadows for others. You should not have to stay willingly hidden at the cost of your own happiness."

My confidence grew as I said the words. It was how I had felt my entire existence, from the moment I had bloomed. Those around me would prefer it if I stayed hidden amongst the shadows, and I obliged for the safety and happiness of my family.

But now I understood that it was all a ruse, and none of us were pleased living that way. Not me, Ornella, or *Mãe*. We had been so busy trying to make the elders, priests, and villagers content that my family had suffered.

No creature or species should have to bend to the will of others because of how they are perceived. A monster is made by their choices and character, not their powers or scales.

A tingly sensation gently brushed my skin as my eyes connected with the sapphire dragon. I observed her *Gavinhas* flicker, and I was overcome with an awareness that we had mysteriously synchronized.

It must have been Obsydora's doing. Dragons were among the most revered species, having been one of the original creatures to walk the five kingdoms, long before the monarchies existed.

Another heated discussion was had between the dragons in their tongue before she answered. "We will offer you and your sister passage alongside your companions," Obsydora stated. "It is only because the *Creator* has blessed you with gifts that our kind extends a helping hand. And our horde must find sanctuary elsewhere now that it is confirmed that the *Thereon* will return."

I relaxed my shoulders and nodded in appreciation before standing.

"How soon until we leave?" Nox responded, itching to depart the barren islands. We did not know when the *Thereon* would return, possibly with an army.

"Early morning tomorrow, before sunrise." Terragorn began to march forward to the ocean, towering over the large boulders, not entirely happy with Obsydora. "I refuse to fly without a proper meal." We observed his massive body from a distance as he disappeared beneath the water, beginning his hunt. Other dragons followed suit, accompanying him with the hatchlings clumsily scampering to join in.

Our crew set up camp to rest in the flat patch of land before us. The journey to Erebus would take several moons. Ornella lay beside me, and it almost felt like we were back in our garden at home, watching the clouds overhead as *Mãe* sang in the kitchen. Almost.

"Are you okay?" I asked her softly. She had drifted off to sleep, only to be woken by the sounds of herself weeping. Tears were still fresh inside her emerald irises.

She gave me a halfhearted smile and hugged me tightly. "We're so close, Sayah. To where *Mãe* wanted us to be." Her arm was slung across my chest, and the rise and fall of her breathing slowed as she fell back into her slumber.

"I'll always be here, you know," I murmured, brushing her white waves of hair out of her face. She flipped over, sleeping soundly with only the occasional whimper.

Now truly alone with my thoughts, my heart fluttered in anticipation at what the morrow would bring.

We had found a way off the Isles of Cadogan. Tomorrow, I would travel to Erebus, where *Mãe* wanted us to find refuge.

And I would travel amongst the clouds on top of a *dragon*.

It felt too good to be true—that we would be rescued. I decided not to think much about it, afraid I might jinx the miracle we had discovered.

I held my hands up in the air, temporarily imagining that my fingers danced across the ivory and ebony keys of the grand piano inside the academy.

I rolled over to my other side, glancing at Nox, who was still awake and conversing with Silas. He leaned against a boulder, and he was rummaging through his pack. His laughter was like music to my ears, and my eyelids drifted closed, grateful for the little moments like these.

In my tired state, I began to dream of being in the clouds. Maybe I would be high enough in the atmosphere to see *Mãe's* soul watching over us, nestled into the moon, waiting to accompany my sister and me when it was our time to depart from this world and enter the next. As I drifted to sleep, the warm sun caressed my thoughts, and fond memories of *Mãe* inside our cottage in Alizeh comforted me.

The hatchlings were the first to wake the following day, the sky a misty grey just before the sun dripped its liquid gold over the horizon and onto the never-ending seas. They interacted like fowls, prancing along the sand, playfully whipping their tails at one another. Several mature dragons groggily hissed at the bright-eyed adolescents, and I now knew why Terragorn insisted we leave before sunrise. Our crew had slept for the remainder of the previous day and throughout the night; the horde's presence made me feel safe for the first time since leaving Alizeh's borders.

We were well-rested and ready for the day's plans.

"Which dragon will be escorting us to Erebus?" I murmured to Brom, who was standing along the shoreline's edge, scanning the horizon.

"They are deciding that now." He gestured to a group of dragons speaking in their dialect. From their tone, it gave the impression of a group of adults bickering. "We will have to split our group, and from what I understand, they are arguing over who will have the privilege of carrying the *Marked Ones*. It seems you and your sister are a hot commodity." Brom grinned, and I smirked, giving him a side-eye.

"Will you be okay?" I glanced around the area, concerned that someone may hear. His fear of the revered species was evident, as he kept a considerable distance from their horde and still refused to make eye contact. Brom's usual chipper demeanor had slightly dimmed, and only those who knew him well enough would notice the minor change.

He chuckled, his eyes meeting mine. "I'll be all right. They chargrilled some fish for me yesterday, so I think we've come to a truce." Worry lines creased his face. "I'm afraid of accidentally falling. And, of heights in general."

"Wait, aren't you from northern Alun? The landscape is primarily mountains."

Brom exhaled, turning away from me before speaking. "An ogre's pride is a prickly thing to behold. From a young age, we were taught that showing any pain is considered a weakness."

I carefully mulled over his admission, thinking. "Elves are taught something similar." The recollection of my past experiences with both the villagers and leaders came to mind. "But it is not so obvious; our teachings have us believe that we must be of service to one another. That we are not individuals in our wants and needs."

My mouth formed a hard line, and I glanced at him as he examined my expression.

"And you disagree."

It wasn't a question; it was a statement. He crossed his arms and leisurely beheld the sea. I dared not voice confirmation out loud, so I just nodded.

"Our *mãe* believed we were meant for something far greater than our priests and elders had planned for our lives." Tears formed on the corners of my eyes, and I quickly wiped them away with the back of my hand.

The dragons, deep in conversation moments prior, now headed in our direction; it was clear that Obsydora must have gotten her way. The sapphire dragon held her head confidently, her chest pushed outward like a bird.

Nox made his presence known to the sapphire dragon, jogging up to her eagerly. "What's the verdict?" His voice was sharp and alert. The day had just begun moments ago, and he was already vigilant.

Terragorn stomped by before Obsydora herself could make an announcement. "I, along with Obsydora and Fraener, will fly you over The Dark Waters to Erebus." The orange dragon cleared his throat, and his sharp eyes shot daggers at the small jade dragon beneath him. "Fraener is only willing to escort one of the *Marked Ones.*"

Obsydora briefly lowered her head and nipped at Fraener. He managed to dodge her bite. Though he was small, the jade dragon was incredibly quick. Maybe that was why he had such self-assurance combined with an ill temper.

"I will be escorting a *Marked One* as well," the sapphire dragon hissed.

Terragorn was evidently not only the largest but also the wisest. He practically rolled his eyes over their bickering. "Very well then. I will be taking the majority of the group. But be warned"—his yellow eyes glistened from the sun creeping off the horizon—"if you fall, I will not save you. If your bones break upon your descent, do not curse me in this world or the next." His voice was low and raspy as he lowered his body for those to climb up from his side. "I am not to blame for the choices you have made up until this point." The orange dragon mumbled a few chosen words under his breath and changed to his species' dialect. He was irritable, as he should be. I felt sorry for the old grump stuck carrying all that extra weight across the ocean.

Ornella walked up to me, her boots in her hand as she experienced the smooth, wet sand underneath her feet.

"Which will it be, Fraener or Obsydora?" she asked, and I looked between the two squabbling dragons, their tails twitching as they exposed their canines to one another.

"Sayah is riding Obsydora with me," Nox replied in my stead. The thought of being pressed against his broad chest for several moons was enticing, but my sister's comfort came before my desires.

"She was asking *me* to answer." I raised a brow.

He sidestepped in front of me as I approached the two dragons, who were impatiently waiting to proceed to our destination. "Obsydora specifically requested that *you* be the one to ride with her, Sayah. And Fraener is only willing to fly a *Marked One*."

Nox watched as we processed what he was saying. The sapphire dragon requested *me*. My chest would swell with pride if it weren't for the fact that Ornella looked deflated.

Thank the vine that my sister was there to reassure me.

Her face was neutral as she leaned in tight for a squeeze. "If Obsydora requested you, that is who you should ride with—it's best not to argue with a dragon."

I reciprocated her hug, embracing her before placing a kiss on her cheek. "Be careful, Ornella. I'll tell Obsydora to fly close and keep a lookout for you." I didn't want to say in case she fell.

"And I will do the same for you." Ornella halfheartedly smiled as she walked toward Fraener, her white hair swaying in the breeze.

I looked up at Nox, his eyes gleaming as he waited for me to move. But I was too busy marveling at his sharp jawline. His brown curls were pulled back, no longer cascading over his handsome features.

Bless the vine; this man is fine. And now I had the pleasure of being within his smoldering gaze for several moons.

"After you, my jewel." Nox bowed his head and winked while gesturing me onward. There was a playful look in his expression, and his presence was suddenly overwhelming. I twisted away, unable to meet his gaze as he slid into step beside me. The sky was a clear blue, and nature's optimism was quite infectious. Freedom from this desolate place was just a simple flight away. I could feel the weight on my shoulders being lifted, the stress of our situation dwindling. But before we were within a few paces of Obsydora, he leaned in to whisper in my ear. "A warning, Sayah." His tone was low, barely audible above the sounds of the ocean lapping against the rocky terrain. "Any dragon can become corrupted, a *Breeder of Thereon*. Remember that as they fight over you and your sister. Greed is an easy emotion to give in to."

The sapphire dragon lowered her head for us to climb up, and my heart ached. I was already fond of her and wondered if it had something to do with our *Gavinhas* being synchronized the night we met.

I did not want her to become a *Breeder of Thereon*.

Nox and I wordlessly sat on Obsydora's back, waiting for her to depart into the clouds after the rest of the horde of dragons. Fraener had taken off moments after Terragorn was up and soaring the sky, watching over the hatchlings with caution. My sister had barely climbed onto his spine before the jade dragon began moving upward, flapping his wings in earnest to catch up.

They were now a speck above our heads, and a wave of anxiety overcame me as Fraener recklessly flew too close for comfort between the other dragons' wing spans.

"Sit between the crevasse of where her neck and spine meet; it'll be easier to hold on from there." My riding partner nodded to the space before him and patted where he wanted me to sit.

My face flushed, and I eagerly joined him where he suggested. "How do you know where the safest place to sit is?"

Obsydora began to snort, her chortles shaking her body as she flapped her wings. "While you were sleeping, this werewolf kept me awake with his incessant questioning." Her head arched slightly, and we made eye contact before she turned her body to face the direction of the icy kingdom. "Better do as he says, *Marked One*. I might be more inclined to catch you than Terragorn, but I'll make you regret it later."

She flapped her wings, quickly gathering the strength to rise into the clouds above. The wind pressure from our ascent into the sky was immense as I pressed my backside into Nox for stability. My entire figure was rigid as I tried to find my bearings and keep a firm grasp on her body; her sapphire scales were slippery to the touch.

Nox was right behind me, with his firm grip on my waist. We soared above the ocean, the *Ligação Mágica* hidden below its luminous exterior.

"Before I met you, I didn't know elves' ears turned red when they blushed." He chuckled, causing the rose color on the tips of my ears and cheeks to darken several shades. "It's cute."

I suppressed a smile by biting my lip. "What are your plans once we arrive in Erebus?" I straightened my back; my muscles were still tense from the movement of Obsydora's wings.

"I'll show you around my favorite town, Flykra, of course," I could hear the smile in his voice from behind me. "Then I suppose I'll head back to Alun to regroup at my family's vineyard. At least I can bring my father back vital information on what compels the *Thereon* and how beings are transformed. However, he won't be thrilled to hear how I sunk one of our clan's vessels."

We were quiet for several moments, and a lump formed in my throat. I glanced at Nox's hands, still holding me firmly in place, and studied the scars left from the ancient magic on his forearm.

"Where is it that you'll be staying?" he inquired, his voice muted.

I cleared my throat, answering vaguely. "At a friend's place." He did not need to know all the details, that Ulfred's cabin was located beside the lighthouse. The handsome werewolf would soon leave, and my heart would be left in tattered bits.

It was obvious that I liked him, I made that clear to him and everyone else. But what those around me didn't understand was how much his kindness meant to me. He didn't flinch away at my touch, and didn't think of me as solely a *Marked One*. Nox was the first being to view me for who I was, and who I wanted to be.

I was not my powers, and I was not someone chosen for a higher meaning. I was simply a young woman who craved the acceptance of another, an elf who had been viewed as an outcast by her own kind simply for existing.

He did not reply, and the lump in my throat grew tighter. The atmosphere between us was stifling; I could feel his hands tense around my waist.

"How did you end up in charge of everything? Hunting down the *Thereon* and freeing your sister?" I was desperate to change the subject, to think of anything rather than our time together being numbered. Tears started forming, and it was not from the constant wind.

He barked a short laugh, his husky breath in my ear. "I was the only one willing to do anything. When Tabitha disappeared, I thought my father would immediately act and try to rescue her." A low growl reverberated in his throat. "But the only ones who cared were Silas and me. The two of them have been joined at the hip since they locked eyes with one another."

"Kind of like you and me, right?" I twisted around to face him. Nox's soft brown curls had been pulled back into a bun, accentuating his strong features. There was a mischievous glimmer in his russet irises, and the dark circles beneath them added to his mysterious lure.

"Yes, exactly like you and me." He laughed, sending butterflies throughout my chest. The pitch in his voice then changed, deeper than before as he continued. "I will never stop trying to rescue her. She has always been my family, through thick and thin. Tabitha means more to me than my own blood."

I nodded, understanding. "Is that why you're also trying to find a cure?"

He shifted his weight before answering; a long exhale escaped his lips. "Sort of. I'm not looking for a cure because I'm some amazing guy, Sayah." Nox continued as if he was revealing a dark secret. "I want to find a cure because the *Thereon's* shields of dark magic are impenetrable. My crew has endured loss after loss, and it wasn't until you and your sister joined us that I could see the light slowly coming back into their eyes. Their will to fight had dwindled, and almost all hope had been lost."

"We were sure that all the *Marked Ones* had been captured until we tracked down a group of *Thereon* in Danu, who were hunting you two." His chin grazed my cheek; he was so intimately close. "And when I strolled into the music shop that fateful afternoon, I witnessed the most beautiful woman confessing her soul with music, blessing everyone around her with such an ethereal performance."

I tightened my grip on Obsydora's spine as my heart raced. If I wasn't careful, he would have not only my attention but my heart in the palm of his hand.

And I couldn't afford to love him, not when I knew what we had was fleeting.

"Such swoon-worthy words from a tall drink of water," I taunted him, lightening the mood. "I'm sure you had all the females lined up at your parent's vineyard back in Alun."

His abrupt laugh, followed by a brief pause, made me smile. I was right.

"And what about you, my rare, one-of-a-kind jewel? All the boys in Alizeh were at your beck and call, whisking you away to some meadow to gift you bouquets of roses." His words, although innocent, made my breath catch.

"That would've been my sister." I giggled halfheartedly. "The boys in Alizeh were afraid of me. There are rumors that I am cursed." I twisted my face to the side so he could hear me over the roaring wind flowing over the sapphire dragon's wings. "I never found the boys in my village attractive or any males of my species. I've always been slightly taller than most and never felt compelled to pursue someone."

My heart fluttered at my following words, admitting them out loud. "You are the first man I've ever been attracted to. The relief I experienced when I met you was overwhelming—it confirmed that nothing was wrong with me; I just hadn't been introduced to you yet."

Nox's hands gently squeezed my waist, and he pulled me closer to his toned figure. I leaned back on his chest, gazing at him as we bathed in the warm sunlight. He kissed the top of my head before resting his cheek there.

"The boys in Alizeh were just that—boys." He took my hands into his, letting go of his grip on my hips as he tightly hugged my waist. "It's their loss; they didn't appreciate a woman who is rarer than all the treasures in the five kingdoms."

My mind raced, and a knot formed in my chest as I realized how much I would miss him when he was gone. The lingering happiness I felt was like that of a fully blossomed cherry tree. We silently traveled through the sun's rays, dodging the dispersed clouds in the blue sky. The once ominous sea now glistened beneath us like an oil painting, and the world around us was once again a canvas of intricate colors.

Obsydora's sapphire scales reflected the morning light as I took turns resting my head against her spine, squeezing her tightly, afraid of letting the fleeting moment pass us by.

Nox did not once loosen his grip on my waist as we traveled to the icy kingdom.

The flight to Erebus was three days of consistent flying, and it was obvious Obsydora and the other dragons in the horde were exhausted. The hatchlings would periodically rest on the backs of their elders, who shouldered the task of keeping the little ones on a steady course with the rest of their kin.

"Do you need to rest?" I tenderly brushed her scales.

"Nay, we are close to making landfall." She yawned, displaying a complete set of razor-sharp teeth. Her wings were spread at full length, and she used the wind to her favor to coast across the sky as she descended. I shivered as the climate drastically shifted, the temperature dropping. Nox hugged me close, and I snuggled into his core for warmth.

He pointed straight ahead through the last layer of clouds. "There it is, Sayah. Erebus."

As soon as my vision cleared, I exhaled at the wondrous sight. The scenery of the frozen kingdom was not what I had expected. Its beauty rivaled Alizeh's canopied forests. The familiar green-and-gold magic gracefully climbed the snow-capped mountains and roaming hills. The snowy landscape contained fir trees, with wildlife scampering about between the thick branches. Icy roads shimmered like stars, and lights of various colors decorated the city of Flykra.

A lighthouse, covered in ice and snow, was perched just outside the bay.

"Our horde will make camp somewhere near the coastline. If you need us, this is where we will be. But please do not need us." She barked a laugh, and I could see the steam rise from her mouth and nostrils. "Fraener might make a snack out of you the next time you show up; he is not particularly fond of other species."

Obsydora followed Terragorn and tucked in her wings at the final descent when making landfall.

"This is . . . unexpected," I said breathlessly as Obsydora landed on the other side of the lighthouse near large ice caps that easily floated in the shallow water.

"What were you expecting?" Nox responded as he held his hand and gingerly guided me down Obsydora's side so I wouldn't stumble onto the snow.

"A cold, dark, bleak kingdom with no vegetation or viable landscape." My breath was visible, and I shivered profusely.

"You're right about one thing." He rubbed his arms to create friction as he shivered. "It is cold."

The rest of the crew dismounted Terragorn as my twin bowed to Fraener in thanks.

I shouted across the small distance, giddy that we had reached our destination, "Ornella, you truly blend in with the landscape." Her hair whipped around her face, no longer in its braid. She grinned, her emerald eyes sparkling.

"That was fun." Her voice was a pitch higher than usual. "And Fraener said he wouldn't mind if I joined him again sometime."

"Really?" I raised my brows in surprise. My gaze shifted to the jade dragon, who was currently being nipped at by the hatchlings. "It seems you two have bonded."

She glanced at the small dragon and smiled. "Yeah, I think we did."

Fraener's attention was still on my sister, his emerald scales glimmering against the piercing white tundra. He snorted when he caught me staring, puffs of smoke leaving his nostrils.

A warm smile etched across my features despite the cold, and I grabbed Ornella's hand, gently squeezing. "Isn't this place lovely? I now only need a fur coat paired with a thick scarf."

"And you can't forget a cup of hot tea," Ornella added as we giggled in unison.

I placed my arm over her shoulder as we briskly walked to find shelter from the cold longing for my old routine. Back in our cottage, I would stare out the crescent-shaped window *Mãe* had carved, holding my chipped mug of hot tea, utterly content with life's ordinary, mundane, and trivial moments. I wished for another tiny instant where Ornella and I could bask in its quiet.

"Where are you two headed?" My mind returned to reality as Nox called out from behind, followed by Brom, Enid, and Silas. Kazumi was nowhere to be seen.

"To find a man named Ulfred," Ornella chirped.

"And someplace with a fire and blankets," I added.

We stood awkwardly, unsure how to say goodbye to the group of misfits who had kidnapped us but also saved us from being captured by the *Thereon*.

My heart skipped a beat as I looked into Nox's russet eyes for the last time, trying to remember every detail of their flecks of crimson and gold.

He grabbed my wrist as I was getting ready to leave. "I said I was going to show you around, remember?" He genuinely smiled, his fangs protruding. "My friends and I are also looking for someplace warm—with a fire and blankets."

"Let's get on with it then. Kazumi is turning into an icicle." Enid walked between Silas and Ornella, heading up the sloping hillside. Her mood was irritable; Ornella's expression was etched with concern while intensely watching the ogress.

The tiny fairy, irritable and shivering, popped her head from Enid's vest pocket. Her black beady eyes were shooting daggers at the entire group. Our boots crunched under the snow, and we spotted a small log cabin beside the weathered lighthouse. Smoke rose from its chimney, its black fumes drifting high into the sky above.

A light was on, that much I could see from a short distance away.

My chest tightened; it was suddenly hard to breathe.

My last connection to *Mãe* was before me as we approached the lodge, made of durable wood with a snow-covered roof. The lights inside flickered, and a shadow of a figure moving inside was visible from the front window.

Ulfred was home.

Ornella and I stood in front of the door; the shifting of feet behind us only added to the immense pressure.

"If someone doesn't knock on the door, I'd be happy to." Kazumi's raspy voice echoed out from Enid's vest. We were urged forward, a gentle push from behind as we stood beneath the porch light in the cold.

I took the first step, knocking on the door loudly with false confidence. For a moment, there was silence. Shuffling noises could be heard from the other side of the wooden door frame. The door pried open an inch, and I was met with glowing ruby eyes.

"Who is it?" a deep voice grunted from inside the shadows.

"D—do you know a woman named Aster?" Ornella whispered adjacent to me. "She is—or was—our *mãe*." When the man did not reply, she explained further. "She told us that she had contacted a man named Ulfred and that he would take us in. Is that you?"

He squinted through the doorway, and a shiver ran down my spine as I tightly tucked my arms, rubbing them for warmth. The man looked between my sister and me through the light snow that began to decorate the just-plowed walkway. He shut the door, temporarily causing my heart to drop. I heard several locks turning before the entrance to the tiny cabin swung open wide.

"Come in." The large man stepped to the side, and we obeyed. Our friends followed behind us, relieved to be inside somewhere with heat. We waited, unsure where to sit or stand now that we were in a stranger's living quarters.

The cabin was quaint; the walls painted a hunter green, a perfect accent to the arched wooden ceiling. His decor consisted of surprisingly beautiful works of art—handmade acrylic paintings mounted on all three walls. The fourth wall contained a red-brick fireplace, with several logs currently ablaze inside. There was a small kitchen in the far lefthand corner and a dining area to the right. A thick white sheet covered the large table in the space, and sunlight infiltrated the area from the two large windows—containing the perfect view of the lighthouse and the ocean. Two quarters were located adjacent the sitting room. A worn leather couch with a matching recliner were on display, and between the two was a hand-carved, round coffee table.

"I wasn't expecting company," the man murmured. He gestured for us to sit before entering the kitchen. Ornella and I sat along with Enid, the men deciding to remain standing; we waited several moments, unsure how to proceed.

The older gentleman turned around and addressed us as a group. "Do you like beef?"

We nodded, our stomachs thankful for any meal, regardless of the flavor. I absorbed every detail about his face, from the laugh lines beside his eyes to the subtle grey in his jet-black beard. He was a giant werewolf towering over the stove, tossing several vegetables into a large pot. We watched the man cook; a familiar smell made Ornella and I perk up. I sniffed the air again just to be sure.

"That smells like *Mãe's* recipe for beef stew," I stated, finally breaking the silence.

He cleared his throat. "That's because it is." Pain flickered across his face, and his hand hovered over the pot. "Is Aster here with you?"

My hands fluttered up to above my heart. His deep, ruby eyes met mine, full of pain and hurt. I didn't have the heart to say it out loud, as this man hurt for a woman who he had not seen in several hundred lunations. Ulfred turned to the stew, his back facing us.

"Her soul no longer resides with ours; she has moved on from this world to the next." Ornella delivered the news of *Mãe's* passing. I gave her a grateful nod, my eyes focused on one of the many paintings along the walls.

Ulfred was quiet as he froze above the beef stew, his body shaking beneath his soundless tears.

The room was heavy as we ate our first meal together since the vessel had sunk. He took bowls out of his cabinet, poured a serving for each of us, and brought it to where we sat. Ulfred took in our unkempt appearance and frowned.

"Your *mãe* left something for the two of you." He gestured to Ornella and me as he began rummaging through a chest just inside his bedroom door. "While I search for it, why don't you clean yourselves up and head into town? The *Grato Amizade* festival is continuing for the next three moons."

Ulfred scanned a wardrobe through the entryway, pulling out several garments on hangers. "I still have several of Aster's winter coats. You girls are welcome to come and take a look." He eyed Enid, sitting on the edge of the recliner. "And that goes for you too."

I savored my bowl of stew, listening to Ulfred converse with the men in the room, willing to share any of his unused garments. Fortunately, he was so large that Brom could wear his spare clothes comfortably.

As I looked around the room at the paintings, it dawned on me that *Mãe's* presence was still in this house, from the decor to the matching vanities and dresser. My pulse stuttered as I looked at Ulfred in a different light.

"How long were you and our *mãe* together?"

Ulfred stopped mid-conversation with Brom and walked over to kneel beside Ornella and me. I was still cupping the empty bowl in shaking hands.

"We never parted from one another—we simply existed for many lunations at a distance. I still love her, and she loved me."

Our mãe and this man had been two souls fully bound together. Distance only an illusion; their love transcended all space and time.

Tears flowed like a raging river, silently down my cheeks. My sister next to me was in shock, the tears collecting in the corners of her eyes.

"If that is true, just know that she still loves you ardently in whatever world she is in now." I placed a hand on my cheek, trying to calm myself. His crimson irises were watery, and I realized I was desperate to know the man *Mãe* had secretly loved from a distance for hundreds of lunations. "May I hug you?"

A choked sob nearly strangled the massive man. "Of course you can." He opened his arms wide, and Ornella joined me in embracing Ulfred. I finally understood why *Mãe* never took a partner in Alizeh. She had met her soulmate during her adventures in Erebus.

I pulled away from Ulfred, a question burning in my mind. "Why didn't you go to Alizeh with her? Or why didn't she stay here with you in Erebus?" I looked around the cozy cabin; every inch of it felt like home. "She would've been happier here."

He gently released us both from his grasp, helping us to our feet before he stood. "I'm afraid that I can't be the one to tell you." He looked back toward the chest of knickknacks in his bedroom, his bushy eyebrows knitting together. "Aster wanted to tell you herself. That is what I've been searching for—a letter she sent me soon after you both bloomed."

"Have you read the letter? Could you perhaps tell us what it says?" Ornella asked in anticipation. Her emerald eyes were hopeful.

Ulfred shook his head. "No, I'm afraid I cannot. I promised Aster that I wouldn't read what it contained." He stood and began rummaging through all the cabinets and drawers in the house. "Please forgive me; it's been so long that I can't remember where I placed it."

"No, no, that's all right," Ornella quickly replied as she stood, gesturing to our companions. They all were watching, including Kazumi, who had left Enid's pocket at some point. "We can all clean up before heading into town to experience the festivities."

Ulfred nodded, his expression relieved.

"What is the kingdom of Erebus celebrating?" Ornella's face blushed in delight, and I smiled, knowing she wanted to head into the city to sightsee and shop.

"It celebrates the kingdom's friendship between Alun and Erebus," Brom quietly chimed in. "Each year, those who reside in Alun travel to Erebus to experience the local food and culture here."

"And Alun also acts as a host for anyone from Erebus; it's an entertaining holiday," Nox responded. He looked at me, his eyes beaming with excitement. "And I can't wait to show it to you."

My face flushed at how he looked at me from beside the fire. His intense gaze did not break mine until someone cleared their throat, and we moved to take turns washing up and looking at the available clothes Ulfred had for us to choose from.

It was unanimously agreed that Ornella would rinse off first. My sister eagerly took a towel and a change of clothes to head into the washroom.

The man who had given his heart to our *mãe* approached me while I was still on the couch and gifted me several handfuls of large gold coins.

"I can't accept this." I studied his kind face, and his crimson eyes showed so much love and compassion. It was easy to see why *Mãe* had chosen Ulfred as a life partner.

"Oh yes, you can." He smiled with his eyes and gestured around the room. "I've been saving for many moons, waiting for Aster's return with the both of you. Go ahead and feel free to share some of the wealth with your friends." His smile was sad, and he looked away for several beats before finding my gaze. "We had planned to live a life together, the four of us here."

Ulfred choked on a sob and quickly got to his feet once again, wiping away tears with his shirt sleeve as he pretended to dig for something in a kitchen cabinet. "You and Ornella can stay for as long as you need, Sayah."

The kind gentlemen looked at me earnestly, and I held my breath.

That was the first time he had said my name, and I wanted to engrain every detail of that moment in my soul. *He would have made the best papa*, I thought, my heart wistful as I returned his look with a genuine smile.

I wondered what happened to take away such happiness.

To stop myself from crying, I left the sitting area and went to Ulfred's room, where he had laid the clothes out from *Mãe's* wardrobe in small piles on the bed. Shifting through the clothes, I tried to find the most worn items. There was a cobalt-blue winter jacket, in near-pristine condition but with a few marks on the sides, and I could see where someone had sewn several buttons back onto the front where they had popped off at some point.

I gingerly picked it up and, ensuring no one was watching, I sniffed the coat's collar. My eyes went wide; even through the dust and many lunations that had passed, it still smelled of her. She had always smelled simple and clean, with a hint of lemon.

I smiled as I looked at my newest and most cherished item, grinning from ear to ear. Whispering to myself, I gave the coat a big hug. "It's perfect."

Chapter Twenty-two

The city of Flykra was more of a small town buried beneath several inches of white powder. Even so, it was a magical place. The festivities for *Grato Amizade* had the frosty square buzzing with creatures. There were ogres, goblins, centaurs, werewolves, dwarves, and other species all strolling about the sidewalks caked in snow. They were equally dressed for the cold, united by their wool coats and scarves, all with similar smiles. Enchanting strips of garland were hung with precision outside of the shops. Every building was strung with blue-and-white lights, and street performers were at the main entrance, using magic to ignite the imaginations of the little ones who watched in awe. The smell of delicious food wafted through the chilly air, and my stomach responded with a growl. I had consumed some of Ulfred's beef stew but was still hungry for more.

We all walked into the city together; I was arm in arm with both Ornella and Enid, giggling while walking past several storefronts. Kazumi had chosen my shoulder to sit on—a feat I took pride in. All of us had found something to wear in Ulfred's collection of clothes; he said that over several hundred lunations, he had ended up with multiple items from his friends for safekeeping while they were still traveling between kingdoms. The smell of delicious baked bread wafted beneath my nose, and I turned to see where the aroma originated.

"Are you hungry?" Nox looked at me expectantly. The group was starting to disperse organically. Ornella was conversing with Enid as they meandered toward the shops. Brom, Silas, and Kazumi, I could only assume, were going to find the nearest open table to play a game of cards. I was tempted to join them; watching that prickly fairy play a game of cards was enticing. However, my stomach growled, and I wondered what pastries tasted like here in Erebus.

"A little." I shifted my weight awkwardly under my feet. I did not, however, want to confess my huge obsession with sweets in front of Nox.

We walked along the brick path, strolling beside the businesses decorated for such a wonderful occasion. A pang of grief flowed through me at the reminder of Alizeh's celebrations for the changing of each season.

The bakery sat before us, sparking a hint of happiness. Nox, to my surprise, strolled straight through the shop's front entrance. He paused, holding the door open with an amused expression. "You coming?" The man's smile alone was delectable, a dessert I could forever feast my eyes on.

I beamed. "Absolutely."

The entire shop had a warm glow around it despite the snow trying to sneak in from the shop's entryway. Plants hung from the ceiling, and the display on the back wall had handwritten prices of the day's creations. Bottles of wine sat behind the register, along with an entire wall full of jars of jelly and honey. The shelves were filled with various types of baked goods, including loaves of bread, croissants, and custard-filled pastries. Several cakes sat on the back counter, the long list of orders growing as customers shuffled in and out.

As he boisterously recited the spell, *Fria*, I spied the baker cooling off several dozen cookies he pulled from the industrial-sized oven. The flames flickered as several logs were tossed onto the fire, causing ashes to jump up momentarily from the abrupt movement.

And, *bless the vine*, that glorious aroma of dough baking in the oven had my mouth watering.

Nox beckoned me forward, snapping me out of my thoughts. "What kind of pastries do you like?" He stroked his chin, looking at the vast menu of options.

I bit my lip, unable to choose. There were too many choices, unlike the bakery back in my village. "All of them," I admitted, causing us both to laugh.

"What did you like to order back at your bakery?" His soft, brown waves framed his face as he waited patiently for my response.

My cheeks and the tips of my ears turned red from blushing. "I would always order the same thing: a chocolatey, gooey-filled pastry."

"Ah, a girl after my own heart." He grinned, turning to get in line with the cashier. I went to stand next to him in line, but he shook his head and pointed for me to wait on an indoor bench. "I'll pick something I think you'll like—it'll be a surprise." He winked and shooed me away, chuckling.

I stepped out of the doorway to the bakers with a fresh, warm croissant in my hand. Nox carefully studied my facial expressions as I bit into its mouthwatering center, revealing the melted chocolate inside.

My pleasure was audible; it was better than any pastry I had ever tasted from my village's bakery. "Mmmm, this is *so* good." With him absorbing my every movement, I was suddenly conscious of the chocolate on the side of my mouth that I went to wipe off.

"Wait." He held my hand back, and I froze. To my shock, in front of a crowd of beings on the crosswalk and beneath the luminous holiday lights strung across the cobblestone streets, Nox deliberately licked the gooey chocolate from the corner of my mouth. Time appeared to slow. My heart was racing. In a daze, I observed him through the same warm glow that emitted from inside the bakery, even out in the colorless snow. He intertwined his fingers with mine, and we held hands while exploring Flykra's enchanting landscape.

The *Ligação Mágica* was the most fascinating here in this icy kingdom; the flecks of green-and-gold magic swirled and danced across the soft pillows of snow. Flakes of the iridescent powder fell gradually onto the ground as I began to absorb the culture that was the staple of Erebus. It was similar to Danu, with multiple species intermingling. But I adored how we all dressed in coats and warm, fuzzy attire. The beings here were all under the same magical spell, adorned with similar smiles and chapped lips from the cold.

I could see this being home.

"My family would travel here specifically for the festival. Tabitha and I had a list of fun activities we would do together that week." His voice gradually deflated as we walked toward the street vendors on the city's edge.

I had just finished my pastry and was licking the gooey contents off my fingers. A clever idea began to take shape, and I beamed at Nox while lightly tugging on his hand. "Let's celebrate like you did with your family when you were little. I want to experience *Grato Amizade* the way you and Tabitha used to."

He scratched his chin, deliberating. "Sayah, I may have to take you up on that offer." The two of us began to snake through the maze of onlookers as several displays and booths selling blue-and-white gifts were for sale.

"What do the two colors represent?" We had stopped at a table containing several ribbons. He scoured the various decorations before finding a blue laced ribbon with an intricate design of the starry sky and a crescent moon embroidered into the fabric.

"The white represents new beginnings and the blue stands for loyalty. Our celebration is from a time shortly after the original monarchs of the kingdoms fell; despair spread like a plague as resentment between the kingdoms grew. But both Erebus and Alun put aside their remaining conflicts and were officially recognized as allies, which started the tradition of *Grato Amizade*, lasting for seven moons." He looked around the stone buildings and to the sky.

The sun began to set on a meaningful day, the atmosphere turning somewhat melancholy.

"I don't want this day to end," I murmured, my time feeling rushed.

Nox kissed my forehead before spinning me around to face the snowy hilltops more inland. "May I touch your hair?" His innocent question caused my heart to flutter, and I bobbed my head to answer yes. My cheeks felt hot as he slowly unbraided my woven locks, and a few raven strands fell forward around my face. I could feel delicate tugs on my scalp, and he flipped me back to face him.

"Now you're celebrating like a local." His russet eyes twinkled as he winked, and I instinctively reached back to touch my hair. He had pulled up a few strands and tied the ribbon into a bow, giving me the accessory.

"What does it mean?" I scanned the area, suddenly aware several young women had bows in their manes.

Nox's cheeks lightly flushed as he looked at me in earnest. "Men gift the woman they have feelings for with a ribbon during the festivities. If she accepts his confession, she wears the ribbon to let others know she has been spoken for."

My entire body turned red as I felt the fabric between my fingers in a new light. "Thank you, Nox." I started to twirl the ends of my hair around my finger. "So, I'm off the market? How formal." I blew a kiss at him, giggling.

He picked me up off the ground and twirled me in the air in the middle of the crowded walkway before planting a kiss on my forehead. "Let's head down to the frozen lake, or we will miss our chance to ice skate before the fireworks start." His lips were in my ear, tickling me with his breath.

This had to be the best night of my life; I had never felt so loved before. We walked the remainder of the way in silence, enjoying each other's company as we ambled through the magical landscape. The shimmering snowflakes danced on their descent in the slight breeze. The *Ligação Mágica* swirled in delight and weaved between the trees and brush. At dusk, the stars in the sky were bright as we approached the lake's glassy exterior.

The body of water was aglow with several hundred lanterns strung overtop, connecting the nearby trees. I marveled at the scenery as beings glided across the surface, enjoying each other's company.

"I'll go grab us some skates," he said, letting go of my hand. I felt his absence as he sauntered over to another local vendor. I carefully moved close to the lake's edge, nervous. Winter was my favorite season, but not because of the exclusive activities one could participate in. It was the season when the villagers hid away in their cottages, leaving me the ability to meander in the streets alone. With all the vegetation lacking life, I did not have to worry as I roamed through the cold and their absence. I rather enjoyed the quiet and peaceful serenity with only myself as company.

And it was always winter in the kingdom of Erebus. I want to stay with Ulfred and Ornella for a while in this frozen place of joy and light.

"Here, let's put these on." Nox appeared behind me, handing me a pair of matching skates. We went to a nearby park bench, and he assisted me into my skates and laced them properly for me. His skates were on in a matter of seconds, and he was on the icy lake, moving fluidly.

"I don't want to fall." My legs were shaking. I had zero experience balancing my weight on top of the ice with two blades on the bottom of my feet.

"I won't let you. Trust me, *my jewel.*" His voice deepened as he tauntingly wiggled his brows, and I laughed at the silly nickname. Nox's distraction was successful and the tension in my shoulders lessened. I glided across the ice, using his arm to steady myself. "You're never completely ready for anything, Sayah." His crimson eyes bore into my own with intensity. "Sometimes you just have to take a leap of faith."

A loud pop rang in my ears and overhead, and we both tilted our heads to the sky as a rainbow of colors shimmered for several seconds up above before dissipating.

"The fireworks are starting," I said in amazement before turning straight into his chest. His tribal markings were swirling with miniature orbs of light beneath the collar of his shirt, and I reached out to touch the small, exposed swirls poking out along his neck.

"Today counts as one of my favorite memories." I kissed his cheek, and my lips lingered. I took in his familiar husky scent before another pop rang overhead, temporarily frightening me. I playfully frowned as he heartily laughed, his hand caressing my cheek before pulling me in close. My head tilted toward his, and he kissed my lips tenderly, savoring every second we were together.

"Nox." I whispered his name with a grin plastered across my face.

"Yes?" We were still on the ice, now gliding in slow circles.

"My *mãe* would have liked you."

He twirled me underneath the stars, and I threw my head back, giggling up at the moon.

Chapter Twenty-three

The next three moons passed in pure bliss. The blue ribbon was permanently tied around my wrist. It was the first gift I had ever received from a male. Throughout the day, I marveled at the embroidered design, showing it to anyone willing to look. The past few moons, Ornella had spent every bit of spare time with Enid in the kitchen, and her cooking and baking skills had slowly improved. Slightly. I was buried into the sofa cushions, listening to the lively commentary in Ulfred's sitting room. Shouts and laughter filled the cabin, echoing off the highly decorated walls.

"Cheater!" Kazumi spat as she held up an ace of spades. It had magically appeared from inside Silas's coat sleeve. The card was amusingly the same size as her.

"I thought this was just a practice round—you said you were teaching me." Silas grinned, brushing his sandy hair out from his eyes. "I can't lose all my gold to you."

"Toss three more coins into the pile, or I'll steal what's left in your sorry sack of change before morning." Kazumi spat. "And this time, I better not catch you stuffing cards in your pockets. Unbelievable."

Silas responded by throwing gold into the center of the coffee table while smirking.

266

The poker game continued as I unstuck myself from the pillows and left my comfortable position for a front-row seat to the entertainment.

Nox had gone out to town for ingredients requested by Ulfred and Enid, and I assumed it was Ornella's fault we kept running out of the spices in his cupboards. Brom had recently joined Kazumi and Silas for a game of cards at the coffee table in the center of the floor. I scooted forward, leaning over the edge of my seat.

They were crammed together in the confined space, and the only one who appeared comfortable was the spritely pink-haired fairy. I eyed the large table, the white sheet strewn across it covered in a thin layer of dust.

"Why don't you three move the game to the table?" I tipped my chin toward the kitchen. My elbows rested on my knees, my face in my hands. "Brom would have enough room to stretch out his legs, not to mention breathe."

Laughter erupted from the ogre, and his warm brown eyes pulled up at the corners before he laid his cards on the wooden surface, face down.

"We already tried, elvish girl, but the large werewolf refused." Brom shook his head, exhaling before pushing several gold coins to the center of the table. "And I'm about done, anyway. Kazumi will take my entire savings if I don't quit."

I laughed as Kazumi fluttered her wings and sweetly smiled, shrugging her shoulders.

Ulfred had overheard the discussion from his room and strolled straight into the kitchen. "Sayah, it's not a table." He whisked away its covering, and dust flew about the room. We all coughed, and I rubbed the debris from my eyes, nearly choking on my words. "Sorry, I should have thought that through. It's been years since I've played."

"It's a grand piano." I gaped at the beautiful instrument before me, immediately on my feet, circling the piano in awe. The sleek black shine was perfect for the room's creative atmosphere.

"It was your *mãe*'s," Ulfred murmured from beside me.

My heart nearly stopped beating at his words.

"She never told us that she had another piano," Ornella said incredulously. She was still in the kitchen with Enid and covered in flour. We watched, entranced, as he pulled out the bench and sat facing the keys.

It felt as though we had traveled back in time and were getting a peek at the woman *Mãe* had been in her youth.

Ulfred raised his brow, looking at her dubiously. "Who do you think taught her how to play?" He straightened and played a few keys for practice. He paused momentarily before his fingers danced along the ivory and ebony keys with vigor. It was easy to see how *Mãe* had fallen for him; not only was he kind, but they both shared a love of music that transcended the barriers built by our culture's beliefs.

"Do you have any of her old sheet music?" I asked when he finished his performance.

"Certainly." He strolled to a cabinet, pulling out an old picture album. "I have a few of her songs tucked away in here."

"I've never seen anybody with this many paintings before." Ornella had left the kitchen to join us at the piano. She gestured to the art along the walls and the album in his hands.

He laughed heartily and placed the album between us. "That is because I painted most of them." Leisurely flipping through the intricate works of art, we studied the beautiful pieces—each one more detailed than the next. *Mãe* was in most of them, and he had painted her likeness flawlessly.

"I wish she could be here with us." My lip quivered. She had deserved happiness too. Whenever I experienced a moment of joy, I felt an overwhelming sense of guilt. A question would burn in the back of my mind, seeping into my thoughts like an unwanted plague.

Am I allowed to be happy now that she is permanently gone?

Ulfred left Ornella and me to walk into his bedroom. We continued looking at the beautiful pictures and sheet music, he returned with a sealed envelope in his grasp. His forehead creased, and he stroked his beard, deep in thought. "This here is almost the same age as you two." He placed the letter into my palm, his features solemn.

"It's addressed from *Mãe* to the two of you." His voice cracked, and he averted his gaze to one of the paintings on the wall. "Why don't you both go to my bedroom to read it, where you'll have some privacy?" Ulfred's eyes were a puffy red as he gestured to his bedroom.

Ornella and I left the album open on the piano and hesitantly walked by our friends. Nox's presence was immediately known as he leaned casually against the wall next to the front door, his eyes boring into my back. I gently caressed the vital letter, afraid to wrinkle the paper.

"Do you think we're ready?" My twin whispered next to me.

I carefully unsealed *Mãe's* last words to us before I had time to consider my answer.

"We'll never be completely ready, Ornella. Sometimes, we have to take a leap of faith." And at that, I started reading.

Chapter Twenty-four

Aster's Letter

To my dearest daughters,

Two things you should take away from this letter: you should not trust the Ligação Mágica, and your existence is a miracle.

You are reading this, which means I am no longer with the living, and I have sent you to my darling Ulfred. This information may come to you as a shock, but it is essential that you find this truth one day, for it may very well save you. I want you to know that every decision I have made thus far and will make has been for your safety and well-being.

I do not know if I have made the right choices, but I do know that I have loved you both from the moment I first laid eyes on you.

I had a family once. A papa, mãe, and an older brother, named Ciaran. My parents were kind, but they believed everything that our elders and priests taught with an iron fist. There was no other way of life for them. I left soon after my rite-of-passage ceremony with dreams of traveling the five kingdoms and having the adventures only few would experience. I did not realize that Ciaran had followed me to Ascelin, where I planned to depart for my journey. I told him I would not turn back, and he said he didn't want me to. So, we left Alizeh together.

Along our voyages, Ciaran and I slowly formed a group of friends. My dear Ulfred was among them, and during the first several years we knew each other, our friendship grew into something much more. Ciaran was outgoing and had a kind spirit, but he struggled to find a companion who wanted to travel and leave the comfort of their home.

That is until one day while traveling to Erebus, we found a passenger overboard with no ship in sight. We rescued the mysterious woman and were shocked to discover she was of an unknown species. Ciaran was instantly smitten with her, and she was indeed beautiful. Her name was Etienne: she had ears similar to an elf, but they were sharper, and more elongated. She faintly glowed in the sunlight. Or so it seemed to me. Her eyes were a greyish hue, with long blonde locks. Etienne had a soft, elegant, quiet demeanor and could command a room with barely a word. We all traveled in pure bliss for a few more years, but that was the end of our peaceful times.

One day, Etienne quietly confirmed her suspicions with Ciaran, Ulfred, and I. She carried Ciaran's child in her womb. We were beyond shocked. This shouldn't have been possible. No elf had ever procreated with another species; we only bloomed from the Videira. But Etienne revealed that it was possible, because her species could mate with whomever they chose. She was worried that her kind would eventually come for her, furious that she had procreated with Ciaran. Etienne did not reveal her past with Ulfred and I, only that her child is a direct descendant of a vital bloodline. She was afraid that our lives would not be spared if we knew any other information.

Ciaran was delighted to become a papa, and his focus changed to protecting his unborn child. We devised a clever plan to perform a forbidden procedure. We would remove the infant from Etienne's belly when she was close to delivery at the next rite-of-passage ceremony. Ciaran and I would make it look like the baby had bloomed from one of the pods.

It was a perfect plan but terribly executed, and unforeseen woes must have been in fate's design. I instructed my dear Ulfred to stay in Erebus as a backup plan in case we needed one. It was the most difficult choice I made up to that point, to leave Ulfred behind. Our parents found out about Ciaran and Etienne's engagement and made the decision to reject him, and me for supporting the two together.

On the night of blooming and rite of passage, we performed the risky operation and took the infant from Etienne's womb—we were shocked to find not one but two infants. The discovery overjoyed Ciaran and Etienne as I quickly hid the two infants in a woven basket and ran with them to the ceremony grounds. My arms ached as I used the forest's vegetation for camouflage to find a just-bloomed pod at the Videira. I watched as two chosen parents followed their orb to a pod and patiently waited as it bloomed, and they excitedly met their child. I carefully placed the infants into the same pod as soon as they left. I turned expectantly to see my brother, who was no longer accompanying me. Ciaran should have been not far behind me with a fake orb we had created using elemental magic to follow my location.

So, I waited. I waited until I could no longer stand the cries of the two infants I had placed inside the pod whose petals now drooped. One of the nurses on sight approached me, and I lied and told her that I had followed a Meir, and the pod had bloomed before me with the two infants resting inside. I was welcomed by the elves, who were attending the joyous occasion, with confusion as they had not witnessed me follow a Meir to a pod. Their suspicions immediately disappeared, however, when the priests and elders determined that you both were Marked Ones. After the ceremony, you both were determined to be healthy. I rushed with you both, cradled in your homecoming basket, back to where I had last seen my brother and his partner, Etienne.

The scene before me was one that I know will haunt the back of my mind for the rest of my days. Etienne lay on the soft grass, lifeless. But I did not have time to grieve her departure from this world because of the pure horror of what lay next to her. My brother, Ciaran, had been beheaded. I remember whimpering as I clutched the basket tightly and surveyed the area. I did not doubt that this was the work of Etienne's species. She had lived in constant fear of them, and they had now taken Ciaran's life. I looked over at Etienne and realized that she had most likely died from blood loss, not from an attack. My heart was in pieces as I ran back to my cottage and decided to move farther out into the country, where I hopefully would not be found. I packed my things the night after and moved to a village on the outskirts, taking both infants with me.

I wish I could say that your birth parents had a chance to pick out your names, but it was I who named the two of you. Ornella means "flowering ash tree," and Sayah means "shadow." I gave you these names standing underneath the old ash tree on the outskirts of the sacred vine.

I am so sorry that I plan on keeping the truth from you until you are older and can comprehend precisely what this means. I want you both to know you are an elf, but you are so much more than that. Your birth mother, Etienne, was born with gifted powers, and the two of you inherited your gifts from her. There's a lot still to be discovered, and I did not have the chance to ask. But if you wish to seek answers, you must look beyond the Uncharted Waters and into the Unknown. This is where other beings like her reside. I am hesitant to tell you to go forward in your search because of how much your mother feared her kind. I must also warn you that those who have crossed the mysterious waters never return.

I love you both ardently and am grateful to have a family again. I pray to the vine daily that I will be able to teach the both of you to become loving, open-minded, and strong women. Sayah and Ornella, please know how much you are still loved, even if I can no longer tell you personally. Etienne, Ciaran, and I will always be with you in spirit and heart. I am in the stars, watching from the moon, always cheering you on. So, if there is ever a time when you need encouragement, you only need to look up. I will be waiting for you inside the moon's luminescence.

With all of my love,

Aster

PS I am so sorry, my dear Ulfred. I could not risk leaving the safety of Alizeh's borders to come to you. The kingdom of Erebus is too close to the Uncharted Waters, and I can't risk bringing Sayah and Ornella that way right now after what happened to Ciaran. I will come for you, my darling, when they are old enough and ready. I love you, my dear. I hope you understand. And when they come to you, please accept them with open arms.

Chapter Twenty-five

Ornella and I stood together in disbelief, staring at *Māe's* letter. The words jumbled together on the old parchment paper as I tried to make sense of what I had read. We did not bloom from the *Videira,* the sacred vine. My mind should have been overflowing with questions, but instead it was empty. All I could think was, *what now?*

Aster was my *māe.* No amount of information or truths could be revealed that would change that fact. Sweat creased my brow, and I pressed my palm against my temple.

The truth had always been obvious, sitting right under our noses. Our ears were sharper and slightly longer; we were taller than the average elf and lean with muscle. And the most apparent evidence was when the *Videira* did not respond to our touch immediately at our rite of passage.

We were not elves, not entirely.

The sacred vine only responded to our touch because we are *Marked Ones.* The need to know our origins was beginning to plant its seed of curiosity inside my soul. Until now, our entire existence was just a mass of deception and lies woven together to keep the truth hidden. Heat filled my face, and a fire of determination sparked its first flame.

But before I could speak, Ornella interjected.

"Sayah, I need a moment to myself." She whimpered, continuously wiping tears with the hem of her sleeves. "I'm going to step outside, to get some fresh air."

Stricken, I did not step to the side, my body blocking the doorway. "You shouldn't be alone." I examined my twin, who was on the verge of falling apart. Her rosy cheeks were pale, the color drained completely from her skin. Fresh tears decorated the floor beneath us as she willed me with her eyes to *move*.

"I am *going* outside. If I spend one more moment in this house that used to be *Mãe's,* I'm going to suffocate." Her voice was no longer pleading, as she was now telling me what would happen.

I sighed, neatly folding the letter and shoving it into my coat pocket. "Fine. But we need to talk about this after you've given it some thought, okay?" I raised a brow, holding her hostage in Ulfred's bedroom until she answered.

Ornella bobbed her head, pushing past me and into the sitting area where our friends were curiously waiting. I did not turn to face them until I heard the sound of the front door creak open and shut with a heavy thump.

Enid had moved away from the kitchen; her hands still covered in ingredients. "What did the letter say?" Her features were etched with concern, and she began to wipe her fingertips off on her apron. "Shouldn't someone go with her?"

Everyone's focus shifted to me, waiting for an answer.

"Ornella needs a minute alone," I stated to the crew. My eyes fell to the floor when I was only met with silence, and I bit the inside of my cheek.

Kazumi flew over and perched on my shoulder. Her wings tickled my neck as she continued. "It's not safe for her to be alone. You two are the only *Marked Ones* left. Your powers are highly coveted."

Silas bobbed his head in agreement. He pushed his shaggy hair away from his eye, revealing the scar over his eyelid as he spoke. "Kazumi is right. Ornella may want to be alone, but it's not safe."

An exasperated sigh escaped my lips; I was stuck between a rock and a hard place.

"What information was in the letter?" Ulfred inquired, and I pulled the crumpled paper out of my pocket.

"There's a part written for you," I replied tenderly, before handing it to him.

The room was quiet as Ulfred read the last words written by his soulmate. I studied him as he sat bent over in his chair, his greying hair and beard were a frizzy mess, and his crimson irises were riddled with tears. I imagined what life they would have shared together, if they had been given the chance to grow old in each other's company.

But fate could be vile, cruel to its core even.

I scanned the room until I found the one being that I was looking for—Nox. When I held his gaze, I started to speak. "My sister and I, we—we are not from the *Videira*."

Several gasps erupted around Ulfred's cabin, and Nox's russet eyes temporarily widened.

"You need to explain further, Sayah." Silas sat on the piano bench now, facing me. The smell of a burning dish wafted into the room, and Enid mumbled under her breath as she ran back into the kitchen to check on the dessert. He was staring at me with an unfiltered fascination, and both my ears and face reddened.

From across the room, near the doorway, Nox moved to sit on the couch. He stared intensely, beckoning me with the curl of his finger.

I went and sat, keenly aware of his presence next to me.

"Don't forget I'm still on your shoulder." Kazumi snickered. I rolled my eyes at the sound of her taunting and fought the growing urge to swat her off me. She was worse than the pesky bugs buzzing in your ears in the middle of summer. I clasped my hands in my lap and began summarizing *Mãe's* words.

"We are half elf, and half something else entirely. Ornella and I had a birth mother and father. Our father was an elf, *Mãe's* brother. For safety reasons, our birth mother's full identity was kept hidden. We were created inside a woman's womb and did not bloom from a pod like all elves. She was of a different species from those in the five kingdoms of Aksel. Her origins are from the Unknown." The silence around the room was deafening, so I continued with the revelation. "*Mãe* said we come from a vital bloodline. We are direct descendants of someone vital to my birth mother's species, and they would eradicate our existence if my sister and I were ever found."

Pots and pans crashing down onto the tiles startled everyone in the living space. Enid ran out of the kitchen, throwing off her apron to grab her coat.

"Your sister is *that* important, and you willingly let her go out by herself into the cold?" The ogress was so angry she looked like she could dismember me from where she stood. Her brown hair was tied back, and her usually green skin was a deep red with worry.

I shot up to my feet from the couch, stopping Enid before she could move any further.

"I was just giving her a few minutes of fresh air," I answered reassuringly before strolling to the front door. "She can't have gone far. Knowing my sister, she's more than likely sitting outside on the porch. Don't worry." Fastening the few buttons on my coat, I half smiled, and her brown eyes did not reciprocate. She twisted away from me, grunting before walking back to the kitchen counter.

The heavy wooden door swung open wide from a gust of wind, pushing me with its force. A figure appeared behind me, standing in my shadow.

"I'm not letting you out of my sight." Nox closed the space between us, his warm breath now visible in the frigid cold. Fingertips caressed my chapped lips, their soft touch sending waves of electricity down my spine. He leaned into me, and the smell of oak and cinnamon euphorically filled my lungs. "I wouldn't want a thief to steal my most precious jewel." His husky tone was playful, but his intense gaze made my heart flutter. A fleeting kiss was left on my jaw before he abruptly shut the door, leaving everyone inside while we were coated with snowflakes.

I examined the beautiful scenery before me. The sun had just started to descend, and the sky was a mixture of both day and night. Stars twinkled high from above, blending in with the pink and orange horizon. The winter wonderland before me enhanced the beauty of the green-and-gold swirls of magic. All that was missing was Ornella.

"She can't have gone far; I need to speak to her *alone*." I emphasized the last word, raising my brows at Nox whose expression was lively. "We didn't get the chance to talk before she ran out the door. Ornella is hurting, and I want to be there for her without prying eyes."

Nox stepped forward, and his callused hands reached for mine, their warmth calming. "Please let me stay with you."

Twisting to face the frozen path, I exhaled, exposed to more than just the elements. "Not until I talk to my sister. Please respect my wishes, Nox. I want to respect my sister's boundaries, and no one will let me." I pleaded with him.

After a short pause, he answered roughly. "You won't even know I'm there, Sayah." Nox smirked; a light danced across his eyes. "Did you forget, my lady? I'm a werewolf. I know how to stalk my prey silently." And with a wink he had disappeared before I could reply; he was nothing but a shadow against the white blankets of snow as he took shelter in the dense fir trees.

My heart was easily moved by Nox, and he knew it. And that alone terrified me. I wasn't ready for our time to end, and for him and his crew to return to Alun. They were going to need a new ship. A lump formed in my throat, and my vision grew fuzzy as I focused on the iridescent lights in the near distance, inside the picturesque town that was Flykra.

I brushed off the sinking feeling inside my chest and concentrated solely on finding Ornella.

Chapter Twenty-six

My sister had vanished. Snowflakes obscured my vision, the scenery now an iridescent blur. Ornella's white hair had always been easy to spot in the dense forest of Alizeh. But not here, where the icy kingdom's landscape camouflaged her delicate features. I weaved between the crowded walkways, the celebration of *Grato Amizade* in full swing. Carolers passed by blissfully in song as I retraced my steps from the few previous outings. But at each establishment, I was met by my lonely reflection in each storefront's glass window.

The local storefronts in Flykra had started to close up shop for the evening, and I remorsefully trudged back to Ulfred's cabin empty-handed. My boots crunched in the fresh layer of snow, and the tangible magic flowed with a gentle ease beside me. Despite the cold, sweat began to form on my brow as I rubbed my palms together, fighting the urge to bite my nails.

Where could she have traveled to in that short time if she had not gone into town?

A memory of Fraener from when we first landed in Erebus flashed across my mind, the jade dragon puffing out his chest and blowing smoke through his nostrils as Ornella smiled fondly in his direction. Perhaps she had run directly to the beach to find answers from the wisest creatures in existence. Ornella could be timid sometimes, but she would go straight to the source when she wanted answers. And, in this case, to the horde of dragons camping near the shoreline.

Right then and there, I abruptly left the road to cut across the encompassing trees. The thick firs brushed against my coat as snow toppled off their branches, and birds flew from their nests in my hurry. Squinting, I observed the area, and it was obvious that no one had been on this side of the forest for ages. Nature was completely untouched, and a herd of reindeer scattered amongst the foliage a few feet away at my unwarranted presence.

I could hear the ocean before I could see it. The sounds of the waves crashing against the sea cliffs and salty air filled my lungs as I stepped out from the tree line to examine the terrain for a familiar head of white hair.

Familiar green and gold flags rippled in the wind, and I nearly fell to my knees, gasping. Nox appeared at my side, holding me steady to keep me from falling off the cliff's edge.

"This can't be," I choked on my own words, my voice strangled. "Please tell me that I'm envisioning things, and those ships are not real." My arms and legs shook violently. He said nothing; the shadows across his features in the dim lighting were ominous.

They had found us. I had forgotten to protect Ornella's mind from all of those in power in the kingdom of Alizeh. We did not cast the *Escudo das Almas* spell to protect her *Gavinhas*. *Mãe* had warned me the day of the ceremony that my sister had been spied upon countless times. Our village's healer and prized possession. Her tendrils of light would be easy to navigate inside the *Ligação Mágica,* especially for those who had synchronized with Ornella numerous times before without her knowledge.

We had been leaving a trail of breadcrumbs.

Nox spun me away from the cliff's edge and, in one fell swoop, had me cradled in his arms, racing back to the cabin.

"We have to warn the others." His tone had an edge, and fangs protruded from his mouth. The man's eyes were nearly black from heightening his senses. From beneath his coat, Nox's tribal markings glowed fiercely along his arms and chest. The wind whipped around me, the movements jarring as the sun faded from view in the distance.

"Nox, stop!" I shouted, my heart pounding. But his pace did not slow. This was all too much; everything had changed in an instant. I had been holding myself together for the sake of Ornella, for everyone else.

But my world was beginning to crumble, and the military was here to whisk me away from the little bit of happiness that I had left.

"Let go of me!" The panic in my tone was evident as I fiercely fought his tight grip, wiggling until the landscape around me was no longer a blur. However, he did not stop moving until the cabin and lighthouse were in view.

"Sayah, we need to leave Erebus," Nox said in a strained voice, a growl deep inside his throat. "We must get back to the cabin and warn the others."

I fidgeted again, and he gingerly put me down in the blanket of snow. "No, you don't." My vision began to haze as I choked on my words. "They are here for my sister and me, not anyone else. Go and find your crewmates; I'll continue to search for her here."

The *Ligação Mágica* flowed next to me; its green-and-gold, fluorescent swirls had tempted me to use their tangible wavelengths to synchronize with Ornella from the instant of her disappearance. But *Mãe's* warning of the rooted magic being a double-edged sword was deeply implanted in my core, and I did not want to rely on it.

A vast fleet of Alizeh's military ships had arrived at Erebus's coastline in unison. There was only one reason they would travel this far from the *Videira* and willingly relinquish a massive number of resources, leaving their kingdom exposed. The elven soldiers were here to retrieve my sister and me. *Mãe* was no longer around to protect us, and as *Marked Ones,* we were to fulfill our purpose and serve those in authority.

"That's not fair." His expression was soft as he extended his hand, but I swiftly turned my face to the side. My own rejection stung, and heat flushed my skin as the guilt sent a wave of pain throughout my chest. Nox's arm fell, and he was quiet for several beats before murmuring, "Both you and Ornella are a part of our crew, Sayah. And when one of us is in trouble, we look out for each other."

A sudden noise off in the distance made us turn our heads in alert.

He briefly took my hands in his and gave them a gentle squeeze. "I'll be back in a few minutes and will let you know if she returned to the cabin." His lips then grazed my ear, and he softly spoke. "We are *all* in this together." He planted a kiss on my forehead before vanishing into the wintery mix.

As soon as Nox had left, I fell to my knees, determined. My hands grasped at the physical magic, their swirls tickling my skin as I let my mind be vulnerable inside their interconnecting wavelengths.

Bursts of images of her white mass of waves along with her striking emerald eyes played behind my eyelids. I recalled us as children playing in the creek beside our village, eating supper together as a family, grateful for another meal on the table. My sister's melodic laugh rang in my ears, reverberating inside my soul. Little tidbits of her trying on a rare lipstick shade in our shared bedroom inside the cottage. The way she stood beneath the traditional elvish carvings *Mãe* had engraved herself above the entryway to our home after opening the gift for her rite-of-passage ceremony. Ornella had been overcome with emotion; her green eyes glistened as she told *Mãe* we couldn't accept such a generous gift.

The tug on my *Gavinhas* was gentle as they trickled into the green-and-gold swirls, traveling up the intricate design in search of her. The tendrils of light weaved their way amongst the vast inner webbing, halting as they arrived at Ornella's soul.

Instinctively, my eyes flung open wide, my grip now tight on the magic. I snapped my fingers, shouting, *"Ligeuro,"* and threw myself forward, stumbling in the pillows of snow before gathering my bearings.

In the present, Ornella was squirming in the arms of a bloodthirsty *Thereon*, screaming.

The man who had murdered our *mãe* was also there.

A cruel grin was etched across his wicked face.

Every second mattered. The abrasive wind stung my face and hands as I moved at a blinding speed to the beach where my sister was about to board the *Thereon's* vessel. They had strategically hidden their ship directly on the outskirts of the lighthouse—black sails whipped in the brittle night air, the full moon now out on display. Ornella's hair tangled as she fought the soulless creatures with all her strength, but to no avail.

The scene was all too familiar as I came to an abrupt stop directly in front of the man kidnapping my sister with his vile beasts for henchmen. All of it was the same as it had been on the Isles of Cadogan—except this time, the *Thereon* might actually succeed in our capture.

"Sayah!" she screamed, blood dripping down her arms. Their claws dug into her arms, tightening their vicious grip.

"Get off of her!" I screamed, my power shooting from my fingertips directly across the sand, but the man with silver *Gavinhas* stepped forward, grinning.

"I learn from my mistakes, dear child. There won't be a second time." He drew his sword and came at me with a vengeance from across the sand, unflinching.

My eyes darted around the landscape, in search of the iridescent scales. The dragon horde had vanished, and with a sinking feeling I realized I was alone in this fight. I dodged him, barely, as I fell with a thud and rolled across the earth, grabbing fists full of sand in the process. There must've been five or six *Thereon* escorting Ornella onto their vessel perched on a nearby sandbank while she sobbed uncontrollably, slung across one's back.

Panicking, I threw the sand in his face, a poorly executed diversion to reach her before she disappeared from my sight for good.

"Did those pathetic elves teach you nothing?" In one fell swoop, he had me on the ground again, close enough to the water that it nearly drowned me as the tide came rushing in. Suddenly I was pinned under his boot as he applied a forceful amount of pressure. My arms thrashed as I desperately tried to remove his weight from my neck, wheezing and gargling as I became lightheaded.

My vision was blurry as the salt water repeatedly stung my eyes. The bright moon in the sky was all I could see; everything else was fading to black.

Until he let go of his hold on my neck, and I heard the wretched man sigh.

"Things would be much easier if I could just kill you."

I coughed, spitting up blood and wiping it with the back of my hand. A sudden punch to the gut winded me, his snicker ringing in my ears.

"How pitiful. You don't deserve those powers, yet here you are." The man smirked, his green and gold eyes staring at me in disgust.

Tears fell from my red, swollen eyes, and for the first time since *Mãe's* death I truly felt defeated.

I've spent my life fighting against all odds for a sliver of happiness, simply because I was blessed as a *Marked One*. All Ornella and I wanted from the beginning was a chance to experience a normal childhood and have an uninteresting existence deep in the Woodlands. Where we were free to spend our time in leisure, planting fruits and vegetables in the garden and visiting the academy where *Mãe* would be waiting for me, sitting at the grand piano's bench with a grin, her violet eyes sparkling.

And we would've played beautifully together.

But she wasn't here, and my face contorted in agony. "We didn't ask for this." The words barely escaped from my mouth; it was an effort to keep my eyes open.

I could feel the man's cool breath on my cheek as he whispered into my ear. "You're paying for the sins of your parents; your existence is a disgrace."

His sharp tone cut through the night, and I knew that he meant every word.

A scream erupted from my mouth before I could comprehend what was happening; my eyes bulged from an overwhelming pain in my side. A sword thrust through my clothes cutting into my flesh. I clutched the sharp blade, slicing my hands like butter. The blade began to twist inside of me, and a feral scream traveled into the ocean's waves, where the sound faded into nothing.

"You both stole my birthright and destroyed my family." He pulled the tip of his sword out from my side, the steel slicing my palms again with the sudden motion. I whimpered. "In turn, I will destroy all that is *yours* and take everything from the two of you."

I screamed in pain as he started to stroll along the shoreline to his vessel, leaving me a crumpled mess in the moonlight. The ocean nipped at my side, the cold saltwater soaking my wounds. The pain was enough to keep me alert, the piercing silence quite ominous. I could no longer hear my sister's wails.

He turned on his heel just before entering the ship, shouting back at me, "I'll be expecting you, *Marked One*." His wicked laughter mixed in with the sounds of lapping water, and I saw their anchor slowly being hoisted back onto the *Thereon*'s vessel.

"No," I pleaded, forcing my body forward, crawling into the water as the eerie quiet consumed me. Their black sails shrunk in size as the ship left Erebus, taking my sister hostage.

The thuds of feet stomping along the sand washed a wave of relief over me as I sat in the waist-deep water, anxiously waiting for assistance.

"Please, save Ornella. They've taken her!" I croaked, struggling to my knees. The elven army had come to collect us, their familiar green armor contrasting harshly against the white background. But at this point, I was relieved to see their harsh expressions.

Ornella was their prized possession, who they adored nearly as much as their maker, the *Videira*. They would rescue her.

The fleet of soldiers encompassed me in a large circle, the sounds of their swords being drawn cut through the quiet. A brute soldier stepped forward, pointing his blade directly at my chest. He formed a signal with his free hand, and the others mimicked his movements.

Weapons from all directions pointed at me.

"Sayah, daughter of Aster, you are hereby charged with the attack on a unit of soldiers, a deliberate and calculated attempt to eradicate the elf population." He barked the accusation, spit flying from his mouth.

I froze, my mouth agape as the weight of his words sunk into my battered skull.

Was the kingdom of Alizeh blaming me for the attack on the ceremony grounds? Why . . . how could this be?

The soldier pressed the tip of his sword into my chest, a clear warning. "You are under arrest and will be escorted back to the kingdom of Alizeh, where you will stand trial for your crimes. Rise to your feet and we will escort you peacefully, if you comply." There was no kindness in his hardened eyes, and the elders must have given them the order to bring me back alive.

I sat dumbfounded, my brows knitted together. The world was spinning, and nothing made sense.

Why would they blame me? What was their motive?

And then it all clicked, and my shoulders slumped further.

The elders and priests did not reveal the existence of Thereon to the rest of the population.

I was their scapegoat. The *Marked One* who was cursed, the one who's fate was of only ruin and misery. I bowed my head, unable to respond. They had molded me into a monster, because that was easier for their simple minds to accept rather than revealing the harsh truth.

Several swords jabbed my sides, but I no longer felt their pain.

"Stand up and comply, or we will use any means of force to make you obey." The man's voiced wavered, as he gave the final warning. I slowly stood, my eyes downcast to the black shimmery water beneath me, its icy temperatures numbing my feet and legs. Snow began to fall again, the white puffy flakes blending in with the blood that trickled down my legs and into the water.

"What about my sister?" I muttered softly, shifting my glare to them. "Will you recue Ornella from the *Thereon*?" Fear reflected in their eyes; some trembled and faltered backward onto the sand.

The soldier in front of me cleared his throat and responded. "Your sister, Ornella, daughter of Aster, was found innocent, and several eyewitnesses reported seeing her aid the soldiers after your planned attack."

Ah, there it was, the same distain that the ruthless man expressed before sailing away with the only family I had left. *Our species,* as in, I am not a part of elven kind. It didn't matter that my entire existence breathed the elven culture; being a *Marked One* with an undesirable gift made me an outcast.

I inched forward, fists clenched. The circle surrounding me collapsed as the soldiers in front of me cowered.

I was beyond listening. I was far beyond reason.

My battered face tilted toward the moon, and a tear trickled down my face as I whispered to her luminescent glow, "I'm sorry, *Mãe*, for what I'm about to do." With palms facing outward, my eyelids closed, and I inhaled for the last time, before giving complete control over to the power buried deep inside my core.

If they wanted to paint me as a monster, they should have been prepared to endure my wrath.

It erupted like a hurricane, its immense strength bursting through the seams and out into the world on full display. An animalistic cry rang out from my mouth.

The soldiers trembled in the sand, shaking in terror. Their *Gavinhas* made themselves known to me, and the dark whisps of my power coiled around them like a snake toying with its prey. I had the entire fleet of military whimpering at my feet.

"Death is nothing compared to what I can do to one's soul. Do not fear death—you should fear me."

I could faintly hear shouting from a distance as I extended my hand.

My vision faded to black.

I had discovered the beast that lay dormant inside of me, and I unleashed her full glory.

ORNELLA

If evil were to ever escape from the dark abyss, crawling out of the crevices from which fear and sorrow were born, then the kingdom of Adara was such a place. Never had I witnessed anything so ghastly and sinister. The *Ligação Mágica* endlessly tremored on the bleak mountains and landscape that welcomed only death and misery with a spiteful eagerness.

The gold-and-green magic that usually imbued the kingdoms in gentle waves was violent near the *Breeders of Thereon*. It was in constant disarray, jagged and angry as it approached the soulless beasts' confinement. Mount Auberon was a place of desolation, and my heart stuttered in pain. I was shackled in a rusty cage high above the chaos of hordes of shrieking monsters raging down below. Their cries echoed into the cave's shadows. There was never a moment of peace or quiet. Several other beings were in the iron cages adjacent to mine, their faces void of any remaining emotion.

Tears were useless, yet they painted my cheeks as I clung to the cage bars, rust staining my palms. I knew from the instant of my capture that fate would treat me cruelly. My time on the *Thereon's* ship haunted me beneath closed eyelids. So, I remained awake, wide-eyed, my nightmares blending into reality. Chains looped around my wrists, preventing me from any hope of escape. I was riddled with bruises, cuts, and scrapes. My hair had come unraveled from its braid on the journey here; my white waves were matted and dirty.

My small prison was encompassed by ancient magic, its electric blue volts crackling and sizzling, a thunderstorm of lightning surrounding each individual cage. Its touch was painful and served as an effective barrier. After much contemplation, I believed the unknown magic rendered my power useless.

A young woman had caught my attention in the cage next to mine. She was unmoving on the filthy floor, even as morsels of stale bread were thrown her way by the *Thereon* guarding the only escape.

"You should eat." I tried to call out to her, but my voice was hoarse from screaming; all desperate pleas to be rescued had gone unanswered. She did not move, and her stubbornness reminded me of—

Sayah.

I sucked in a ragged breath, clutching my chest. The existential dread of not knowing what had become of her; the memory of her features contorted with pain as she was stabbed in the abdomen unwillingly replayed in my mind until the torture I endured at the mercy of the *Thereon* invaded once again. As they kidnapped me, I saw the fleets of Alizeh's ships on Erebus's shoreline. Their massive presence had sent another set of shivers down my spine. Nightmares of Sayah had overwhelmed my dreams every night since the day of our ceremony, and my twin was utterly oblivious to her destructive nature. She believed *Mãe's* death to be the reason I was unable to sleep peacefully. The truth was far more disturbing, and it was a truth that I had been determined to keep from her.

Finding my sister deep inside the forest had been easy. A trail of dead foliage was left in her wake, and several woodland creatures had unfortunately been caught in her path, falling limp to the earth. She had painted a colorless world, filled with only black and grey. The leaves from the pines had begun to fall, along with spring's newly bloomed flowers. They recoiled before turning into crumpled ashes, sucked dry of all vibrancy.

When I stumbled upon Sayah, I did not immediately recognize her. She was encircled by dozens of Alizeh's soldiers, sent from the city of Ascelin as the second wave of our military's defense against the creatures cloaked in black, now known as the *Thereon*.

They were still at her feet, and large tendrils of black whisps stretched out from her being, slowly crawling over their bodies. My heart raced and limbs shook, but I could not move forward. I was paralyzed as fear gripped my core, and my voice was strangled as I repeated her name, calling out to her. She slowly turned, and I nearly fainted when she whipped her head in my direction, making eye contact.

Sayah's usual mischievous grey eyes were shockingly black, matching her raven hair. We stood in the middle of what appeared to be the aftermath of a battle, though the only sign of blood stained my sister's hands and her ripped ceremony gown. The forest around us was quiet; the only noise came from my desperate cries. My lips quivered. She held the look of a predator—her dominant presence overwhelming.

The soldiers' auras were growing faint, and the mysterious tendrils of light emanating from their beings trembled. Dread spread throughout my body as I realized that she was draining the soldiers of their souls—not only their energy.

She had transformed into the monster of nightmares.

The creature she had fought so desperately against, the vile beast that the villagers in the Woodlands made her out to be. This was not what she wanted, and I ran to her, desperate to remind her of who she was. Embracing her, I shivered as my sister unknowingly began to drain me of my energy and life.

"Sayah, please!" I sobbed, pleading. Her skin was cold and rigid. I buried my face into the matted mess of her hair, no longer in the intricately woven hairstyle that *Mãe* had braided earlier that day. My legs wobbled, threatening to give out beneath me as I clung to her to hold myself upright. I noticed my aura was draining at an alarming speed, the white light encompassing me dimming. I whispered into her ear; the only truth I knew was certain. "*Mãe* wouldn't want this for you."

There was a brief pause as she deeply inhaled before her chest began to shake, and small noises of heartbreak escaped her lips. She was crying. I faced my sister head-on, her chilling black irises staring vacantly at mine. Tears formed in those unfamiliar eyes, and she blinked them away before murmuring, "She's left this world and taken all the joy of living with her."

The whisps of black slowly pulled back into her core from around us, and her eyes returned to their familiar greyish hue.

I gently stroked the top of her head and closed my eyes, overwhelmed with relief that Sayah had returned to me. "That is not true, moonflower." I tenderly called her by the nickname that *Mãe* had given her as a child. "Happiness is something you create; it cannot be taken from you."

And with that, my sister collapsed in my arms, and I grunted at her sudden weight. I laid her carefully on the dry, brittle grass where we stood. New waves of panic flowed over me, and I stumbled to the first few soldiers before me to check their pulse. The fleet of the military took shallow breaths, asleep. Their auras were all faint; nearly a hundred of Alizeh's best soldiers were wiped out in a matter of minutes by Sayah, singlehandedly.

I did not have time to grieve *Mãe's* death; I could not afford to feel anything. Instead, I called to my powers, their gentle touch comforting as it flowed underneath my skin. In haste, I made a selfish decision, one that the entire kingdom of Alizeh wanted me to pay for.

Sayah had little energy left; her aura was dim. The energy I created from my fingertips seeped into her body, and the color returned to her cheeks as she soundlessly rested on the forest floor. After tending to my twin first, I turned to the soldiers and nearly used all the strength I had left to keep them from the brink of death.

This was when the startling recognition of my limitations were made apparent.

Sayah was by far more powerful than I. The elders and priests had honed my gift for years, keeping my twin's power locked up inside her because they were afraid. And they had every right to be.

She had the ability to drain someone's life, stealing not only their energy but also their soul. I had heard soldier's heartbeats fade and witnessed the tendrils of light above their auras flicker.

My muscles screamed in pain as I awkwardly pulled her forward inch by inch to a nearby cavern, before falling to my knees. We nearly wasted away in the thick part of the forest, its only inhabitants wild animals and creatures that did not want to be found. My energy at this point stemmed solely from my anxiety; I was terrified of the military finding us, being attacked by the creatures cloaked in black, and my sister never waking. Several moons passed overhead while I nursed Sayah to the best of my abilities. When her eyes miraculously fluttered open, she was completely unaware of the events that had transpired after *Mãe's* passing.

She inquired once about the military's aid, wondering when we would cross paths with them. I lied out of fear. My words had been rubbish about traveling too far east. Her cunning eyes saw through my fib, not entirely convinced, but she dropped the subject. My twin knew not to ask questions you didn't want answers to.

My sleepless nights were haunted by my guilt and the startling awareness that I was frightened by my own flesh and blood, my other half.

I loved Sayah ardently, but who she transformed into when shrouded by her fury was terrifying. I did not know that version of her, and I did not want to find out what she was truly capable of.

The army of *Thereon*'s rabid howls broke through my thoughts as more beasts funneled in from every crack and crevasse inside the mountain's heart. The soulless creatures danced in a circle, creating a blasphemous ritual rising from the depths of their greed and desires.

The cavern shook, and I felt the vibrations inside my prison as rocks crumbled and crushed several *Thereon*. That did not stop the celebration, and a mighty roar reverberated off the cavern walls, exciting the mindless creatures beneath me even further.

The woman in the cage next to mine moved for the first time, shifting to her feet to grip the iron bars as she peered out into the darkest depths of Mount Auberon. Her arms shook, and she hissed angrily as she bared her teeth. The thunderous noise of footsteps approaching had my skin crawling in terror.

She whipped her head drastically to face me, and startling blue eyes filled with hatred and loathing met my stare. "He is evil reincarnated, crawling out of the deepest depths of the abyss." Her breathing was haggard as her pupils dilated. The stranger shifted her awareness to where the loud sounds were originating.

"He is here to greet you." Her tone had an edge that caused me to sit up straight. The woman did not meet my gaze, but I knew it was a warning. Her eerie tone made the hair on my arms and neck stand straight. Impending doom headed our way.

All at once, the area was consumed by an ominous silence; even the *Thereon* had paused their movements. Beads of sweat formed on my forehead, and I held my breath, waiting. Every being was suspended in time; none dared to move. We all felt it. Whatever was coming, its presence was nearly suffocating.

And from the darkness, serpentine eyes appeared, their irises blood red and full of poisonous rage.

I released my grip on the cage, falling backward, when the *Breeder of Thereon* homed in on my presence, speaking directly to me. "Your power is quite pure, *Marked One.*" His voice shook with excitement as if it had been melded from thunder itself, crackling with strikes of authority.

The predator slithered into the light, and I involuntarily flinched.

His scales still resembled those of his brethren, a vibrant red shade. But the black parasitic magic now crawled over them, creeping over his wings and spine as separate entities. The dark magic encompassing him was aggressive, and his massive aura emitted the feelings of a ravenous wild beast. With each movement, gemstones and gold stuck to his scales clanked to the cave's hard surface. Bakunax had risen from his slumber amongst his mountains of hoarded treasure.

Steam rose from his nostrils, and sharp fangs protruded from the corrupted dragon's mouth.

This beast was the origin of all nightmares—the shell of what was once a dragon, now something petrifying and hideous. Masked inside the black fumes of dark magic, Bakunax stalked forward, his shoulders low to the ground. Squeals of the *Thereon* fleeing the area cut through the painful silence as even they feared their maker's wrath.

I shrieked and crawled backward, pushing against the back of my cage. My wide eyes, however, never left his gaze, the sole instinct to survive revealing itself as I yanked at my shackles. They cut deep into my wrists, the fresh scent of iron filling the air as I continued to pull on my chains with urgency. Blood trickled down my wrists and dripped onto the cage's base. I needed as much distance between myself and the original *Breeder of Thereon*, whom the *Creator* decided was too evil to be attached to the land's magic.

"There is no escape, *child of the vine*," he sneered; his mocking tone pierced like daggers to my already torn pride. "Now that I have you in my grasp, the final piece of my treasure will soon arrive."

I felt my soul drain from my body. He meant Sayah.

Bakunax stretched his translucent wings, the parasitic magic traveling their entire length as they lashed the sides of the cave, nearly causing the foundation around us to collapse.

"I will at last break free from the magic that has condemned me to this mountain for centuries. With your and your kindred's assistance." The corners of his mouth tugged upwards, revealing a complete set of sharp fangs before he lunged in my direction.

An earth-shattering scream ripped from my throat, and I threw my hands above my head defensively as my knees smacked onto the iron cage's floor.

This was it; I was done for.

There would be no stopping my sister's fury from consuming all living things inside the five kingdoms of Aksel.

And the *Breeder of Thereon's* obsession to devour all power was now focused solely on me.

Chapter Twenty-eight

Out from the trenches of the darkest abyss,

He slithered his way into our world ravenous,

Hunting for something to satisfy his utmost desires,

On a quest to devour all power.

Fate observes indifferently,

Two sisters intertwined with the hands of time to meet the same unfortu-

nate

E

N

D

I

N

G,

Only to be reborn again to choose the same path;

An infinite cycle, wretchedly repeating.

THE END

This letter is for you. Thank you, from the bottom of my heart, for giving my book a chance. There is nothing more enchanting than hearing that someone has read your story. You may have enjoyed it; maybe not. We all have different opinions on art styles, including writing styles and genres. But the fact that you picked up my book to try is truly meaningful to me. So, this is a letter specifically to my readers who helped make my dreams a reality.

You are highly inspiring.

Magical, even.

Yours truly,

Victoria M. Sorenson

Hi there, and welcome! I am Victoria M. Sorenson, a debut author, longtime poet, and vintage book collector. My specialty is forging worlds full of magic and mystery in the young adult genre. When not writing enchanting plot scenes or poetry, I homeschool my three daughters and feed my fat cat, Chili, his second breakfast. My day-to-day is filled with fun and chaos, and I absolutely revel in its pandemonium. When you begin to let yourself experience all that life has to offer, your writing and imagination will start to flourish.

This is where you can keep up with my latest adventures and all the juicy details—

www.authorvictoriamsorenson.com

Instagram & Threads: @victoriamsorenson

TikTok: @authorvictoriamso

YouTube: @VictoriaM.Sorenson

Facebook: Victoria Sorenson

There are never enough words.

I could write an entire book on how much I love and appreciate every single person who has helped me on my journey to publishing. It's not easy, not in the slightest. I feel as though I have climbed a treacherous mountain and finally reached the top, only to discover that it was never my publication or book waiting for me at the end of the adventure—but rather all the new friendships I've made ready to escort me across the finish line.

Parker Sorenson, you have always been my rock. I love you and thank you for helping me stay positive even in times of doubt. You know me better than I know myself, and you always show up like the knight in shining armor that you are, with a pint of ice cream in hand to make everything better.

If you ever see my parents out in public, pat them on the back and thank them. Their help was crucial to my dreams coming to fruition. They babysat my daughters on Friday nights and during the summer so that I could type this bad boy. And then retype it twice. Thank you and I love you both, Mom and Dad.

Vivienne, Sophia, and Rosalie, your existence alone has made me a better person. You three are my number one motivation in life and in seeing this dream to the end. Thank you for your unwavering kindness, gentle words, and hugs. Thank you for making me a mother.

I am shouting from the rooftops a big thank you to my illustrator, Rena Violet. She is my fairy godmother, granting my wishes for beautiful artwork. Her highly advanced skill set and bubbly personality have made marketing my book a breeze.

Thank you to my editor, Heather Hudec. Her sprinkled words of kindness throughout my manuscript instilled confidence in me, and I am incredibly appreciative and grateful to have an editor who's in my corner.

I want to give a special thank you to my arc readers, who not only made me feel important but also loved. They have supported me and met every bump or hiccup in my plans with stride. This would not have been possible without their guidance and feedback. Now, to force them to be my guinea pigs for the next few books . . . *insert evil grin here.*

Abbey Peterson, thank you for being you. Our friendship knows no distance. I love your daily voice messages and being a part of your publishing adventure too. I can't wait to be there for you on your release day in the near future. Sending lots of love and silly memes all the way to Canada.

Last but far from least, I want to mention specifically my friends Raeah, Kaitlyn, Courtney, Alyssa, Sam, Reenu, Niamh, Shelbie, Sara, Jessica, and the many others who helped spread seeds of encouragement in my times of doubt. This book would not have been possible without you all.

With Love,

Victoria M. Sorenson

www.ingramcontent.com/pod-product-compliance
Lightning Source LLC
Chambersburg PA
CBHW071358300726
48976CB00006B/1919